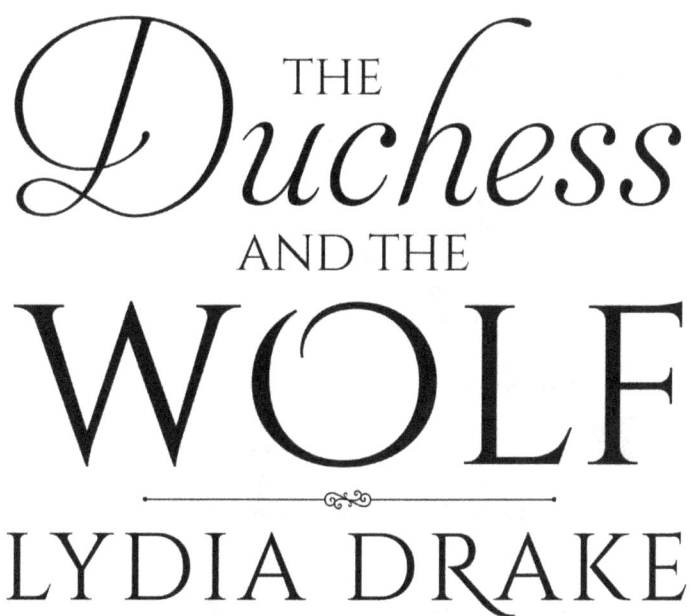

This book is a work of fiction. Names, characters, places, and incidents are the product of the author's imagination or are used fictitiously. Any resemblance to actual events, locales, or persons, living or dead, is coincidental.

Copyright © 2023 by Lydia Drake. All rights reserved, including the right to reproduce, distribute, or transmit in any form or by any means. For information regarding subsidiary rights, please contact the Publisher.

Entangled Publishing, LLC
644 Shrewsbury Commons Ave
STE 181
Shrewsbury, PA 17361
rights@entangledpublishing.com

Amara is an imprint of Entangled Publishing, LLC.

Edited by Jen Bouvier
Cover design by Bree Archer
Cover photography by Period Images
Ranta Images/Getty Images

Manufactured in the United States of America

First Edition September 2023

At Entangled, we want our readers to be well-informed. If you would like to know if this book contains any elements that might be of concern for you, please check the book's webpage for details.

https://entangledpublishing.com/books/the-duchess-and-the-wolf

For John, who knows all sorts of things, including how to make me laugh.

Chapter One

London, 1816

Susannah Fletcher was lost in the woods of Mayfair.

She could have sworn she saw her friend, Annabelle, standing before her but a mere moment ago. Though everyone here was masked, including Susannah, she knew her friend by her distinctive purple velvet gown and mass of gold hair. But in the space of a heartbeat, a man had passed in front of Susannah and Annabelle had vanished.

"I should never have allowed her to talk me into this," Susannah muttered. She looked around. "Who on earth decided a forest should be the ambiance for a gentlemen's club?"

Annabelle had convinced Susannah to leave the house without her mother's knowledge and traipse down to the Wolf's Den, Mayfair's most elegant and notorious club.

Normally, gentlewomen could not enter, but tonight was the Hunter's Ball, an event in which everyone was masked and prey for sensuous delights. Ordinarily, the club must resemble any other in London, with crystal chandeliers, silk curtains, and a bevy of beauties available to the most eligible and infamous gentlemen of the *ton*.

Tonight, they'd transformed the club into a silvery glen, a forest by moonlight.

They had constructed the trunks of silver trees to crowd one in, pushing the attendees together. Servers dressed as forest nymphs and rather virile satyrs moved through the space, enchanting and enticing whoever took their fancy.

Susannah wished now that she had chosen a more threatening animal than a fox for her mask. While the creature's coloring matched her own coppery hair, it left her open for a swarm of wolves and bears to chase after her, slavering for a taste.

"Who's this little beauty?" someone asked, leering toward Susannah. She almost laughed when she saw his badger's mask. What an erotic sight. "What are you doing here, my sweet?"

"Looking for my husband," she replied, and immediately, the fellow left her alone. *Thank God*. Of course, Susannah was not yet married, though she was very nearly engaged. Her mother waited every day to make an official announcement.

Susannah should have been happy. So why was she here, parading around a debauched gathering, something no marriage-minded young woman should dare to do?

It was Annabelle's fault, really. After she'd married a marquess's son last year, Susannah's formerly prim school friend had undergone a devilish metamorphosis. She was no longer Annabelle Wembley, a wealthy merchant's daughter, but Lady Henry Douglass, part of the aristocracy's most elite circle. Her new status allowed her to get away with all manner of risky behavior, and she took full advantage. The London season was only a week old, and already, Annabelle imagined the wild time they would have in Susannah's last moments as an unmarried girl.

Honestly, if the duke knew she was here, what would he think? Even Julia, Susannah's beloved stepsister, would disapprove of such shameful behavior. Susannah had always been the sweet and dutiful child, the girl without a single cross word for anybody. Only when she played at the pianoforte did Susannah show even momentarily the spark of fire that dwelt inside her breast.

She had what every young woman dreamed of, didn't she? The Duke of Huntington had been most attentive this past year. He was handsome, charming, and astonishingly rich and powerful. Julia and her husband, the Duke of Ashworth, were his great friends, and ecstatic at the thought of his and Susannah's union. Everyone agreed it was a happy ending written in the stars.

So why did Susannah risk her reputation and future? Why did she feel every day like she was in a cage whose bars were growing nearer and nearer?

Perhaps it was because every night, she dreamed of playing before crowds of people in gilded opera houses throughout Europe. She dreamed of foreign ports and alien languages, a world in which she could choose where she went and whom she met with and how she felt.

Susannah stepped into a clearing beside a pond made of glass, diamonds encrusted upon the top of it. Lord, this club owner had extravagant taste, didn't he?

Most of all, more than anything, she wanted to feel alive only once before her life became entirely about her husband and his estate.

"There you are!" Lady Henry bashed into her, giggling riotously. She wore a purple owl's mask, and, unlike the bird, had not demonstrated a drop of wisdom this evening.

"How much champagne have you had?" Susannah hissed.

"Ugh, you sound like my mother-in-law. Henry and I are thinking of moving to Milan to escape the incessant questions and reprimands." Annabelle stuck out her tongue, impish as ever.

"Milan? That'd make a nice change of scene."

"The benefits of being second born. Henry never has to worry about managing a title, so all that's left for us is pots of money and fun." Annabelle sighed in happiness. "I do feel for girls who marry titled men. Their lives become *so* regimented."

"Mmm." Susannah knew her friend meant nothing by it. Annabelle could be thoughtless when she was tipsy.

Lady Henry winced. "Lord, sorry. The duke's grand, though. I'm certain he'll let you have as much freedom as you like."

"He is indeed grand." Susannah pulled the edges of her red cloak tighter about her shoulders. She should have taken it off at the door, but she felt so exposed in the rather daring cut of dress Annabelle had insisted she wear. "Now, is it me, or are we lost?"

"Nonsense. The path leads right that way." Annabelle pointed in what Susannah thought was the wrong direction. The lady evidently had the same thought. "Or this one?" She pointed in the opposite direction.

"It's left, I think," Susannah said.

"No, right."

"Either way, there's nothing to fear. It's not like there are actual bears running around these woods."

"Don't be too sure." Lady Henry wore a wicked grin. "There are men here tonight who'd gladly ravish you if they saw your face beneath the mask."

"Which is why I'm keeping it on."

"You're dull. Come on, Zan! We must enjoy ourselves while we're still young and fresh." Annabelle disappeared into another crowd of animal-masked men. She'd gone right, which Susannah knew was not the correct way. Or perhaps

Annabelle wanted to lead them farther into the heart of the deep, dark, sinful forest.

Susannah groaned. "That girl will get us both in serious trouble," she murmured, then set off in pursuit of the blasted purple owl.

Susannah had to marvel at the ingenious beauty of the place as she went.

They had hung stars made of crystal from the fake wooden boughs of trees and set candles in the proper place to make them glitter. Up ahead came the lilting sound of strings as musicians played a spirited waltz in the grand ballroom.

The largest chamber in the club, it boasted ceilings twenty feet high and several chandeliers.

Tonight, they'd turned it into a proper faerie glen, crowded on all sides by dark trees while costumed sprites and will-o'-the-wisps cavorted about, dancing with the guests. Susannah blushed beneath her mask seeing how little clothing the dancers wore. The men were bare-chested, dressed in mere loincloths, while the women pranced about in shimmering gauze and satin. They might not even be wearing stays beneath their clothes.

Susannah felt a pang of longing. She knew how fortunate she was to be a rich heiress with a duke seeking her hand, but she sometimes would trade it all for one night as a girl on the stage. Not a dancer, no, but a musician.

Susannah hovered on the edge of the ballroom, watching the young male dancers lead swooning gentlewomen around the floor in a waltz. Tonight, no one knew one another by face or name. Tonight, even society's women were allowed to indulge their most decadent fantasies.

Susannah froze when a young, bare-chested man in a stag's mask came over to her.

"A lady so lovely should not be forced to watch the dance," he said.

Susannah bit her lip, feeling shy even with her mask and cloak protecting her. That was the frustrating thing about her, how she dreamed so wildly and yet was so timid in real life. *Then stop being timid for one night. No one knows it's you, after all.*

Susannah took the young man's hand and let him lead her to the floor. She was a good dancer, and they merged with the other couples easily. Susannah's heart pattered as she turned around and around in the dim, candlelit ballroom.

This was no strict and starched ball at a society dame's home, with mothers chaperoning and gossips whispering behind fans. This felt wild, and sensuous, and free. Susannah couldn't contain the laughter that bubbled up out of her.

"Enjoying yourself, my dear?" the young man asked. His voice was rich and low.

"Yes. I didn't think I should come tonight, but I'm awfully glad I did."

"So am I." He held her a bit closer. "You're the loveliest girl I've danced with."

"Oh. Well. You don't know what I look like."

"That can be fixed. Come with me to a private room after the dance, and we can both take off our masks."

Susannah's eyes widened. Oh no. She was daring, but not *that* daring. "Erm. Not sure that's the point of a masked ball."

"This is the Wolf's Den, love, and the Hunter's Ball. Tonight, everything's on the table. Whatever you want can be yours."

Susannah became tongue-tied as the waltz stopped, and the partners bowed to each other. The stag escorted her off the floor.

"You've been terribly nice," she said, stammering. "But I think I must find my friend. She's probably frightened being on her own. She's, um, the nervous type who faints at random. I might find her sprawled out upon the floor somewhere, and

I should hate for anyone to trip over her."

The stag winked at her from behind his mask.

"A shame, pretty one. You make a sleek little fox indeed."

"I should say so," a man said next to them. He was obviously a guest, a gentleman with graying hair and a bear's mask. He grinned at Susannah, displaying his "fangs." "Dashed prettiest fox I've ever laid eyes on."

"Thank you." Susannah made a quick curtsy and fled the ballroom. She wandered down a smaller corridor, which was rather quiet. *Finally.*

She paused beside an oil painting of some Venetian courtesan from two centuries ago. The woman lay bare upon a sofa, glancing at the viewer over her shoulder. There were pearls and peacock feathers in her hair. Lord, how would it feel to be an artist's model like that? To remove your clothes and not give a damn what strangers thought of you?

In the elevated circles of the *ton*, rigid conformity to popular taste was everything. But that wasn't the case here at all, and Susannah loved it.

Every inch of this club was decadent and sensual. It all felt like some amazing dream, a forest she could have imagined only in her fantasies. Wasn't that the best way to live, wrapped in whimsy and art? Again, Susannah felt the overwhelming urge to leave her safe, privileged life and go after what she wanted most. Travel. Music. Adventure.

She did have the means, really. Her dear father, long since departed, had left behind a substantial fortune for her. The only drawback was that the terms of the money had been strict. Susannah would not see a penny until she either married or turned thirty-five. And once she married, her money would be her husband's, and she doubted that even a man as tolerant as the duke would approve of her gallivanting across Europe.

But to wait to really begin living until she was thirty-five seemed intolerable. Fourteen years! And while Susannah loved her mother, she did not want to picture living with Constance while she endlessly groaned about Susannah's spinsterhood.

No. The sensible thing would be to marry the duke. She had to take in all the delights of the imaginary forest tonight, and tomorrow return to the real world.

"I say there! Little fox!"

Oh damn. That bear-masked fellow had decided to follow her. He swaggered back and forth as he lumbered down the hall.

Susannah had no wish to find herself in any kind of unpleasant or compromising scenario. Opposite the painting, there was an alcove that housed a marble statue of a naked woman with her hands raised overhead, flowers in her hair.

A red velvet curtain hung to one side of the alcove, and Susannah stepped behind it in a hurry. She peeked around the edge and watched the bear as he arrived, looking about for her in every direction.

"Hello?" He turned in wobbly circles and put a hand to the wall so as not to fall over. Susannah bit back a laugh. "Oh, I say. Do excuse me," he slurred, bowing to the painting of the naked courtesan. "Dashed pretty, aren't you? Such lovely…feathers."

Susannah forced herself not to giggle. The drunken man was totally captivated by the naked woman in the picture. He reached out to stroke a rather sensitive part of her, and Susannah felt indignity on the fictional lady's behalf. Some men had no sense of propriety!

Susannah wondered what Julia would do if she were here. She wouldn't be hiding behind a curtain, for one thing. Susannah's bold duchess of a stepsister would probably lob a few choice words at the fellow. If he tried to approach her, she'd likely kick him square between the legs. Susannah wished that she wasn't so eternally *nice*.

"Oh, I do say. You're a pretty one, aren't you?" The bear turned from the painting and ambled toward the naked statue. Susannah held her breath. This was much too close for comfort. "Now, now. Don't go wobbling all over the place." The man scolded the statue while he himself lurched back and forth. He reached out to molest the poor work of art. "Now jus' hold still while I—"

"*Oi!* What do you think you're doing?"

Both Susannah and the bear froze at the sound of another, deeper male voice. Susannah pressed her back to the alcove's wall and watched the drama unfold from her hiding place.

The man's every step was accompanied by a blunt tapping sound, which she quickly identified as a cane. She shivered once as he sauntered into the candlelight, revealing the jagged edges of his wolf's mask. The wolf confronted the bear. He was one of the tallest men Susannah had ever seen, even with the cane.

"You. Ponce. What were you doing?" the man growled. His voice was smooth as whiskey, and his accent placed him on the lower end of society's spectrum. He was from the streets, yet Susannah noted he dressed exceedingly well in a fine dark suit with a pristine cravat. The handle of his cane glimmered like pure silver in the light. Perhaps it *was* genuine silver.

"I, er, that is..." The bear backed away from the formidable wolf. "Now see here! I don't know what you're insinuating, but—"

"You had your greasy paws all over Venus."

"I assure you, sir. I am not acquainted with a young lady of that name."

"Venus is the statue, you dolt. She's a goddess of love. Cost a fortune. She deserves better than to get felt up by some goon."

"I, sir? A goon, sir?" Now the bear was growing enraged. "I'll have you know I am a gentleman."

"Same difference, isn't it?"

Susannah's eyes bulged as she clapped a gloved hand over her mouth. She almost barked out a laugh, which would have given her hiding place away at once.

"And who are you, anyway? An art dealer?"

"I own the place."

The bear flinched. "Oh. The Wolf of Mayfair?"

"The very same."

Wolf of Mayfair? That would explain the mask, at least. So, this was *his* club, then. The man seemed a bit wild and dangerous; the Wolf's Den suited its master perfectly.

"Stick to drinking and dancing. Leave the girls alone, sculpted or otherwise." The wolf walked past, his cane thunking with every step. "Good evening to you."

The bear clenched his fists. Evidently this wolf had wounded his pride, and that could not be borne. If the Wolf of Mayfair had belonged to the *ton,* maybe the incident could have passed, but he was a man of low birth. Gentlemen like this bear did not accept anything but reverence from common people.

Susannah gasped as the bear leaned back, preparing to kick the wolf's cane out from under him. It was the gesture of a petty bully, and she couldn't allow it to stand. But before she could shout out "behind you!" the wolf spun about with the grace of a dancer.

The wolf used his cane to jab the bear right in the stomach. The other fellow bent over before collapsing to the floor. He clutched his midsection and groaned in pain.

"Should've guessed you were the type to play dirty." The wolf sounded like he was sneering. "But so am I. Now get up and get out of my club. I see you around here again, you'll find out I've been playing nice up until now."

The bear didn't need another warning. He wheezed as he crawled to his feet and bolted back down the hall. Susannah waited for the wolf to leave, but he paused in front of the statue. She held her breath again, not wanting him to realize he'd enjoyed an audience this whole time.

Heat rose to her cheeks as she studied the man. She could not see much of him through the mask, but his eyes glittered as they beheld the statue of Venus. She wondered what he looked like beneath the wolf's façade.

"You're too good for the likes of him, girl." He spoke almost kindly to the marble goddess, so different from the way he'd talked with the man. The rough, low sound of his voice made the hair on the nape of her neck stand at attention. "Too good for both of us, really."

He finally walked away. Susannah listened until she could no longer hear his cane, then emerged from her hiding place. She hurried back down the corridor, hoping to find Annabelle and get out of here. She didn't want to run into this wolf again.

Chapter Two

Rafe reclined in his office chair, his booted right foot slung over his desk.

It was a good position to take when his knee was a bastard, as it was this evening. He'd laid his wolf's mask aside the moment he entered the room. Damned nuisance having to wear that thing, but as his business partner, Jacks, had pointed out, the Hunter's Ball was *his* idea. Even he had to abide by his own rules.

So now Rafe relaxed, letting his knee unknot itself a little as he tapped his cane against the floorboards rhythmically. The silver wolf's-head handle grimaced at him, the candlelight glinting in its ruby-chipped eye. The Wolf of Mayfair they called him, and he'd named his club to match his persona.

There were three in the office right now for this meeting. Rafe at his desk, Jacks leaning against the wall, and Lord Sackville-Chambers perched at the very edge of his chair. His Lordship did not seem to think Rafe's office clean, though it was spotless. He paid extra to have every bit of it scrubbed; he couldn't abide a mess. But as he was gutter trash that'd clawed his way up into good society, he was and always would be filthy in the eyes of Lord Sackville-Chambers.

"Enjoy yourself tonight, my lord?" Rafe tried to keep himself from growling, but it had become a habit of his. Particularly when dealing with rich vermin like this man.

"I've found your club intriguing. It is an exceedingly opulent establishment." The lord sniffed, letting the suggested insult linger in the air, though Rafe had no idea what the slight was supposed to be. He hated not knowing anything that the toffs knew.

"Mr. Winters and I wanted to thank you again for coming to visit us this evening," Jacks said. "As you can see, the Wolf's Den is rated the most luxurious gentlemen's club in London for a reason. Anyone can open an establishment and have some alcohol and pretty girls slotted about for the guests, but Mr. Winters approaches his enterprises with an artist's eye. It's that quality what will make his proposal for your building truly exciting."

"Indeed." Lord Arsehole scanned Jacks from head to toe with one withering look. "He certainly surrounds himself with eccentricities."

Rafe squeezed the handle of his cane, the old instinct in him flaring up to rise and beat the man bloody. But Jacks laughed it off, as she always did.

"I admit I make a strange man of business," she said. Jacks dressed as nattily as Rafe did, in a fine velvet suit and cravat, and her yellow hair was cut like his as well. They'd known each other from the age of fourteen, when she'd joined his crew of pickpockets. "What are you?" he'd asked in bewilderment when she appeared in her trousers and cap. "I'm Jacks!" She'd shaken his hand and laughed, utterly without fear. Rafe had liked her at once, against his better judgment. Always smarter to not like people, since they usually disappointed. Still, Jacks had made a good investment. She was savvy with numbers in a way even he wasn't, and she had a better manner of talking with people.

So when snooty lords and ladies looked down upon her, Rafe wanted to break skulls.

"Shall we get down to the discussion?" he asked the pompous lord.

"We shall. I've reviewed your offer to purchase my property, and I admit I'm delighted to finally have an offer. In some ways, I feel almost guilty entertaining it. Frankly, Mr. Winters, it is a grand old building, to be sure, but rather derelict and in need of a great deal of restoration. I can't imagine that will be cheap."

"It won't be," Rafe said, turning his cane slowly. "But I can see what it could really be worth. I'm getting a good deal here, all things considered."

Sackville-Chambers owned a large property directly across the street from the Wolf's Den, an enormous house that had belonged to an illustrious ancestor a hundred years ago or so. But as was usually the case with rich tossers, the family had no head for business and eventually squandered all their cash.

Lord Lickspittle here was trying to sell off the family properties he didn't need to keep himself and his brats in their accustomed luxury. The Corner Castle, as it was known around Mayfair, was beautiful and ostentatious but also rather rundown.

But Rafe saw beyond what was right before him. It was that quality that had allowed him to rise from obscurity to his current position. Well, that and his ability to be the last man standing in a fight.

Rafe saw a luxury hotel, grander than the grandest yet built in London. A destination so pristine and perfect, fancy clientele would come over from the Continent just to spend the night and see the wonders he'd create.

He saw those riches feeding into the Wolf's Den, into its gambling halls, and he saw the surge of cash it would all bring. He saw more properties bought around London, fancy properties he'd let to the second sons of aristocrats and other wealthy knobs.

But above all, Rafe saw a vision of himself accepted by the *ton*. Seen as a man of business, a man who was their equal, not merely a peddler of liquor and flesh. He'd rub their faces in his success. He wanted that so much, his throat would tighten when he thought of it.

"You said you wish it to be a hotel, correct?" His Lordship sniffed again, a sign of disgust. "It will be hard to imagine my ancestral home as such a common place."

"Tourists will sleep in your beds and piss in your chamber pots." Rafe shrugged. "Which is what your folk were doing for hundreds of years before. It's all the same."

"I say." His Lordship's cheeks paled, astonished at Rafe's crude tongue. He and the rest of the perfumed gentlemen could get used to it. Rafe wasn't changing.

"Mr. Winters aims to make this new establishment something unseen before," Jacks said. She shot Rafe a look and made a gesture with her hand. *Calm down*. "It's more than an inn or a tavern. It'll be a whole world of luxury. Imagine a hotel so comfortable and its food so excellent that you never want to venture outside. That's Rafe's vision. Your family legacy won't be tarnished, my lord. You have our word on that."

"I know that your offer is more than adequate." Lord Sackville-Chambers downed the glass of nice port Rafe had poured him. He savored it a moment before swallowing. "And I must say, you understand the importance of good wine. I've had a look at your cellar, and it's most exceptional."

"I hired the best experts I could find when I started the Wolf's Den," Rafe said. "They recommended wine and everything else. I spent more than I should have, they said at the time, but my investment paid off. My standard of quality is one that people will pay extra to enjoy. I want only the best, you see. Life's not worth anything without it."

"Indeed. You are not a cheap con artist, Mr. Winters. I grant you that. And it would be nice to know the Corner Castle would have a second life as a London landmark, if you have your way, of course. It won't be pulled down for new flats, which I appreciate."

Rafe nodded, turning the handle of his cane again and again.

With every rotation, the wolf's ruby eyes met his. *Almost there. Keep going until the job is done.*

Those were the words that'd run through his head as a child on the streets, picking pockets. When he'd graduated as a young man to home burglary, he'd stayed calm by repeating those words over and over. When the boss of a rival gang had him held down and had his knee busted years back, Rafe had soldiered through the pain, envisioning the day when he'd have that boss kneeling in the street before him.

And when that day came, Rafe had reveled in his victory and then pictured the day he would be rich. Powerful. A businessman.

Years later and he was thirty-one with a thriving establishment and a fashionable flat on the top floor. He'd his own carriage, accounts at fine tailors. All he needed now was respectability. Lord Sackville-Chambers was about to bestow that upon him. *Almost there, Rafe.*

"However," the lord said.

No. No. We're almost there!

"However?" Rafe growled.

"You could introduce me to the most refined and beautiful Venetian courtesan, fluent in five languages and adept at philosophy and music. You could dress her in the most lavish silks, but that would not change the fact that she is a whore. Would it?"

"What are you implying, sir?" Jacks sounded short now.

Rafe's vision began to blur. If this lord had taken a meeting only to rub Rafe's low birth in his face, this man was going to learn what a poor decision that was.

"I imply nothing. This club of yours, this Wolf's Den, is a brothel and a tavern. You may dress it up with artistry all you like, but it is a gilded veneer. I don't believe you know true class, Mr. Winters. If you could display some understanding of real culture, I'd consider selling my family's property to you. As it stands, though, I see nothing here that is truly art. Only fancy baubles, the taste of other, more refined men filtered through your own cruder sensibilities."

Rafe gripped the handle of his cane and rose slowly to his feet. Jacks made a nervous sound, a half laugh that begged him not to be rash.

"I can show you the plans I've drawn up for the hotel," he said. "They're not cheap."

"Nevertheless. I've my family's legacy to consider as well as my own pocketbook." The snooty lord rose, about to take his leave. "My ancestors should never forgive me if I allowed their home to be turned into some vulgar attraction."

"You might've told me this in a letter and spared me the time of this meeting." Rafe took one, two steps closer, delighting in the obvious discomfort in the other man's face. Even with his cane, Rafe was six feet tall, and while he was lean, every inch of his body was muscle.

"I wanted to take a look at the club's interior to judge for myself."

"You'll go back, then, and sell for less money to someone who'll tear the bloody place down? If you get another offer, that is."

"As I said, my ancestors would rather the place be razed to the ground than polluted with tawdriness."

"Your ancestors are quiet in their graves," Rafe snapped. "I doubt they care overly much about what kind of man you're selling their house to. It's the living who tend to be snobs, not the dead."

"You're an eloquent man, Mr. Winters." The lord sneered, turning Rafe's vision to fire. "Unfortunately, your taste doesn't suit mine. Good night."

Before Sackville-Chambers could leave, Jacks negotiated herself into the conversation.

"My lord, is there anything we can show you that'll set your mind at ease about our intentions?" She kept smiling that charming Jacks smile, polite as ever. She'd easily been the most charismatic thief Rafe had ever met back in the day.

"Hmm. Well. Your offer *is* most attractive, as I've said." The man pondered; Rafe wanted him to ponder faster. "If you could show me a change in the culture of this place, a sense of your own evolving taste, I might reconsider my position."

"The culture's what people come here for." Rafe sneered in turn, and his sneer, he knew, could chill blood.

"Nevertheless. You asked me my conditions, and I gave them. And as I said, your offer is most generous." The lord knew a good deal when he saw one, then. Common greed warred with fruity ancestral honor. Rafe knew which one mattered more in the end. "I'll tell you what, Mr. Winters. I'll agree not to entertain any more offers on my property until the end of the Season. In the interim, show me that you can evolve into the man of culture in whom I can invest. If your establishment can become something other than the overly glittered tavern it currently is, I might reconsider selling to you."

Rafe knew he should tell this man to piss off and then go find another property in London to transform into his dream, but he realized at once that it was impossible. The location of the Corner Castle was half its appeal, directly in the heart of Mayfair and opposite his club. Its beauty and its history were another part of the charm.

If he was to do this, make this final move into respectability, he must have that building and none other.

"Changing the look and tone of the place could alienate

the customers I've already got," he muttered.

"What is it you men of business often say?" Sackville-Chambers gave a smug smile. "That's not my problem. I've given you my challenge, Mr. Winters. Will you accept?"

Rafe wanted to break his smile in half, one firm whack of his cane to do the job. But he was too smart for his own good sometimes, and he knew this was the only way forward. *Almost there. Keep going until the job is done.*

"Fine," he rasped.

"You're invited to revisit us anytime you like, my lord. That way, you can keep up your inspections and be involved in the process. I'm sure we could use your expert opinion." There Jacks went, smiling and sly as ever.

The poncy lord puffed himself up with her compliments. "Well, that might be arranged. I'll take my leave now."

"I'll walk you out." Rafe gripped his cane and stumped toward the door.

"Oi, Rafe! Forgetting something?" Jacks held up the wolf mask.

Sackville-Chambers gave an amused and condescending noise. Right, he probably saw masked balls and fancy-dress parties as the province of children and tasteless hacks.

"I own the place, Jacks. I can do as I please, eh?" He led Lord Sackville-Chambers out the door and into the crowded forest.

Rafe's scowl allowed him to cut a clean swath through the crowds milling about his foyers, drinking his wine and ogling his dancers. As he went, Rafe scanned the people around him, always looking for an attack. In this world, you stayed alert, or you wound up with a mouthful of broken teeth.

But it was possible to reach a place of greater safety, and Rafe was almost there.

Chapter Three

Well, *this* hadn't been the right corner, either.

Susannah made an exasperated noise as she came face-to-face with her own reflection in a gilded mirror. Another dead end, one that was lined with art and mirrors and sumptuous couches for, er, passionate meetings. She blushed again as she hurried back the way she'd come, making a left this time.

"Let's go to the Wolf's Den, Zan. We'll have such fun, Zan," she grumbled to herself, mimicking Annabelle.

A few masked women in fine gowns giggled as they raced past her, a bottle of champagne in one of their hands. They wavered back and forth, tipsy already. Susannah looked to see if Annabelle were among them, but no luck.

They really ought to be getting home by now.

Susannah's mother had allowed her to spend the weekend with Lady Henry in the hopes she would meet and mix with the most elite society. Constance thankfully did not know that Annabelle and her husband were two of the wildest members of the English peerage. Henry often came home at all hours, and he and Annabelle had once gone to a house party in the country and stayed nearly two weeks. The hosts had tried everything to get them to leave. Rumor had it they'd set their own hedgerows on fire to make the location less desirable to their immovable guests.

But Lord Henry's father was one of the most respected men in England, and thus all his son and daughter-in-law's intrigues were hushed up.

Lucky them. But even Henry might grow worried if his wife never came home tonight.

Susannah turned a corner, sure this time it must be the main path.

"Bloody hell." She stomped one slippered foot in irritation.

She'd come upon another room, nearly abandoned save two drunken people snoozing at a table. This was a theater of some kind. The lower level had tables and chairs, while the upper level hosted rows of more conventional red velvet seats. There was a small stage at the front of the room, and on it was…a pianoforte!

The tips of Susannah's fingers tingled as she imagined climbing onto that stage and touching that instrument. She could pretend she had an audience. In a way, she did. Those two drunks might be asleep, but they could likely still hear.

"Oh, why not? This whole night's like a dream. One more before we're done," she whispered to herself. Susannah mounted the stage and sat upon the bench, tracing one finger along the keys.

It was a handsome instrument of polished rosewood and ivory. It might even rival the one at Lynton Park, her brother-in-law's estate. Whoever had chosen this had fine taste indeed.

She struck a few keys lightly, enjoying the notes' perfect pitch. It had been well tuned, too.

"Would you like to request anything in particular?" she asked the drunks.

One of them snorted and pitched forward until his head was on the table.

"I choose, then? Very well."

Susannah loved Mozart's music above all the composers she'd studied. His seemed the brightest and sweetest, the most playful. She decided the Piano Concerto no. 21 would do nicely and began to play.

She'd meant to play softly, as not to draw too much attention to herself, but the instant she touched the keys, she felt as if she'd been framed in a beam of light.

Susannah could forget time when she played, lost in a world of beauty. Soon her fingers ran up and down the keys, the music floating through the air as if on a cloud. Susannah could picture a grand Viennese orchestra playing alongside her.

When she'd finished the first passage, she decided to play it again at a faster tempo, just for fun. It felt as though her hands didn't belong to her any longer, her fingers worked so quickly. She leaned back and forth, letting the music surge its way through her with an energy she adored. When she came to the very end, Susannah even added a few of her own flourishes. There was no improving on Mozart, of course, but she was having fun.

Finished, Susannah sat back and took a breath. Music inspired so much passion in her body that she sometimes forgot to breathe. She laughed…and then stopped when she heard applause.

The two drunks had woken during her performance and now staggered to their feet as she finished, clapping and whistling for her. One of them still had his rabbit mask on, while the other had removed what seemed to be a skunk's face. Probably for the best. Why should anyone want to be a skunk, anyway?

"Tha's beautiful! Beee-yooo-tiful!" The rabbit tried

to whistle with two fingers in his mouth but fell to the floor instead.

"Give us another, love! You play so pretty!" The former skunk took a swig from a tankard of ale. "Only could you maybe do 'Little Mary Beth Lost Her Spoon?' I like that fast busy music you play, but I'd love to hear li'l Mary Beth again." He sniffed. "Reminds me of me mum, so it does." Then he sat down and started to weep.

"Hooray!" The rabbit got off the floor and applauded again, oblivious to his friend's tears.

"Thank you!" Susannah gave a small curtsy and wondered if she should tell the poor man she'd never heard "Little Mary Beth Lost Her Spoon." But then another, harsher male voice sounded in the theater.

"Oi! What're you doing on my stage?"

Susannah froze as the man with the cane strode toward her, blue fire in his eyes. Her heart beat faster, and not only because of his fearsome look. Earlier, he'd been the wolf, but now she saw his human face. And even though he scowled, she could easily call him the most beautiful man she'd ever seen.

His hair was pitch black and curled in a devilish way about his face, rather like pictures she'd seen of Lord Byron. His eyes were pale blue, their gaze sharp and cold as a dagger forged from ice. His jaw was lantern-shaped, the cheekbones high, and dark stubble coated his chin. He looked rough, this man, like he could take on the world in a fight and win. The cane didn't make him look infirm; rather, it added to his air of menace.

Susannah couldn't help comparing him instantly with the Duke of Huntington. How different they were. The duke was golden-haired, his shoulders broad and his muscular form healthy, his jaw strong and his bearing regal.

This man was strong as well, but in a leaner and hungrier

way. She doubted there was an inch of fat on his body. It was, she thought, like comparing a lion and a wolf. One was a creature of sunlight, the other of shadow.

Susannah knew the duke was handsome, but this other man… She'd never been this desperate to touch a man before. She wanted to trace her fingers along his stubbled jaw, feel the proud line of his throat, and even run her hands along the steel and sinew of his arms. His chest. And…everywhere else. What did it mean?

Well, she'd have to figure that out later, because this sinfully beautiful man looked like he was about to berate her again.

"No one was using the instrument. I thought this was the Hunter's Ball." She decided to be quick and unafraid, so he wouldn't be able to bully her. "Aren't we allowed anything we want tonight?"

"I meant liquor and dancers, not my property."

True, she'd seen how he'd dispatched the man fondling his artwork. But Susannah was doing nothing so lewd! She squared her shoulders.

"It's not as though I'm about to steal the thing, and I've certainly done no damage to it."

"She plays—*hic*—beautiful!" the rabbit cried. The surly man shot him such a look that he ducked beneath the table.

"She does, indeed." A fourth man entered the room, one who also did not wear a mask and who bestowed upon Susannah a thin smile. She froze, recognizing him as Lord Sackville-Chambers. She knew every member of the *ton* on sight, and they knew her. Susannah thanked God above that she was still masked, or her reputation might have been gone on the spot. "Mr. Winters, this is precisely what I meant earlier." He gestured to Susannah. "A lovely musician with talent and taste is exactly the sort of creature you should employ."

The black-haired man eyed the lord. "That so?"

"That was Mozart, wasn't it, my dear?"

"Yes." Susannah tried to pitch her voice lower in case he recognized it.

"And you did all that with no sheet music? Incredible."

"It is?" The rude man cleared his throat. "Of course it is."

"Think on what I've said tonight, Winters. I'll show myself out if you don't mind."

Susannah exhaled in relief as Sackville-Chambers left the room. Her relief was short-lived, however, as the man, or Winters, as he'd been called, came to the edge of the stage and glowered up at her.

"You, girl. Come down. I want to talk to you."

"I…" What would Julia say? Probably that Susannah should stand her ground and not allow a man to order her about like that. "I prefer it up here, thank you."

"Fine." His ice blue eyes traced down her form. "I can get a better look up your dress at this angle."

Of all the insolence! Susannah strode off the stage and down the steps, cheeks flaming. The handsome, horrible man stopped her exit.

"If you didn't want anyone playing the instrument, you ought to have blocked off the stage." Susannah had to force herself to be, well, forceful. But she believed she was managing it.

"You got a little fire to you." He nodded. "I like it." Once more, he looked her up and down. "For a prim society miss, you seem to handle yourself well."

"You don't know anything about me. How do you know I'm from good society?"

He gave a sharp, predatory grin. "Trust me, Red. You speak posh, and you played some fancy music like you've been practicing your whole life. None of the girls from down the rookery know their Mozart."

He was a quick man, but also hard. There was an edge of

danger about him that Susannah knew she must reject.

"And no true gentleman would have ever spoken to a lady as you've been speaking to me, so we both understand each other."

Where had *that* come from? There was something about this dreadful Mr. Winters that ignited a fire inside of Susannah. She did not feel so afraid to speak her mind when in his presence. After all, why should she? They would never meet again after tonight.

"I'm no gentleman. You can be sure of that." He took a step nearer, looming above Susannah. Her heart thrilled at the low, husky quality of his voice and the obvious strength in his body.

Even though it was not proper, for a moment she wondered how his stubble might feel against her skin if she kissed him. Susannah had never kissed a man before. Until tonight, she'd never wanted to. What would it be like?

"But what I am," Winters said, "is a businessman, and a good one. My club here's proof of it."

True. The Wolf's Den was a well-run establishment if nothing else.

"Congratulations. Now I really must find my friend." She made to leave, but Winters stuck his cane before her. That snarling silver wolf's-head handle was so very…him.

"I've an offer for you," he said.

"You must be joking. I could never entertain offers of any sort from strange men." His suggestion, whatever it was, had to be scandalous. Susannah would not be shoved around. "In fact, my *fiancé* would rather I did not." Granted, the duke had not yet proposed, but it was only a matter of time.

"Oh? Fiancé, is it?" He smirked. "Terrible shame. A girl like you ought to have some fun before getting locked away by a husband."

"He would never lock me away. He's no jailer. He's a duke."

Now the man outright laughed in her face. The nerve! "Don't you believe me?" she snapped.

"Oh, I do, Duchess. I do. I'm sure you'll have a grand life." The way he looked at Susannah, it was as if he saw straight through to the bone and marrow of her. "But you're not married yet, are you?"

"What are you suggesting?" Her throat swelled and her entire body tingled as she pictured this man offering some scandalous affair. She could imagine the two of them meeting in secret, his hands caressing her body, his lips burning upon hers.

She must refuse! She would refuse. She hoped he'd ask her so she could do just that. *Immediately.*

"I'm suggesting you might like a job."

Well. She hadn't expected *that.* "Excuse me?"

"I need to change up my acts around here for a while. About a month, say, until the end of the Season. I need a girl to play music nightly, but she can't be any old musician. I'm looking for someone posh and talented enough to draw in the new crowds I want. What do you say, Duchess? Care to earn your own money for once in your life?"

Now Susannah knew she must be dreaming. This scoundrel wanted her to play for crowds? Nightly? She imagined playing upon this stage for a whole audience, the lot of them captivated by her sound.

It was…too marvelous to be true.

And it was also impossible.

"If you know I'm from good society, then you know I can't entertain your offer. I've my reputation to consider."

"I can make it worth your reputation."

"I doubt that." She began to move around him.

"Five thousand pounds, say. That's a lot of cash in exchange for a month's work. What would you say to that, Duchess?"

Susannah had nothing to say; in fact, she was lucky not to

have fallen over on the spot. *Five thousand pounds?* While it was only a fraction of her dowry, it was more than enough to secure her independence.

She could leave England on her own, travel on her own, see the world and meet the people in it without having to be conscious of class or race or any of the other ridiculous things that kept people apart. And to earn her freedom, she had only to do a month's work, a job she would have happily done for free.

It was a beautiful offer. It was perfect. And that meant it could never be.

Susannah knew that her loss of reputation would affect her mother and even Julia. She would not bring scandal on them for anything. Even if it meant giving up everything she'd ever wanted.

"Goodbye, Mr. Winters." Susannah hurried for the door.

"You'll come back, love. I saw that look in your eye." His voice was rich as sin and warm with laughter.

Susannah dashed out of the room and down the foyer. She looked behind her to make certain the man was not following, then collided with someone.

"Oof!" Annabelle fell backward and sat upon the floor. Her mask was askew on her face, and she'd splashed her glass of champagne all over her gown. Dripping, the young woman appraised herself with a sigh. "Well, that's a shame. But perhaps a fourth glass would've been improper."

Susannah helped her friend to stand up, then hurried along with her arm about Annabelle's waist. The other girl giggled and talked nonsense as they finally found the right path and headed out of the forest.

"What's got you so bothered?" Annabelle nudged Susannah. "Did you find a handsome bear or something?"

"No." Susannah shivered. "Just a wolf."

Chapter Four

Susannah had little sleep that night. She tossed beneath the blankets and thought of Mr. Winters's offer, not to mention the brooding Mr. Winters himself. She thought of travel and freedom, then of shame and social ridicule. Over and over, she pictured cold blue eyes and midnight black hair. She was exhausted the next morning, yawning on the bench before her pianoforte. Annabelle had dropped her at home so Susannah could receive callers, and just now the young woman could not make up her mind what to play.

Her mother, Lady Beaumont, was parked upon a sofa and embroidering a cushion. Susannah took after her mother in petite size and delicate features, but their coloring was totally different. Lady Beaumont's hair was ashy blond, her eyes a chilling blue gray. Susannah's mother dressed in the apex of fashion, and always kept an eye on everyone in the *ton*, waiting for the smallest slipup that she could snatch for gossip. The only person who had Lady Beaumont's total admiration was the Duke of Huntington. Susannah's mother always insisted the girl be around in the morning in case the duke should call. Every now and then, her mother would glance at the morning room door with longing. The occasional rehearsed sigh punctuated the quiet.

"I do *so* hope we'll have some visitors," she said for the fourth time in half an hour.

"I believe there's only one visitor you want to see, Mamma." Susannah began to play a fugue by Bach. Her mother pursed her lips in disapproval.

"Must you choose something so morbid, Susannah? At any rate, you should be the one excited to see him, not I. You're the one who's marrying him, after all."

"The duke hasn't proposed yet." Susannah almost missed a note. Oh, why couldn't Julia be here right now? She'd have a few choice words to lob at Constance, and then Susannah would be free to play music and dream while the melodrama continued in the background.

"I'm sure he will. Nevertheless, a little encouragement on your part wouldn't hurt matters, my darling. You don't smile at him near enough when he visits or when you dance with him."

"The duke is a friend of mine. He knows well enough that I like him," Susannah said, growing cross. He was indeed her friend, and one she valued.

For two years, she'd seen the duke often at Ashworth's estate. The Duke of Huntington was a charming and agreeable man, attentive to every lady in his presence. Susannah and he had got on well, and she liked him tremendously. But she'd never felt any burning desire for him and had been certain he felt the same. Until this past summer, when Susannah had felt his attention start to change. He began looking at her more than any other woman in the room. He lingered by the pianoforte in the evening, complimenting her playing and making light conversation.

Constance had been wild with joy when she saw what was happening. Julia had been elated. And Susannah had tried to feel as excited as they did.

The door opened, and Constance shot to her feet. The cushion went flying.

"Yes, Hodge?"

"The Duke of Huntington to see Miss Fletcher."

Constance looked like *she* was the young miss on the threshold of a fairy tale marriage. She hurried to Susannah, adjusting her shoulders to make her sit straighter.

"There's no time to add extra curl to your hair." Constance tsked. "We'll have to hope it's good enough."

"The duke's seen my hair many times, Mamma. We're such old friends, I'm sure he wouldn't mind if I wrapped my curls in rags while entertaining him. If we're to marry, after all, he'll have to see me like that often."

"I don't like the influence Julia has had upon your thoughts. No one likes funny women."

Susannah could have discussed how her brother-in-law, the Duke of Ashworth, certainly did like her stepsister. But Huntington entered the room, and Susannah had to rise and curtsy along with her mother.

The Duke of Huntington caused a minor commotion wherever he went for good reason. He was a full six and a half feet tall with golden hair, sky-blue eyes, and the muscled physique of a modern Hercules. Women from sixteen to sixty often fanned themselves vigorously when he walked by. Susannah found it all humorous, because while she appreciated the duke's handsomeness—indeed, who wouldn't?—she admired him as she would a statue in a museum. She felt no burning desire to touch him. To her, he was for display purposes only.

Yet a wife ought to feel more excitement about her husband as a man, surely. Susannah liked to talk with Huntington, but she never thought of him when he'd left after a visit. She never yearned to see him again. So now that he was courting her, she found herself a bit tired whenever he entered the room, for it meant she would have to pretend more enthusiasm than she felt. A shame, for she did truly like being his friend.

If her mother had any notion of Susannah's thoughts at the moment, she'd scream. Susannah forced herself to wear a smile.

"Your Grace, how charming to see you." Constance accepted the duke's respectful bow over her hand. "You caught us completely unawares."

"Yes. My mother throws her embroidery around for fun," Susannah said, eyeing the abandoned cushion. She giggled, and the duke smiled in his usual charming way.

"I hope you ladies are well. Miss Fletcher, it's always good to see you working at your music." He bowed to her, and his lips brushed the back of her hand. Susannah waited to feel that spark of excitement that everyone said a woman in love must experience. Again, she was left wanting. Ah, well. Perhaps next time. "I hope you don't mind. The roses in my hothouse are in full bloom, and they rather reminded me of you."

He offered her a bouquet of red and cream roses, which Susannah accepted with an expected charming blush. Really, he was a terribly good man.

"Will you take some refreshment, Your Grace?" Constance smiled as she began to ring the little silver bell beside her with vigor. Susannah had to strike a few keys on her instrument to disguise the sound of her laughter. "I'm certain we can have something put together."

The door opened and Hodge bowed through a footman who set a tea tray upon the table. The tea was from China, which the duke preferred, and Constance had ordered the cook to make the raspberry scones Huntington had mentioned in passing he liked. Once. Two months prior.

"How very spontaneous," Huntington said. This time, Susannah had to slam her hands on the keys to disguise her giggling. He winked at her, charming as ever. She did like him so very much. Why couldn't she seem to love him?

That's what marriage is for, I suppose. Learning to love your husband.

But Julia had loved Gregory almost from the moment they'd met. Susannah sighed and played a simple tune, reproaching herself. Her stepsister had been deprived of nearly every advantage with which Susannah had been blessed. After her father died, Julia had been left virtually penniless. Constance had tried to keep her stepdaughter from marriage so she could retain Julia as a perpetual nursemaid and companion. Julia had become a duchess through sheer will and determination. Susannah was being given such a position on a platter. Any other woman would be delighted.

"What are you playing?" Huntington asked, putting down his cup. "It's lovely."

"Something I've been noodling with." Susannah would sometimes sit at the pianoforte, let her mind wander, and allow her fingers to travel across the keys in search of a tune. "I'm no composer, of course."

"Yes. Composition is a man's territory." Constance chuckled as though she'd been amusing. Sometimes Susannah wished she could roll her eyes at her mother.

"I believe women should be encouraged to create as well as to copy." The duke smiled at Susannah again. "Also, I should love to hear you play upon our instrument at Moorcliff. The acoustics in our music room are said to be the finest in England."

"Oh. Moorcliff Castle?" That was the duke's family seat, all the way in Northumberland on the very border of Scotland. "That seems an awfully long trek for a visit to the music room." She gave a weak laugh.

"Susannah." Constance's voice was a sugar-laced warning.

"No, she's quite right." Huntington rose and stood beside the pianoforte, one hand laid lightly upon the instrument. "You would need a very special reason to make the journey all the way north."

His implication was clear: when they married. Constance looked as if she might die immediately and dance off to heaven, where she'd rub Susannah's brilliant match in the faces of the angels. Susannah, meanwhile, wanted to run out of the room, out of the house, and keep running until she was out of London. If she could have run across the Channel, she would have been in France by teatime. Though she liked Huntington, he was so upright, so calm, so untroubled, that marrying him really would be like marrying a statue. Susannah imagined she would become something like a statue herself as a duchess. Lovely, immovable, and cold. The thought made her want to scream.

"Ah. Yes. A nice visit might be just the thing." She focused on her playing and prayed Huntington did not notice that she refused to meet his gaze.

"Or perhaps something more permanent." He spoke low, but she heard what he meant. Permanent. Monuments were permanent, as were graves. To Susannah, this particular marriage would be like being buried alive.

"Oh. But surely His Grace would not want to sit up in the country forever. He must wish to return to town at some point." Susannah tried for hope. Maybe it wouldn't be as dull as she feared?

"Not if I had my way." The duke chuckled. "Sometimes I think my idea of heaven is watching the seasons pass through the windows of Moorcliff Castle for the rest of my days. It would be perfect. So long as I'd the right companion, of course."

A lifetime up in the country, barely a soul around. No action, no travel, no adventure. The thought made Susannah hit a wrong note, and she winced.

"Goodness. My mind wanders."

The duke laughed and took her hand, bowing over it again. "I must go, ladies. I hope I'll see you both at the Duchess of Ashworth's ball?"

"Of course." Constance smiled as she and Susannah curtsied to the duke.

"Thank you for the visit, Your Grace," Susannah said.

She continued playing after the duke had left, tuning out all of Constance's exclamations and declarations of joy. While her mother vocally considered what cut of bridal gown would best suit Susannah, the girl herself continued to brood.

The duke had hinted at Moorcliff. He'd as good as told her he would propose, and likely soon. It would be wonderful, would it not? A titled husband who adored her, multiple estates, a grand position in society. A castle of her own, a world of barricaded comfort to keep her safe forever more. A life without action, without danger, without trying what scared and thrilled her.

Susannah felt herself on the cusp of bursting into tears.

"I may need to lie down for a while." Susannah stopped playing. "I feel a headache coming on."

"Of course. You've already entertained the only worthwhile caller, anyway." Constance kissed Susannah's forehead. "A future duchess needs her beauty sleep."

While her mother tittered, Susannah trudged upstairs with weariness growing in her heart. She lay facedown on her bed and considered how selfish and spoiled she was. But it couldn't be helped. When she thought of marriage to the duke, a little voice inside her said the same thing over and over.

Don't do it.

It didn't matter if Susannah *was* the most wretched and worthless creature alive. She couldn't resign herself to this marriage. Impossible. The thought made her want to scream. She moaned and turned onto her back, staring at the ceiling.

The only escape she could see was that hateful Mr. Winters and his offer. But her reputation would be tattered if she accepted, and she could not do that to her mother. Susannah could never knowingly wound someone like that.

She shut her eyes and imagined herself back in the fantasy forest, dressed in her red cloak and mask, wandering aimlessly along the paths. She thought again of Lord Sackville-Chambers, of how fortunate she'd been that he hadn't recognized her. Because of the mask.

Susannah bolted upright. Oh, that was a ridiculous idea. Wasn't it? She'd have to be daft to think it could work.

But what if it did? What if she could protect Constance and Julia *and* set herself free? Susannah rolled off the bed in a most unladylike fashion, then sat at her desk and scribbled off a quick note to Annabelle. There were only two people in the *ton* who could know what she was up to.

...

The following day, Susannah rode with Lord and Lady Henry through the streets of town in their coach. She stared out the window, rehearsing her speech over and over in her mind, tapping her satin reticule with impatience.

"I say, this is damned exciting stuff." Henry, a red-cheeked, ginger-haired man of four-and-twenty, looked the eternal schoolboy whenever he was delighted, which he often was. Annabelle giggled and hung upon her husband's arm.

"We can be the perfect accomplices, can't we, my love?" She kissed Henry's lips, longer and fuller than she should have done before an unmarried young lady.

Susannah shielded her eyes and giggled helplessly. The two were so in love, it was almost sickening.

"We can fool all those snooty *ton* bastards." Henry kissed his wife's cheek...and down her neck. *Oh dear.*

"We can lead double lives, risking ruin at every turn," Annabelle said breathlessly. "Why, suppose we were caught and flung out of good society? Or better still, arrested and put on trial?"

"Why would you be?" Susannah asked. "We're doing nothing criminal at all." But they ignored her, lost in their own private world.

"What fun we could have playing that scenario out." Henry's pink cheeks had turned a flaming red as he nibbled his wife's jaw. Susannah wondered if she could perhaps roll out of the carriage.

"I've just the outfit, purchased from Madame DuMaurier's last week. It comes with velvet manacles."

"You wanton hussy," he growled. Annabelle and Henry became lost in kissing each other, their moans growing more heated, their embraces tighter. The carriage rolled to a stop.

"We're here, milord," said the driver.

"Oh thank God." Susannah leaped outside and hurried for the club's entrance.

"Zan! You go ahead, darling. We'll be along in a moment," Annabelle called before shutting the carriage door and rolling down the blinds.

In the light of day, the Wolf's Den looked like any other posh address in Mayfair. The building's front was of gray stone with Corinthian columns framing the doorway. The large wooden door itself was equipped with an ornate brass knocker. A most respectable gentleman might live here. Only a placard on the side of the building advertised anything unusual about the place.

THE WOLF'S DEN

Liquor, gambling, fantasies made flesh

Well. That certainly sounded unusual.

Susannah knocked, waited, then knocked again. After a moment, someone opened the door. Susannah tried not to look too surprised. It was clear this person was a woman, but she was dressed in men's clothing and looked as if she didn't care a jot about that fact.

"Hello! May I help you?" The woman smiled, an expression as sunny as Mr. Winters's had been shadowy.

"Ah, is Mr. Winters available?"

"Oh. Who's asking, please?" The woman appeared a touch less friendly now, almost wary. Perhaps this Mr. Winters often entertained complaints from affronted young women. That wouldn't surprise Susannah in the least.

"If you could tell him that the duchess from the other night has come to call, he'll know who I am."

"Well. It's just past noon, so he may be up. Come in, Your Grace." The woman made a courtly little bow and let Susannah inside.

Two nights ago, this foyer had been crammed with people in fine silks and satins, drunk on champagne and laughter. Now it was a dingy, rather common-looking corridor. There was a staircase to either side, both of which led to the second-floor landing and the club's main entrance. Two maids were busy dusting and washing up the detritus of last night's revels.

"Can I tell Rafe what this is about, Your Grace?" the woman asked.

"Tell him I've come about the job."

The woman blinked and shook her head. "A duchess who needs a job. What times we've come to." Whistling, she strolled off and Susannah took a seat upon a small velvet bench beside the door.

She inhaled the scents of the club, the lingering cigar smoke and the sharp smell of liquor underneath. It was not the place any well-heeled young lady should investigate, let alone enjoy. But Susannah found the idea of working here was almost too exciting to bear. Imagine playing all night for an adoring crowd, drinking until three or four, sleeping until noon. The freedom of it all stirred her blood.

If I do this and get the money, that's what my whole life could become.

She'd make certain to take leave of England in the least scandalous way possible, to spare her family. Once she was in Italy, no one would give a damn what she did. Susannah imagined playing in opera houses, in grand salons, or even in luxurious clubs like this one. She could have cried with joy.

"So. The duchess comes back." Rafe Winters walked down the steps toward her, leaning upon his cane. In the light of day, his handsomeness had not evaporated. His hair was still black as sin and untidy, his chiseled jaw unshaved. He gave a rather rakish and crooked smile, eyes gleaming with pleasure to behold her. Susannah pressed her legs together tightly, feeling a strange, hot sensation between her thighs.

"I've decided to accept your offer, Mr. Winters. Or should I call you Rafe?"

"Well, Rafe's for my friends. Mr. Winters is for my business associates." He stopped before her, that silver wolf's head snarling in her face. "So how about you call me sir?"

Susannah narrowed her eyes and rose. "So you're rude during daylight hours as well."

Indeed, he seemed to challenge her whenever they met. Susannah rather enjoyed that challenge; most men of the *ton* treated her like she was precious and breakable.

"You should've taken the offer when you'd the chance, Duchess. Think you're the only posh girl in town who needs money?" He smirked, eyes sweeping down her body again. "Though you might be the prettiest."

Susannah ordered herself not to blush. Challenging *and*

complimentary; it was enough to set a girl off-kilter if she wasn't careful. "Who, may I ask, has taken the job?"

"Well. I'm still considering several candidates." He tilted his head to the side, eyeing her carefully. "Tell you what. I'm feeling generous today. Take one thousand and the job's yours."

Susannah chewed her lip, thought, and then crossed her arms. "You don't have any other candidates, do you?"

"What makes you say that?" His eyes gleamed with merriment. Her answers seemed to delight him.

"There aren't many well-bred young ladies with as extensive a repertoire as mine who're looking for a job at a club."

"Times are hard, Duchess. Girls are desperate."

"Oh, I'm sure they are. But no matter how desperate they are, they're not as good as I am." What a conceited thing to say! But Susannah knew it was the truth, and she didn't think it right for women to deny their own talents. She knew that men liked it when women downplayed their achievements. It made women seem "sweeter," for one thing, and it probably allowed men to pay women less than they were worth. She wondered if this wasn't a test on Mr. Winters's part to see if Susannah was strong enough to match him. She'd show him she was more than his equal.

"I don't need a true gentlewoman, you know. I could take a tart off the street or out of a dance hall, polish her up, slap her in front of an instrument."

"And would this woman know every Mozart concerto by heart?" Susannah smiled, knowing she had him. "Would she be able to differentiate between Gluck and Bach, and how each style should be played?"

Rafe appeared lost merely trying to comprehend the names. Susannah suppressed a cheer.

"You make a point, Duchess. Very well. Two thousand

and the job's yours."

"You can't expect me to take such a reduction when you already offered five!"

"That was the offer I made two nights ago. Prices change the longer you wait." This afternoon he'd dressed more casually, in a shirt without a cravat, the top two buttons scandalously undone. Susannah caught a glimpse of a fine, broad chest with chiseled definition. She wondered if she'd have to sit back down; she felt rather faint.

"Why do you need a musician, anyway? You said you needed someone like me to start immediately and play through the end of the Season. Why the haste?"

"That's my business." He seemed reluctant to discuss secrets with her. Well, Susannah could understand.

"Business with the *ton?* Has it to do with what Lord Sackville-Chambers was saying to you, about changing your acts?"

Rafe appeared truly surprised for the first time.

"You know Sackville-Chambers."

"Of course. I know everyone in town." A new angle emerged, and Susannah snatched it. "Pay me five thousand for the performances, and I'll add something else to the pot: my connections and knowledge. I know exactly what sorts of taste the true toffs like Sackville-Chambers have, and I've access to those in his world. I can help you there."

Rafe frowned, looking as though he were deep in thought. Perhaps he was now truly calculating her offer. Susannah felt a little proud. She was negotiating and standing up for herself! Julia would be so happy, that is, if she didn't burst into flame upon hearing Susannah's deal. Even a liberal-minded woman like Julia couldn't countenance a girl from high society working in a gentleman's club.

"All right. The playing with your assistance pays five thousand. Deal." He extended his hand to shake hers.

Susannah had never shaken hands upon striking a bargain in her life. How marvelous. "There's one more thing," she said.

"Let me guess. Champagne in your private dressing room before every performance?"

"That sounds jolly nice, but no. I need to maintain my reputation for my family's sake. No one can know who I am. So, I'll play in your club and gather the audiences you want, but I'll do it while masked and under a different title. It'll lend the whole act an air of mystery, which the upper classes adore. What do you think?"

Rafe considered again, eyes narrowing. Even when he looked pensive, he was the most attractive creature she'd ever beheld. This was going to be a fascinating experience, one that almost frightened her.

"The Duchess. No, the Musical Duchess. Hmm." He cursed. "Something's missing."

Susannah recalled her red cloak and mask of the night before. How he'd called her Red.

"The Red Duchess." She grinned. "And I'll wear that crimson cloak again, so it covers my hair. Some might recognize my hair, after all."

"Long as they can see some part of you, we can work that out," Rafe said. "Oi, Duchess. You're rather good at this negotiating business."

"Well, it could be a family trait. My father was a merchant."

"What's he do now? Swill port and live at his club?"

"No. He's dead." Susannah studied her gloved hands, feeling somewhat wounded. "I don't remember him at all. He died when I was a baby."

"Ah. Well." He frowned and stared at his feet. The Wolf of Mayfair appeared rather sincere. "Sorry about that. It's no good thing to never have a father."

"Mr. Winters apologizing? This is a fine thing."

"Don't grow accustomed to it, Duchess." Rafe loomed over Susannah, and she found she couldn't help smiling. "Five thousand for one month's work. Shows five nights a week. That, and you use your expertise to get the snooty classes into my club. You remain masked and anonymous for your family's sake. Am I forgetting something?"

"I can't do anything during the day. There are too many *ton* engagements, and I'm expected to participate. In the evening, there are too many balls and parties to beg off all of them. I'll need to perform later at night."

"That won't work. If you're headlining my club, you can't take the evenings off for parties and such. You need to be on that stage at eleven nightly."

Eleven was when most balls were only finding their stride. Oh dear. Susannah's instinct was to turn it all down and run away, but she'd come so far. The future she wanted was only a month away if she'd the courage.

"Let me worry about how to get away. You provide the rest."

"Deal." He took her hand, and they shook. Susannah's heart fluttered. Though she wore gloves, she got the feeling his hands were rough, callused, the hard hands of a hard man who had done hard things to survive. She ought to be repulsed, but tingles shot up and down her arm. She was near enough to him that she could even smell the heavenly, masculine scent of him. Tobacco, and brandy, and strong white soap. This man felt like danger and freedom all in one.

Susannah looked up at him and noticed he was staring at her with intensity, a hunger she'd never seen before. Her body felt warm and liquid at the sight.

"I'll need a demonstration of what you're planning, of course. A rehearsal of sorts."

"Haven't you already heard me play?"

"I know you've the talent, but I want us to find a strategy for what your program will be. Never leave anything to chance, Duchess. That's how you rise in the world."

"Very well. Now?" Susannah frowned.

"Is something wrong with that?"

"It's just that I can't linger." Though she wished to, strangely. "I've people waiting for me in the carriage."

A wild knocking came at the door. The woman in the suit from earlier hurried down the stairs and answered.

"Is our friend in here?" Annabelle sounded breathless. "Forgive our rather rumpled appearance. There was, ah, a bee that got into the carriage."

"In here, Annie."

Rafe's face was a treat to behold as Lord and Lady Henry hurried to meet them. They were so well dressed, and yet so utterly disheveled. Annabelle turned her back and seemed to quietly readjust her bodice as her husband spoke.

"We've come to chaperone Miss Fletcher." Lord Henry cleared his throat. "I say, Zan. Nothing untoward has happened, has it?"

"Zan?" Rafe furrowed his brow.

"Yes. My name's Susannah Fletcher. Zan for my friends, Miss Fletcher for acquaintances." She tilted her chin upward, feeling bolder than usual. "So you may call me Duchess."

Rafe laughed. The sound was unexpected and delicious. He put a hand to his face, getting himself under control quickly.

"All right. I need an hour or so of your time in the Rose Room. That's where you were night before last."

"Shall we come, Zan?" Annabelle asked.

Strangely enough, Susannah didn't want her friends to chaperone her with Rafe. She felt energized by being alone with this man. She felt indecent, which should have frightened her but didn't.

Fortunately, Rafe was ahead of her.

"Jacks," he called. The woman in the suit reappeared. "Open the front bar for these two. Give 'em whatever they want."

"Oh, but it is only half past noon," Annabelle said, already following Jacks out while dragging her husband by the hand. "We couldn't possibly."

"Now, now, my love. Champagne is a good starter for lunch," Henry said as they left. Susannah laughed, relieved to have such devoted—and hedonistic—friends.

Then she was alone again with Rafe Winters, and again she felt a touch of blush redden her cheeks. He moved away, leaning on his cane. She wondered if he'd been born with that injury or had sustained it somehow.

But that would be a rude thing to ask. Susannah followed her new employer, trying not to watch him and failing utterly.

Chapter Five

This could be a dangerous idea.

Rafe settled into his seat and watched Miss Fletcher climb the steps to the pianoforte.

Two nights ago, he'd found her lovely even with a mask covering her face and a cloak shielding much of her body. Now that he saw her in the open light, unmasked and in a soft muslin gown, he felt himself spiraling out of control.

He had never seen a woman with such delicate curves before, or such a sweet, high bosom. The girl's eyes were no normal shade of brown, but amber. With her red hair, she seemed to be made of fire.

He wanted her to burn for him. He wanted it badly.

Don't let your cock ruin your business. Rafe sneered at himself, annoyed by his own weakness. So what if he entertained feverish dreams of pressing his lips to Susannah's own, of listening to the delicate moans she'd make as he slipped a hand between her legs and touched the most intimate part of her.

She had to be a virgin, maybe she'd never even had an orgasm before. Young society misses were so repressed. The idea of being the first man to touch and stroke her, to hear her breathless cries of ecstasy as he made her come, almost caused him to lose his bloody sense.

He frowned at the wolf's head on his cane. Its frozen snarl felt like an admonishment. He had to remember who he was, and who *she* was.

"What should I play?" Susannah asked when seated at the instrument.

"I don't know my Mozart from my Back."

"Bach?"

"Him, too."

The girl laughed, which made Rafe's cock stiffen that little bit more. God, this was going to be torture.

She began to play, letting the music rock her back and forth upon the bench. He could imagine a whole ballroom filled with fine people dancing as fast as possible, twirling in perfect synchronization. Very pretty, but Rafe shook his head.

"Stop. Oi! Stop, I say."

She stopped and appeared perplexed. "What's wrong?"

"Sounds too boring and pretty. I want to spice it up a bit."

She glared flatly at him. "This is Mozart's overture to the *Marriage of Figaro*. It's one of the liveliest pieces he ever wrote."

"Play something else. Something more…I don't know, more."

The girl rolled her eyes, cheeky minx. Then she brought her hands down upon the keys and played something that sounded rather dramatic, the kind of music you'd expect to hear as you fell overboard during a violent storm and were drowned at sea while giant whales laughed at you. It was a very specific type of drama.

"Stop! Stop. You got anything more cheerful?"

"You said you wanted something more…more!"

"You should know what I want when I say what I want, even if I myself don't know what I want. It's what I'm paying you for."

"You've paid me nothing yet."

"Go on. Play something that'll thrill the crowds."

"You are an impossible man." She huffed, lacing her fingers together and stretching out her arms. After a moment's contemplation, Susannah began to play once more. This time, it sounded light and bright and quite simple. Too simple, in fact.

"Now what are you playing?"

"That great masterpiece of high culture, 'Pop Goes the Weasel,'" she replied.

Rafe got up and walked over to the stage, wincing as he moved. That right knee was being a regular bastard today. When he stopped at the lip of the stage, Susannah spun to face him with her arms crossed. He realized he could see up her dress a bit from this angle, noticing a white stocking that accentuated a shapely calf. He forced himself to stop looking.

"I need you to play something that'll draw in the high culture crowds," he said.

"I know. That's why I'm playing Mozart and Handel. This is what audiences with fine taste enjoy!"

"But you were different two nights ago. Why?"

"Besides the mask, you mean?"

Oh, she was a clever little beast. He liked that far too much.

"What I heard was you playing what you yourself wanted, isn't that so?" Rafe knew he'd hit upon the truth; he could feel it beneath his breastbone. "Don't worry too much about what the toffs want. If I've learned anything, it's that the real money's in giving people what they want before they know it's what they want."

"That sounds more like magic than business."

"A good businessman's like a magician, only better. When I give people something that's false, they can still hold it in their hand. Drink it, dance with it. Take it to bed, even, and walk away smiling come the morning."

A scarlet blush adorned the girl's cheeks. Fuck, she really was an innocent. It enflamed Rafe's lust while also making him hate himself a little more than usual. And he hated himself plenty on the best of days.

"Well. A good musician's like a magician, too. I strike a few keys upon an instrument," she said, doing just that, "and it stirs emotions that would've slept otherwise."

The girl dreamily played on a bit more, and this time there was a change about her. The music was fine and fancy as ever, but the way she connected to it seemed to heighten everything that Rafe heard.

She tilted her head to the side, her lithe, delicate body swaying back and forth. Her music was the wind, and she was bandied about by it, higher and higher into the air. Rafe didn't know if anyone in the audience would recognize this, but to him, the musician herself was the real show.

"Very nice." Rafe cleared his throat; his voice sounded more hoarse than usual. "What was that?"

"Only a tune I've been working on for myself."

"Compose as well, do you?"

"Composing helps me think." She lifted her chin, defiant again. "But I imagine you're not paying me to think. Isn't that right?"

She was clever. Funny. Bright and sweet, as well as beautiful. She gave him a peace he'd never known with her playing. That bit of music had stirred something inside him. He wanted to hear more. He wanted to hear more of Miss Susannah Fletcher's true voice.

"Go on. Play more. There is more, isn't there?"

She looked surprised. "There is. You don't mind?"

"I like it. It sounds...I don't know. Different."

She returned to the piece. Once again, she disappeared into her work, smiling as her melodies carried her far away. Rafe still admired the graceful motions of her arms, the movement of her head upon her slender neck, but as the music continued, he found himself concentrating less on the girl's exquisite form and more on the girl herself.

She was a good composer; he didn't know much about music, but he knew that. The lilting, almost hypnotic passages felt rather shy and secretive, but then there'd come a tiny burst of passion that would surprise him. It was as if Miss Fletcher had written out little truths about herself in a series of musical notes and was allowing him to glimpse them.

He wondered if anyone else connected the music with the musician this way, or if he was the sole lucky bastard. But to him it was damned obvious. He heard something gentle and yet strong, funny yet somber, lively and dreamy all at once. The whole woman was a work of art, not just her physical beauty or her playing.

Rafe was a businessman, yes, but at heart he was a collector of art. He wanted to live in a world of beauty, a world of luxury and elegance that would blot out every last horrid memory of his youth. To him, life was worthless without the exquisite.

Numb, he thought how this girl, her playing, her spirit, might be the most exquisite anything he'd ever found.

With a few quiet notes that seemed to linger in the air like smoke from a snuffed-out candle, the piece ended. Susannah beamed, looking radiant. She loved to perform; it was as natural for her to be an artist as it was for a butterfly to crawl out of a chrysalis.

"Did you like it?" she asked.

I love it. It's perfect. You're perfection.

"Yeah, that was good," he muttered. But his astonishment

was plain, because Susannah chuckled. Rafe made his slow way up the steps. He wanted to stand opposite her, look her in the eye. "You must've been to some posh music school."

"Sadly, no. I always wanted to attend a conservatory in Vienna, but most of the great schools admit only men."

"This world can be such an unfair place." Rafe had long seen how women in this world were held back on every conceivable level. They suffered for it—he knew from experience how much—and he hated it. Every person had a right to fight for their own life.

"That's a rather progressive view, Mr. Winters." She looked surprised and delighted.

"Well. I'm a progressive fellow." Rafe cleared his throat, trying to get his thoughts in order. He'd negotiated with crime lords and viscounts and never flinched once. Somehow, this small girl had him nervous. "Where'd you learn to play, then? Just your governess?"

"She taught me much, but my true education came from Herr Gruber."

"Her who?"

Susannah giggled. "Herr is the Prussian word for "Mr." My stepsister hired him to come from Vienna just to instruct me. He lived here for two years, and he said I was the strongest pupil he'd ever taught. He told Julia I'd a touch of genius about me."

"That a fact?" Rafe's admiration warred a bit with surliness.

Susannah had a hard lot as a woman, but she was also rich. Being rich could ease a lot of the injustice of this world. It was another reminder of how she belonged to Sackville-Chambers's kind, and not to Rafe's own. There'd always be that barrier between them, one not even a rise in his respectability could ever breach.

No. Susannah was made for this duke fiancé of hers, not

for Rafe. Never for Rafe.

"Well," Rafe said, "it's good but it's not what the *ton* expect. We'll need a safer choice like that Mozart you played."

"I thought you said the Mozart wasn't enough."

"He wrote more than one piece, didn't he? I'm sure we can find something that'll work."

Rafe couldn't allow himself to be too amazed by this girl. She would take from him and then leave; she could never be convinced to stay. As Rafe started to walk to the steps, he had to stop and bite back a cry of pain. He'd put too much weight on the bad knee again, and the hot, pulsating flash of agony obliterated his thoughts.

"Are you all right?" Susannah sounded truly concerned. The thought she might pity him felt like a slap. He glared at her over his shoulder.

"I don't need nursing. I need you to play. I need nothing else, understand?"

He had to keep her at arm's length. He needed to keep her as far away as possible, because while she'd been playing, he'd felt something inside himself opening. Something that had slept for years. If she hurt him right in that vulnerable spot, it'd make his smashed knee look like a scratch in comparison.

"I just wanted to help." The young miss sounded wounded; he'd pricked her pride, eh? Too bad.

"I need no one's help, Duchess."

"If that were so, you wouldn't need me to court Sackville-Chambers's favor, would you?" She played once more, a dynamic and fleet tune that sounded as fancy and arrogant as the musician herself.

"You know nothing about what I need," Rafe growled.

"Fine." She stopped again. "And you know nothing about what I can do. So leave me to my job, and I'll leave you to yours."

"You're a mouthy little thing." He turned back around.

"Why are you doing all this, anyway? Doesn't your duke fiancé have enough money to keep you in pianofortes?"

Susannah bit her lip as she stared at the pianoforte's keys.

"Maybe I don't want to marry him," she said softly.

Now Rafe surely must have heard wrong, because no woman on earth could be so bloody foolish.

"I missed that. What'd you say?" He gripped his cane's handle to steady himself. "Sounded to me like you said you don't want to marry a duke."

"Well, I don't! Is that so wrong?" The girl flushed crimson again.

"What is he, a hundred years old? Short? Poor, ugly, with a lousy sense of humor and the personality of a turnip?"

"No. He's young, handsome, tall, clever, rich, and incredibly kind!"

"Right, I see now why you'd want to run away from all that. Forgive my questions. You'd better charter a boat to get out of the country as soon as possible," Rafe drawled. "Maybe you can make an appeal to the king himself, see if he'll grant you royal protection. What, you're some well-bred-but-penniless girl with a pretty face who this perfect man wants to snap up as a possession?"

"No." Susannah was sulking now, perhaps hearing how ridiculous she sounded. "My father left a fortune for me to inherit."

"You might see why I can't understand what you're doing here." Rafe felt real fire grow in his breast in addition to amusement. The streets were crawling with young girls who'd led hard lives, girls who had been beaten, starved, forced to work in brothels from the time they were eleven years old. They'd all have killed for a single shot at a handsome, wealthy duke, and this girl was trying to run away like she was the victim here. Rich girls always made Rafe sick; it was nice to remember why. "Why are you taking five thousand pounds off me when you've a fortune of your own?"

"I won't inherit it until I marry. And I don't want to marry!"

"So you'll take my five thousand and buy your own pelisses and bonnets, eh?" Rafe approached her again. "You rich girls think you're so daring. Really, though, you're spoiled rotten."

"You know absolutely nothing about my life." Miss Fletcher rose from her bench and faced him. Well, she faced his chest; the girl wasn't that tall. She was small, so slim and delicate and tiny. Yet she was also bold as brass. She was wonderfully complex, and so far above him. He could never reach her, especially not with this bum leg. That thought made him all but wild.

"Tell me, Duchess. Go on. What's so difficult about being some posh girl from the right side of town? The high society life too dull? The rich twats of London too boring? You ought to be happy you've got boring in your life. Where I come from, being bored means you've got everything you need."

"We're not talking about the same sort of thing at all," Susannah said. "Anyway, how is all this supposed to help either of us? Shouting at me won't get the elite into your club, and it certainly won't help our business relationship."

"Business. Tch. What's some green young miss know about business?"

"I don't know anything. It's true." Even though her lissome form was trembling with passion, she would not back down from him. Truly, he'd never seen a society girl with this kind of fire before. "But can't I learn? Learning's not only for the lower classes, is it?"

"No. It's not." Rare indeed that someone with money recognized her own limitations. Especially when that someone was also so sinfully beautiful, with doe eyes and delicate wrists. When she was brave and talented and brilliant. When she was standing so close, he could catch the warm scent of her perfumed hair.

"Then why don't you stop antagonizing me, sit down, and let me finish this bloody rehearsal so I may go home."

"You feel free giving orders, don't you, Duchess?" Rafe grinned, feeling energy flooding his limbs for the first time in God knew how long. "I'll wager you boss your staff about all day long. But here's the thing, sweetheart. In my club, you play when I tell you."

He loomed over her and lowered his face to hers. Susannah was trapped against the bench and had nowhere to go as Rafe drew nearer. He caught the faint scent of honeysuckle and rose. She was all things sweet and natural, and that thought only made him want her more. But he couldn't have her, because this world was unfair and because he had not been born anywhere near her circles. Everyone from her world would see him as inferior; maybe Susannah did, too. Maybe it's why she felt so free to talk back to him.

"I don't boss anyone about," she murmured.

"You think you can boss me about because I'm trash from the street? Because I own a business?" he growled. Rafe knew he ought to back away, but being so near to those pink lips, those expressive amber eyes, that trim waist, and those graceful arms was turning him into an animal.

He'd been called a wolf even back in his days as a thief roaming the London streets. Hungry, ruthless, he'd been the type to lash out and bring down an enemy before they could think to do the same to him.

He'd always taken what he wanted when he wanted it, knowing it might not be there any longer if he waited. Right now, he'd an appetite the likes of which he'd never known before.

"I don't think you're trash." She sounded breathless.

"Well, then you're a fool. I'm a worthless cur, the kind of man all good parents keep their daughters far away from." He leaned closer to her, and Susannah did not faint or sit down or burst into tears. If anything, the girl appeared to waver on the balls of her pretty little slippered feet. Almost as if she wanted to touch him. Reckless girl.

The sight and the scent of her overwhelmed Rafe, as did the warmth of her body. Her music still seemed to float about inside his head, stimulating his soul, what little shreds of it were left.

"I'm not afraid of you," Susannah said.

"You should be. If you knew what I was thinking just now, you'd scream and run."

His heart pumped in his breast, so full and slow, he could hear it. The girl licked her rose-petal lips.

"What are you thinking?" she whispered.

He did not answer with words, only brought his mouth down upon hers and kissed her roughly.

Chapter Six

Susannah forgot how to think as the man kissed her.

It was her first kiss, and Susannah had always assumed that her first kiss would be with her husband, the only man she would ever kiss. She'd expected kissing to be full of affection and gentleness, but that was not this at all. This was an inferno of passion that engulfed her the instant his lips touched hers.

She gasped with the shock, with the sensation of heat rushing through her veins. She lifted onto her toes, heard a pleased growl in the man's throat, and then wrapped her arms around his neck when he pulled her close and crushed her to his chest.

Susannah opened her mouth, only a bit, and moaned as his mouth opened in turn. He kissed her deeply, with finesse and experience that made the foundations of her soul move about. Her eyes rolled back as she kissed *him* now, kissed him with equal feeling as she lost full control of her senses.

His stubbled jaw scraped her cheeks, and Susannah relished the coarse sensation.

His mouth was hot and ruthless upon hers, conquering

her, capturing her as if she were a spoil of war. Nothing should feel this good.

She held him, anchoring herself as the feeling threatened to sweep her away. When they stopped the kiss and she gasped for air, a pleased growl sounded in his throat. As if he were truly a beast. Or a wolf.

"Very nice, Duchess," he whispered, his lips upon her neck. His warm breath tickled her, and Susannah began to feel a sensation between her legs, a slippery and throbbing sensation that threatened to obliterate all common sense. "You're a fiery little thing, eh?"

Susannah ought to scream and cry and shove him away. She ought to race out of the club, sobbing about her lost innocence, going home to hide in her room until the duke arrived to claim her like a little wayward sheep for him to shepherd. Society demanded that she do all those things, but Susannah had little patience for society's rules. Society had never kissed Rafe Winters before; it didn't know what it was talking about.

She kissed him again, all fears leaving her in a rush of longing. Though she was a bit clumsy with her lips and tongue, the man was masterful and soon had her learning the steps as elegantly as she might a dance.

Susannah shivered when his tongue slipped into her mouth, a move so audacious she could have died. But died with pleasure, not embarrassment.

Rafe held her close, so close that her feet lifted from the stage as he straightened up. Her arms were locked about his neck, her cheeks now raw and tingling from being scratched over and over by his stubble. The scent of leather and good tobacco engulfed her, those masculine scents women were not supposed to enjoy but which she adored.

When they stopped once again, permitting them both the space and time to breathe, Susannah kept her arms about his neck, her fingers wound in his black hair.

Her breath was rushed, her heart galloping in her chest, a buzzing in her blood and in her hands. Susannah felt as if she'd woken up from a long sleep, the longest of her life. Hell, it was as if she'd been asleep since she was born, and only now opened her eyes and saw the true colors of the world around her. The fantasy had fallen away. No more dreams, but reality.

"I say," she whispered.

"Mmm?" Rafe began to close his mouth over hers again.

Dear Susannah, may I heartily recommend that you remember yourself and request this gentleman put his tongue back in his own mouth?

Because my sweet, if anyone should catch you in this compromising position, you'll be ruined on the spot, and Julia and your mother would suffer the consequences. Most sincerely, yourself.

Susannah's conscience had managed to send a rather polite message to her, given the circumstances. Lord, what was she doing? Susannah stopped kissing Rafe and pushed away from him. That movement proved a bit awkward, as her feet were still off the ground and pedaled for a while in the air. Thankfully, Rafe set her back upon the stage.

"That was. Ah." Susannah could not think of the proper words, beyond "enthralling" and "earth-shaking." Those might not deter him, however. "That was...very wet. Thank you."

Rafe fought against laughter. Oh, apparently, she was amusing. How delightful.

"Sorry about that, Duchess. I got carried away for a moment." He leaned upon his walking stick, eyeing her as if she were some savory treat about to be gobbled up. "Sometimes I end up mixing business with pleasure."

Pleasure. It had never sounded like such a grand word

before.

Susannah was rather hazy on the realities of men's and women's, er, interactions, but Julia had bequeathed her a stack of Gothic literature that had furthered her education somewhat. Pleasure between a man and woman usually meant heated embraces upon a silken chaise longue, kisses on the neck and eyelids, and a mounting sense of tension somewhere in the body. Well, Susannah could feel something like tension in the center of her hips and between her thighs. It made her feel fluttery.

She'd never imagined that those trashy reads were telling her something true. How incredible.

"We..." Susannah felt herself about to capitulate back into his arms, hungry for more. Thankfully, that polite voice of her conscience hissed at her in a less-than-polite manner to stop. "We shouldn't have done that."

"No. Of course not," Rafe said. She could read nothing behind the ice blue of his eyes, and his gruff, delicious voice gave nothing away. Was he angry? Bored? Amused? She'd no way of knowing. "Sorry, Duchess. I overstepped the mark."

"It's all right. I didn't...not...enjoy it." Susannah was going to either faint or burst into a giggling fit. Perhaps she'd do both.

"Pleased to hear that. I aim to do my best," Rafe said.

She could remember being lost in his arms, pressed to the warm yet rock-hard line of his body, and that memory inspired fever to course through her once more. She could never be alone with Mr. Rafe Winters again. Susannah couldn't trust herself around him, and she must be so careful now for her family's sake if not her own. If she put a foot wrong, her reputation would be in tatters, her dreams of the Continent vanished, and the people she loved would be disgraced.

"But that can never happen again."

"No. You're right, it can't." He sounded so sure of it that she almost wanted to pout, ridiculous though that impulse made her.

Some part of her wished he'd growl that rules meant nothing to him and kiss her again, taking her against halfhearted protests. But Mr. Winters was a good businessman, if not a gentleman, and he had to know that this moment between them posed too much trouble.

"I'm sorry if I gave you the impression your advances would be welcomed," she said stiffly.

"Well. My advances *were* welcomed, eh?"

Susannah could feel her face heating to impossible levels. She must look tomato-ish at this point. "This business relationship between us has to work, for both our sakes."

"Agreed."

"So. Let's chalk it up to a strange moment and move on, yes?" Susannah didn't think further rehearsal would do much good today. She edged past Rafe, afraid to put her back to him, lest he grab her about the waist and ravish her. Well, perhaps she was less afraid and more secretly hopeful.

"Fine, Duchess. Your first show's tomorrow night. Eleven sharp, you're on stage. If you're late, our little deal's off."

"Yes. Fine." She didn't like being ordered about and sought a way to strongarm him as well. "I should also like something in writing, in case you try to renege on our agreement."

"Oh? Miss Susannah Fletcher would like to sign a contract tying her to this establishment?" Rafe gave another of his wicked grins. He had quite a collection of them. "That'd be a juicy piece of blackmail for me, wouldn't it?"

Right. Susannah was a fool.

"Oh, this is a mistake," she muttered.

"I keep my promises. You do the same, and we'll have a fine time of it." The man turned his back on her then, casting a brooding eye upon the pianoforte. "Off with you."

Susannah rushed out of the theater. Her head spun with the events of the last few minutes, so much that the hallways practically swam before her eyes. In her confusion she made a couple of bad turns before she finally stumbled upon Annabelle and Henry at the front bar.

They'd gone through a bottle of champagne already, and Annabelle was seated upon her husband's knee, running fingers through his hair. They were whispering endearing, vaguely filthy things to each other as the woman in a suit stood behind the bar and watched them with amused disbelief.

"Zan! Join us, darling. We're having *such* a nice time." Annabelle hiccupped.

"That was our best champagne. Whose tab am I putting this on?" the woman asked.

"Er. Mr. Winters said all my drinks are on him." Susannah ushered her friends off the stool. Then she had to wait for Henry to get up from the floor. He seemed to be having a difficult time of it. Eventually, Susannah and Annabelle managed to drag him to his feet and to stagger back and forth with him propped between them. In this ungainly fashion, they headed out of the club.

"Something tells me you'll be a headache for Rafe, Your Grace." The woman laughed heartily. "I like it already."

Susannah managed to negotiate her drunken friends out the front door and back into the carriage without all of Mayfair noticing their dissolution.

They rode for home, Henry curled up on his side and asleep upon the floor. He smacked his lips and kissed Annabelle's shoe, smiled, then fell back asleep.

"You had only one bottle!" Susannah said.

"Oh. No. One, *hic*, each!" Annabelle held up four fingers. "Three total!"

"Oh dear."

Susannah was relieved when her friends dropped her off at her mother's home. She made her excuses to Hodge, asking him to tell her mother that Susannah had another headache and needed to lie down a while. Then she went upstairs and lay upon her bed, gazing at the ceiling with thoughts buzzing through her mind. She was horrified at what she'd done today, both the deal making and the kissing.

What kind of ungrateful wretch was she, to turn up her nose at the duke and her family, all so she could live out some selfish dream?

She ought to send a note telling Mr. Winters she'd reconsidered and that she would be obliged if he never spoke of their dealings to anyone. After all, she'd nothing in writing to tie her to the man, and Annabelle and Henry could be trusted. When they were sober, of course, and when they were drunk no one believed a word they said, anyway.

But every time Susannah thought about Mr. Winters—Rafe—and what had occurred at his club, that warm tingling began in her limbs again, that pressure building in a secret place between her hips. She'd wanted more, and more, unable to get enough of him and his lips and his indecency.

If Susannah hadn't been able to regain control of herself, how far would they have gone? He was obviously a man without honor, who used women and enjoyed himself at their expense.

Why did she find that thought so dreadfully delicious?

"I'm a monster." Susannah moaned and buried her face in a pillow, trying to force the exquisite memories of Rafe's kiss from her mind. Half-reluctantly, she admitted that the physical desire between them, while crackling, hadn't been the sole reason she'd yearned to kiss him.

When she'd played her own composition, there'd been something in his eyes. It had been there a moment and then gone, but it had looked in some strange way as though he'd understood her. When she'd played her own music for Huntington, he'd thought it a clever hobby, but Rafe looked as if he'd heard Susannah herself speaking through the music.

Susannah hadn't guessed how astonishing it could feel to be recognized by somebody else. Especially not someone for whom she felt such overpowering hunger.

This was much too dangerous. She'd make certain never to be alone with him again, that's all. She had to be at the club only a couple of hours a night, and just for a few weeks. Then she'd have the money and her freedom.

And the first show was tomorrow night! Susannah would find some way to beg off whatever gala her mother wished them to attend. It couldn't be that hard. After all, this was to be her theatrical debut, what she'd longed for since she was a little girl. Her dreams started to come true tomorrow night.

Tomorrow night…

"Oh no." She sat up with a gasp. "Oh…*bollocks*."

That word was another uncouth thing she'd inherited from Julia. Dear, sweet Julia, whose grand ball was tomorrow night! It was one of the biggest events of the Season, an engagement Susannah absolutely could not squeeze out of.

What the devil was she to do?

• • •

Rafe had never known a kiss quite like it before.

He'd known plenty of women in his time, had sampled kisses from every type of girl in Europe, and none could compare to Miss Fletcher's. How could some green girl have knocked him back on his heels like this?

After she'd fled the stage, he'd ordered Jacks to oversee the preparations for opening tonight. Jacks kept asking after a few bottles of champagne, but Rafe paid no mind. He needed to be alone with his thoughts.

A man in his physical condition perhaps shouldn't live in a flat with several flights of stairs to climb, but he felt truly safe only in the Wolf's Den.

Rafe liked to live on top of his own little world, a secure perch from which he could look down upon all the rich bastards in Mayfair. He could watch over them, collect their dirty secrets, and live off their cash. And Rafe liked to live with gusto.

As a boy sleeping on dirty floors, he'd promised himself that one day, he would reside in a palace and sleep on silk sheets. He'd kept one half of that promise, at least. Rafe's flat took up the entire top floor of the building, a spacious eighteen rooms, most of which he never saw. But he filled every corner of his surroundings with beauty. Even as a young thief, he'd possessed a preternatural ability to sense how much things cost. Jacks might riffle through a lady's drawers and snatch a necklace with a fat, glistening diamond hanging from it, thinking she'd made their fortunes. Rafe could tell at first glance it was paste, only cheap costume jewelry. Meanwhile, he'd come away with a delicate string of small seed pearls that, while appearing utterly nondescript, turned out to be two hundred years old and worth a fortune.

Rafe bought as much fine furniture and art as he could, and what he couldn't purchase himself he strongarmed out of his wealthiest members. If an earl or a viscount had a bad night at the tables and didn't want his wife to know, Rafe could be persuaded to forgive a bulk of the debt provided the nobleman parted with that Rembrandt he was famed for owning, or perhaps that Louis XIV chair upholstered in silk. The mark would bluster the piece of art was worth ten times his debt, but Rafe always walked away with his prize in the end.

He entered the front parlor of his flat, locking the door behind him as he sauntered toward the window. From here,

Rafe had a prince's view of all Mayfair.

He gazed down upon the clean streets and fashionable carriages carrying ladies and gentlemen to supper or the opera.

Rafe poured himself a tumbler of expensive whiskey from a crystal decanter and sat in that silken Louis XIV chair, sipping away. He glanced around his flat and all its treasures. The gilded mirrors, the fine Persian carpets, the silk wallpaper, and the crystal chandelier whose pendants twinkled in the candlelight, all of it was his. He was king of his own fantasy kingdom from up here, a place where no one could ever touch him again.

But the thought of touching brought Susannah Fletcher back to his mind, and he shut his eyes as the memory overwhelmed him. She had tasted exquisite, all rose and innocence, and yet she had ignited in his arms, kissing him back with equal passion.

She was more than just a prim little miss. She was more than just a potential lover, too. She was a fiery little genius, a sweet and stubborn angel. Susannah was something fine, something as rare as the Botticelli hanging in his foyer or the hundred-year-old bottle of Chateau Lafite in his cellar.

And she frightened him a little because, unlike his paintings and wine, he could never own her. She was too perfect to ever give herself to a creature like him. Maybe she'd give herself to him for a night, but Rafe already knew that a taste of her would never be enough. Besides which, he didn't want the girl to sully herself with him.

Rafe belonged with Jacks and the club's dancers, with the other misfits who'd been given no place in society and had to carve out a life for themselves on the margins. He didn't hate it. He'd found a safe haven for himself, a paradise all his own. Even if it was lonely, it was luxurious. But Susannah deserved more. She deserved more than any man could give her, but especially more than Rafe could.

He would have to be a regular monster to let Susannah get involved with something like him. While Rafe was a wolf and a brawler, he wasn't a monster. He couldn't let his own lust interfere with Miss Fletcher's beautiful dreams. She was a girl made for sunlight, and he had been born for the underground. No matter how desirable she was, no matter how sweet and sensual her body, no matter how rare her spirit, he could not let himself be even worse than he already was.

So, he drank his whiskey and resolved never to touch her again.

Chapter Seven

Susannah curtsied to her dance partner, the eldest son of the Baron Wimpole, and applauded the musicians as the quadrille concluded.

Wallace Wimpole escorted her to the side of the room, speaking with a high, excited voice at having had the honor of dancing with her. Not that Wallace wanted to court her or anything. Oh no. He and the rest of the *ton*'s eligible men had stepped back when the Duke of Huntington made his intentions clear.

The duke could have any prize he desired, after all.

I wonder if this would be the ideal time to faint. Hmm.

Susannah needed to choose her moment carefully, but she couldn't wait too long. She needed to be at the Wolf's Den at least half an hour before she went on stage, and that meant she needed to leave Carter House within the next twenty minutes. She felt a twinge of guilt at the thought of deceiving Julia and Gregory, but it couldn't be helped. Susannah's stepsister was her dearest friend in the world, but even freethinking Julia could never condone this plan.

"You look exquisite tonight," Julia said as Wallace

deposited Susannah and bowed to her. The Duchess of Ashworth positively glowed that evening. Julia was a tall woman with golden hair and cornflower-blue eyes that practically sparkled with intelligence. Dressed in the height of fashion, one could easily mistake her for a queen.

"Well. No one can outshine our hostess," Susannah said with a wink.

"Please! It's been a mere two months since Violet was born, and I'm doughy as ever. It's just a relief Ashworth still finds me appealing. Of course, if he didn't, I'd have to lash him to the bedposts in our room to keep him from wandering off." Julia's husband had once been the most notorious rake in England.

"He would never do that! Ashworth adores you."

"Too true. Though the lashing him to the bedposts idea has merit on its own." Julia gave a wicked grin.

"You're supposed to protect my innocent ears!" Susannah laughed.

"A woman should lose her innocence in stages, darling. You're quite old enough for the ears."

Susannah shook her head at her stepsister's silliness.

Julia truly looked radiant tonight. She was the type of woman who seemed to become more beautiful during and just after pregnancy. Perhaps the glow came from being so blissfully in love. Though they'd married for rather mercenary reasons, the Duke and Duchess of Ashworth had become the *ton*'s most celebrated fairy tale love match. Whenever they looked at each other, their adoration was apparent, despite their playful teasing.

"I've found her. The most radiant woman at this ball. Indeed, in all of London." Gregory Carter, Duke of Ashworth, appeared between the two women. The tall, dark-haired man winked at Susannah and slid an arm around his wife, pulling her close. Julia beamed. Decorum demanded they behave themselves, but the duke was permitted a light kiss.

"What were you saying about this radiant woman?" Julia purred.

"Lady Forsythe. She's over by the punch, would you like me to introduce you?"

Susannah stifled a giggle when Julia poked her husband in a not-so-ladylike manner. The Ashworths loved nothing more than to tease each other. Well, they seemed to love something more, but Julia said it would be indecent to perform publicly.

"I have to disagree." The Duke of Huntington appeared beside Susannah, looking down on her with great interest. He was as tall and handsome as ever, dressed in a sleek, dark blue waistcoat that highlighted the color of his extraordinary eyes. Women gazed at him in awe from every corner of the room. "Apart from our esteemed hostess, Miss Fletcher must be considered the incomparable of the evening."

"Thank you, Your Grace." Susannah gave a quick curtsy in greeting. She hated the way her gut twisted when she met with the duke now. There was nothing wrong with the man... apart from the fact that he just felt, well, wrong.

"May I have the next dance? I believe it's to be a waltz."

Susannah checked her dance card, but it was for show. No one ever requested a waltz from her; everyone considered those to be the duke's domain. It was as if all of society were an audience at the theater, waiting for the hero to propose so they could dutifully applaud.

"Ah, you unmarried men have all the fun." Gregory grinned. "I remember my carefree bachelor days, dancing with any pretty girl I liked and getting shot at by their husbands afterward."

"If you don't behave yourself, I'll send you to the nursery with Arthur and Violet," Julia said sweetly.

"Excellent. Have some of those jammy tart things sent up. Children eat so much better than adults."

"You know, if you really miss being shot at, I'm certain we could come to an arrangement."

Susannah and Huntington smiled at each other and shook their heads. It was nice to have another somewhat normal person to talk to when Julia and Gregory were enjoying themselves. If only her relationship with Huntington could stay like this, friendly and amused. The musicians warmed up, preparing for the next number, and couples found their way to the floor.

"Shall we?" Huntington took Susannah's hand and led her to the center of the room.

All the other dancers parted for them, whispering in awe as Susannah tried to pretend they weren't staring at her.

The interest of London society combined with all the gossip columns breathlessly recording every one of Susannah's meetings with the duke made her almost unwell. She was the most celebrated unmarried woman in England. It should have been the great triumph of her life. At least it gave her mother something to enjoy. Lady Beaumont clipped and saved every one of those gossip columns.

"You really are exquisite tonight," the duke said as they began the dance. He was so much taller than she that Susannah had to negotiate her steps with care.

"You're always so kind to say."

"It's not kindness, only truth." His blue eyes crinkled at the corners as he smiled. The duke's eyes were the blue of a summer sky, but now Susannah could think only of Rafe's ice blue eyes. Rafe, that is, Mr. Winters, was cold and sharp where the duke was warm and comfortable.

And speaking of Mr. Winters, Susannah needed to get out of here very soon. She scanned the crowds for Annabelle but couldn't find her. Oh no. If Annabelle and Henry were behaving badly on the veranda right now, Susannah would be miffed. Well, no matter what, she needed to make conversation with her dance partner.

"How are things up at Moorcliff Castle?" she asked and regretted it at once. Inquiring after his ancestral home would only make him think of taking her there as his duchess!

"They're excellent. My sisters say that Northumberland in late spring is lovelier than anyplace else in England. They're quite right, of course. There's so much that needs attending to in the castle after winter passes; I'd rather be overseeing repairs to the estate than enduring a ball or the opera night after night. Too much frivolity, wouldn't you agree?"

Susannah disagreed to the very core of her being. She couldn't say that, of course. "It must be unpleasant, then, for you to be down here in London."

"I'd like to go home, provided I had a suitable companion for the journey."

Susannah felt how he appraised her, and she felt his approval. "You could always get a dog, I suppose."

Huntington laughed. "I'm very selective, unfortunately. It takes me a while to choose anything. But when I've chosen, I'm always right."

Susannah forced herself to keep smiling. "Yes. You, uh, probably want one with a good pedigree. A dog, that is," she said quickly. Lord, her brain was about to fall out of her head. What was she on about?

"Pedigree is important. But so are temperament, liveliness, intelligence, and health. All that makes for a hardy breed."

"Yes, breeding sounds like it's very important to you," Susannah muttered. Her cheeks heated up at once. A silly thing to say.

"It *is* important," Huntington said softly. He seemed to hold her closer. "There's much that needs to be passed down from one generation to the next. It's important to live for something greater than yourself, don't you agree?"

"Well, of course." Loving one's family was among the most important things in the world. But... "Though I think we should all choose what we're best suited to, don't you agree?"

"Perhaps a bit. But I wouldn't want to spend my whole life pursuing only what interested me. My tenants wouldn't thank me for that. I'm what they rely upon for a living, after all. And my sisters need a head of the family to look after their interests." He was utterly sincere, and Susannah sighed. Why did he have to be so bloody decent? "And, of course, I have the future of the line to consider. I'd be a worthless libertine if I didn't."

Her gut tightened. "So that's what concerns you most? Making sure everything continues?"

He smiled. "I do think some personal feelings matter. We shouldn't marry only for duty, after all. It becomes more of a life sentence than a partnership that way. I believe a man should care for the woman he takes as his wife."

Susannah's head throbbed, her throat felt ready to close, and now she actually *was* feeling dizzy enough to faint. She knew what the duke was saying, and she knew he cared, and she knew he was good, but it seemed like no one had ever asked Susannah how she felt about this. Not even the man who likely saw himself as her future husband. After all, shouldn't a wife care for her spouse, too? Besides, Susannah didn't want a man to only care about her; she wanted him to burn for her, as she would burn for him. Maybe wanting that made her an unworthy woman, but she couldn't help herself.

And when she thought of burning, she thought of Rafe Winters's lips upon hers, his hands touching her body.

She thought of how time was passing, and how if she wasn't promptly at the club at ten thirty, she would miss her only chance to have a say in her own destiny.

Her mind whirled as the duke continued speaking of how pleasant the ball was this evening and how well Julia looked and how adorable little Violet was. Susannah made light conversation back, her attention fixed elsewhere, on that stage at the club, on Rafe's hands and eyes and his luscious, sneering mouth.

When the waltz ended, everyone applauded the musicians and Susannah noticed Annabelle making her way around the edge of the ballroom. Lady Henry caught her eye and gave a quick wave. In truth, this couldn't have been better timed.

"Miss Fletcher, are you well?" The duke looked concerned as Susannah wobbled on her feet.

"I feel…rather… Oh!"

She slumped to the side, her knees giving out as the duke caught her. A couple of women around them gasped, but he'd been masterful about it, nabbing Susannah before she could fall on the floor. Susannah roused herself at once, apologizing profusely.

"I felt light-headed suddenly. It must have been the dance. I think it was one too many."

"I should have been more considerate," Huntington said. "Forgive me."

No, Susannah was the one who'd need forgiveness when this was all over. As the duke escorted her from the floor, Susannah heard a woman whisper to her partner.

"Probably swept up in the romance of the moment. Isn't it too perfect?"

It was better for everyone that people were impressed and not scandalized, but Susannah wished she could tell the woman to stuff it. Julia had noticed her almost take a tumble and fussed over Susannah when she returned.

"Darling, are you ill? Perhaps you need some brandy? Gregory, fetch her some!"

"I don't need to fetch anything. She can have a ladylike sip of my flask." Ashworth took the liquor from his pocket as he spoke.

Julia was indignant, naturally. "Hiding liquor at your own party? You have an adolescent's maturity!"

"And stamina. You never complain of that one, my love."

"I'm fine," Susannah said, quickly pushing off the flask. "I think it was simple exhaustion. I fear I've danced too much tonight."

"Would you like to go upstairs and lie down?" Julia asked.

At that moment, Annabelle popped up beside Susannah, her entrance timed to perfection. "Zan, I saw you wobble out there. I must leave a bit early." Noticing Julia, Annabelle made her halting excuses. "Beg pardon, Your Grace. My, er, parrot has developed, ah, mange. I don't trust anyone else to administer his, eh, drops."

"I quite understand." Julia looked like she didn't, but was too polite to pry.

"Anyway. I can drive you home in our carriage if you like!"

"That might be nice. I do feel a bit worn," Susannah said.

"Would you like me to see you home, Miss Fletcher?" Huntington asked. "It would be no trouble."

Susannah froze, ready to scream on account of her nerves. Oh, this sneaking around thing was exhausting. How was she to politely put him off without raising suspicion? Thankfully, her brother-in-law managed everything perfectly.

"Hunt, this is my wife's grand event of the Season. You're not leaving until it's past midnight and you're fashionably inebriated."

"Of course. I'd never disrespect such a cherished friend." Huntington bowed to Julia. "Or her husband."

"You bastard." Gregory chuckled as Susannah bid

everyone farewell, embraced Julia, and let the duke kiss her hand. It would all be so much simpler if she could look at this man and feel excitement. But nothing in her life was ever simple.

"Thank you," she whispered to Annabelle as they left the ballroom together. "I'll never make this up to you."

"Oh, please. Henry's meeting us at the club. I'd rather sip champagne with rakes and badly behaved women than attend one more society ball."

Yes, that sounded like Annabelle. As they climbed into the carriage and headed for the Wolf's Den, Susannah sighed in relief. They'd make it in time.

But the knot in her stomach, the one that grew tighter the more she thought about disappointing her family, was something that she knew would not disappear any time soon.

Chapter Eight

Rafe stood in the hall outside of the ladies' changing room, tapping his cane against the floor with impatience.

The girls were already dancing with clients in the ballroom or performing their more risqué moves in the smaller theaters dotted about the building. Miss Fletcher was adjusting herself in her costume, inspecting the red silk mask and velvet cloak Rafe had pulled out of storage for her.

"Stop scowling," Jacks said, walking past him with a bottle of champagne tucked under her arm. She had dressed with extra flair this evening, in crimson silk breeches with a waistcoat to match. She called it "advertising" for the Red Duchess.

"I scowl when and where I please. Shouldn't you be tending bar up front?"

"I had to get that Lady Henry a bottle of our best. She and her husband are seated at a front table in the Rose Room, and if I don't get them something to drink quickly, they might end up making an indecent spectacle of themselves." Jacks shook her head.

"Lady Henry?" Right, the blond chit who'd brought

Susannah. "This is a gentleman's club, Jacks. She ain't a gentleman."

"She made the point that because she's helping our new star get to and from the theater, she's entitled to a seat in the house."

"Still. She's part of the *ton*, if they notice her here, they might start asking questions."

"Don't worry." Jacks rolled her eyes. "The lady's masked herself, too. Stands out in the crowd, but no one knows it's her."

Rafe was going to have to deal with all these aristocrats mucking about in his business.

Jacks went to deliver the alcohol, and Rafe tapped his cane again in its slow, steady rhythm. Tap. Tap. *Almost there. Almost there.*

Sackville-Chambers had agreed to return tonight, to watch Rafe's little protégé in her theatrical debut. Perhaps having a musician of Susannah's caliber would speed this whole process along. Once His Lordship saw the quality of Rafe's performer, he might agree Rafe's taste had been good enough from the start. Perhaps they could tie up this deal tonight.

And then Susannah could take her cash and step out of his life.

He could probably shortchange her, too. Give her a thousand pounds, or even five hundred, or even less than that. After all, they'd signed nothing binding. The agreement had been for a month, and if she played only one night, she shouldn't be entitled to full compensation, yeah?

But Rafe knew he couldn't do that. He was a hard negotiator when it counted, but he believed in paying women what he'd promised them. Being poor was terrible no matter who you were, but a poor woman dealt with twice what a man did.

His whole life, Rafe had known women who worked for themselves and their families, who had to strive twice as hard for often half as much as a bloke. The Wolf's Den wouldn't be the success it was without his servers and dancers, and he paid them handsomely. More than that, he saw to it they didn't get stuck in uncomfortable situations with customers. Occasionally he'd had a creep roughed up a bit and tossed out, but it hadn't hurt his business any, and it had earned him loyal employees.

No. Rafe took care of his people, no matter what.

"I think it looks all right," Susannah said, emerging from the dressing room. "What do you think?"

Rafe smiled without meaning to. The girl's mask was a cunning little thing fashioned from red silk with crystal beads decorating the eyes for a little extra flash. Jacks had dug out the best red cloak they had, but it was still a little over the top for such a subdued, tasteful young miss. The cloak was of heavy scarlet velvet, with a raised collar that almost lifted clear above the girl's head. It was trimmed in swirling patterns of gold brocade, creating an outfit so heavy and rich looking, it seemed always on the verge of swallowing the young woman whole.

"Looks good," Rafe said.

Susannah harrumphed as she tied her mask tighter. "I feel as if I'm disappearing under this thing."

"Count it as a virtue. If people are paying attention to the costume, they won't be thinking too much about who the girl is behind the mask."

"Won't all this distract from my playing?"

For Rafe, she would always be a distraction. No playing, no matter how beautiful, could cause him to forget Susannah Fletcher for a moment. "Let's see how you do tonight, Duchess. If you can't overcome a bunch of red velvet, you're not much use to me, anyhow."

"Trust you to be charming as ever," she grumbled, cheeky minx. "And it's The Red Duchess, if you please." She spoke the full title with such a sense of over-the-top drama that Rafe had to fight to keep from laughing. The girl was disarming, no doubt about it.

"The stage is down this hall, through those curtains to the left. Wait for Murray to announce you, then walk up onto the stage, sit down at the instrument, and play. Remember, this has to work, or you don't get your money. Give us a show."

"Couldn't you try being a little more supportive?" Miss Fletcher sounded cross.

"Why should I be?"

"We're both in this together, aren't we? We both need this to succeed. You should be cheering me on rather than putting pressure on me."

"You debutantes are such delicate hothouse flowers." Rafe waited for her to go settle herself for the show, but Susannah wouldn't budge. In fact, she crossed her arms and glared up at him from behind the holes of her mask. "The audience is waiting."

"They can wait. We need to have a talk about something."

Rafe had no fast reply; he was stunned by how serious she appeared. Considering the gaudy costume, she'd managed quite a feat. "What is it?"

"I'm not going on that stage until you apologize for your rudeness."

He almost laughed, but she was deadly earnest. Rafe couldn't believe she was putting their whole enterprise on the line over a concern about bloody manners. "This is the theater, Duchess. Bad manners are part of life."

"But we're working together as a team. We're on the same side. I don't want this to fail. In fact, I need it to succeed, and I daresay you do as well."

"What are you saying?"

"If you continue to behave like this, we won't be able to work together. I'll be cross, and when I'm cross, I don't play as well. I know that's not what you want."

"No." He had to admit it. But he also hated to lose an argument. "But life's tough."

"It is. But you don't need to make your own life tougher. Do you?" She had him there. "I'm being honest about what I need to do this job well. I need you to apologize, and more than that, I need you to *understand* why you're apologizing."

Oh, this was bloody infuriating. But the girl stood as firm as any statue. Rafe felt surly, but with himself now. He truly was just trying to trip himself up, wasn't he?

Here he was on the threshold of everything he'd spent his life working toward, and he was about to throw it away on what? The ability to say whatever he pleased? On keeping a woman he craved at arm's length so it wouldn't hurt so terribly when she left him?

If Susannah was going to leave him, better she do it once they both had everything they had ever dreamed of.

"All right, Duchess." He gave a little nod of his head. "I apologize. Truly. We're working together on this. I can't afford to forget that."

"There, now. Not so hard, was it?"

Susannah's merry smile disappeared as they regarded each other with closer scrutiny, and the memory of her lips pressed to his momentarily overtook Rafe. He'd thought of that kiss all of today and had been counting the hours until the girl would be here again. He felt like some ruddy schoolboy, and he hated feeling out of control in any way.

"Play well," he muttered, and shambled away from her.

Sackville-Chambers was seated near the back of the room, a half-drunk glass of Chablis before him. The man had good, and expensive, taste.

Rafe settled himself next to the poncy lord and glanced

around. Jacks had done her job, shepherding a bunch of the more illustrious regulars into the Rose Room with the promise of free champagne. A couple of soused earls were present, even a dissolute marquess. A promising start.

"This is the same girl I saw the other night?" Sackville-Chambers asked. "I congratulate you on your acquisition, if so. She seemed quite unusually fine."

"She is," Rafe said gruffly. Susannah was fine in every respect. Unusual, too.

Up ahead, near the front of the theater, Rafe noticed Lord and Lady Henry giggling and drinking and doing potentially indecent things to each other under the table. He sighed in exasperation as Murray finally took to the stage, summoning everyone's attention. The master of ceremonies made a few opening remarks, gaining some enthusiastic and inebriated chuckles when he added some risqué lines about "a girl who knows her way around a fine instrument."

Sackville-Chambers shut his eyes in pained forbearance.

Shit. Rafe needed to think about presentation as much as performance. For the first time, he wondered if His Lordship, and even Susannah, had been right about him. Perhaps he was just a brute with pretensions to fine taste. The thought made him more sullen than usual.

Murray stepped down, and Miss Fletcher took the stage. There was a smattering of drunken applause, even a few whistles from some of the so-called gentlemen.

"Is that her regular costume?" Sackville-Chambers asked. He sounded like he was trying not to laugh.

Rafe squeezed the silver wolf's head, anger twisting his gut. It wasn't even that the arsehole was amused at Rafe's costuming or tastes. Anyone who laughed at Susannah in any way was bound to get his head knocked in.

"It's a work in progress," he growled. Rafe settled back and waited to hear the girl's incomparable playing. He waited.

And waited. Oh, damn it to Hell.

Rafe bit back a swear when he realized the girl was standing before the pianoforte, staring out at the crowd with wide, doe-like eyes.

Of all the times to get stage fright, this was one of the worst.

...

Ever since she was little, Susannah had loved pretending she was a concert musician.

She would set up rows of her dolls and an amused Julia and have them applaud while she plinked out nursery tune after nursery tune on Pennington Hall's pianoforte. Tonight, her dreams had finally started coming true…only now they were like a nightmare from which she couldn't wake.

A whole room of rich drunkards gaped at her. She caught the flash of Rafe's wolf cane as he turned it around and around, growing more frustrated with every moment that passed.

Must move. Must play music. Must not faint. Must try *not to faint.*

What was the remedy for such paralysis? Perhaps she was supposed to envision the audience in their undergarments, a trick she'd heard once from an opera singer at one of Julia's house parties. But she knew most of the men sitting in front of her, and none were paragons of masculine virility. The thought made her a bit ill.

"Play us a song! There's a good girl!" one of the fellows shouted.

Susannah swayed back and forth, a velvet-clad tree about to fall.

"Have you got 'Once a Fishmonger, Twice a Viscountess?'" someone called, followed by a loud belch.

"What about 'Whoops, Tore My Petticoats in Hyde Park?'"

"Play 'Little Mary Beth Lost Her Spoon!'" This request was followed by copious weeping. "Reminds me of me Mum, so it does!"

If Susannah didn't move, and quickly, her chance at freedom would be lost forever. And in an odd way, she didn't want Rafe Winters to be disappointed.

Not because she feared him, and not because she feared losing his money—well, not *just* because of the money. Susannah got the feeling he was a man used to disappointment, and even if he was a brute, there was something sad behind his eyes. He was, like her, a person who wanted something other than what he'd been given and was willing to work for it.

She wanted this all to succeed for his sake as well as her own, even if that made her a fool.

Finally, she managed to sit herself at the pianoforte and began to play.

It was as if a match had been struck, taking her from utter darkness to brilliant light in a matter of an instant. Susannah began with a piece by Vivaldi, swept up immediately into a world of color and light and beautiful sound.

Pieces by Handel and Mozart began to pour from her fingertips, and she could forget the men watching her, and Annabelle almost falling off her chair in her enthusiasm. She could even forget Rafe Winters as he watched her from the back; well, she could almost forget him.

As Susannah raced through the different passages and felt reality itself dissolve around her, she was aware of only one other person in this room.

Perhaps one other person in all of London, or indeed the whole world.

She could feel Rafe's attention burning upon her skin as

she played and played, the spirit of the music rushing through her. She could have giggled with delight as she merged from one piece seamlessly into the next. It was easy to play when she imagined it was only the two of them in this dim theater.

Susannah knew how utterly she'd captured his attention, and that sent rushes of warm pleasure through her body.

Nearing the end of one of her more difficult pieces, Susannah glanced over her shoulder and out to the room. She looked past Annabelle and Henry and all the other *ton* members, and for a brief second locked her gaze with Rafe's. His eyes were like blue fire, piercing bright in this shadowy world.

Susannah grinned, spirits rising ever higher as she pounded out the final, emotional chords and finished the concerto with a grand flourish.

She'd played for almost an hour straight and never thought to rest. She wasn't sure she *could* rest now, not as filled with excitement as she was. Susannah realized that Rafe had arranged some sheet music to be left out for her, but she'd never touched the pages. She got up from the bench and faced the crowd, curtsying in her triumph.

There was a smattering of applause. Henry and Annabelle cheered so loudly that an older gentleman at the next table shushed them. A few of the men had fallen asleep, and others had been chatting among themselves the entire time.

"That wasn't 'Little Mary Beth Lost Her Spoon!'" someone called, followed by yet more weeping.

In the back, Lord Sackville-Chambers looked around with obvious distaste, and Susannah saw the rotating flash of Rafe's silver cane.

Susannah dropped into one more halfhearted curtsy and walked off the stage. She stood in the wings a minute to let her heartbeat slow and to fight the tears that threatened to overwhelm her. So that was it?

She couldn't entrance a room filled with London's most elite music appreciators, even if they *were* all drunk? Perhaps Susannah had misjudged her own talents her entire life. Perhaps this dream of roaming the Continent and playing for all the great crowds of Europe was only the foolish dream of a silly, spoiled girl.

Maybe this was a sign that she had to get her head together, marry the duke, and finally grow up.

Susannah almost untied her mask, but then quickly kept it in place when Lord Sackville-Chambers and Rafe pushed through the curtains.

"Beautifully played as ever, my dear." Sackville-Chambers bowed over her hand. "You're a bright ornament on an otherwise gaudy stage."

"Um. Thank you, sir," she whispered. Susannah saw Rafe wince at the lord's words and felt indignation on his behalf.

"Like I said. It's all a work in progress," Rafe grumbled.

"Yes. A step in the right direction." Sackville-Chambers screwed up his mouth in a moue of disdain. He glanced around the backstage as though it were secretly filthy. "But your 'select' clientele proved to be as boorish as I'd anticipated. I said I wanted to see true taste on display, Mr. Winters, and you can't merely buy taste. You can't put a true artist on the stage amid sequins and beer-swilling fools and expect her to flourish. It's a noble effort, but I doubt you can reinvent yourself so completely."

"You said I'd a month." Rafe sounded raw, his hand clutching the head of his cane so hard that it shook. "I hope we're keeping to that agreement."

Susannah's heart fractured at the sound of his voice. Underneath the growling and the coarseness, she heard a bruised young boy. Someone who'd been told his entire life he wasn't good enough.

"I keep my word, Mr. Winters. Congratulations again, my

dear. You're a credit to our great English tradition of music."

"I'm a credit to Mr. Winters, too." Susannah modulated her voice a bit lower, so he wouldn't recognize her. His Lordship appeared surprised by her cheek. Rafe did as well. "He knows good music when he hears it."

"Indeed. Well. You're fortunate to have such loyal employees." Sackville-Chambers nodded to Rafe and swept out through the curtains. Susannah and Rafe stood silent a moment. She felt almost shy, unsure how to proceed.

"You…" Rafe cleared his throat. "Oi. You played well tonight. Better than well, even." He sounded honestly admiring. "You're a damned genius."

"Thank you." Susannah studied the toes of her slippers, fighting a smile. "I'm sorry I didn't make a better impression."

"Eh. Drunk sods wouldn't know good music if it clobbered them in the face." He shrugged, that single movement of his shoulders sinuous and powerful. "It's a work in progress, like I said."

"I'm not afraid of hard work."

"No. I don't think you are." Rafe looked her up and down. "I doubt there's much you're afraid of, really."

She wrestled with a smile. "If I could make a suggestion?"

"We're partners in this, aren't we? Of course I want to hear your thoughts." Oh heavens, was that a smile from Mr. Winters? Susannah tried to ignore how warm that made her feel.

"I think you should admit gentlewomen as well as their husbands."

"This is a gentleman's club. Kind of defeats the point if we've got wives lurking about, shaking fingers at their menfolk and what not."

"I can assure you, London's society women are as debauched as any of the men." Susannah shook her head, recalling the Carter Club, a group of women who met to happily reminisce about their long-ago affairs with Julia's husband. "At the very least, have select nights of the week open to everyone. Women care much more about fine art and public performances than the gentlemen do."

"Well." Rafe nodded. "Good point, Duchess."

"Also, I'll see if Lord and Lady Henry can spread gossip through the more elite circles about a bright new talent onstage at the Wolf's Den. It may entice some of the true tastemakers."

"Well. Thank you." Rafe stepped toward her, so near she could smell tobacco and French cologne. It made her weak. "I must say, I'm impressed. You're clever at this sort of thing."

Susannah flushed with pleasure.

Rafe made to say something else, but winced and hissed in seeming pain as he shifted his weight. He almost toppled over, and Susannah cried out as she made to support him. "Don't!" he roared.

She leaped back as if he'd bitten her with that one word. "I was only trying to help! You seemed in pain."

"I *am* in pain," he growled. He was the wolf again, bared teeth and bristling menace. Rafe moved away from her, leaning on his cane. "But I don't need your help, or anyone's. Got it?"

"Everyone needs help," Susannah said without thinking. "From time to time."

"Not me. Not ever." He winced as he shoved the curtain aside. "Be here tomorrow night, same time. We've got work to do."

And he was gone. One instant he'd been sociable, rather kind, and then the pain had changed him. The man was impossible. But it didn't matter how unruly he could be. The fact was, that man held the purse strings to her destiny.

She and Rafe Winters were tied together by fate now, and she had to make certain they succeeded.

Chapter Nine

This double life business was going to murder Susannah.

She'd been fortunate that Constance still wasn't home by the time she returned from the club, and that the servants all adored her and would never, ever mention anything strange to her mother. But the lying and sneaking about wasn't even the most difficult part of this arrangement.

By the time Susannah had been ready and wound down enough to sleep, it had been almost two in the morning. And during the Season, an early start to the day was considered essential. After all, there were so many calls to make and accept, so many appointments to keep.

"Stop that yawning!" Lady Beaumont hissed as they sat beside each other at luncheon. "I've no idea why you're tired, anyway. You left Julia's ball so early."

"Perhaps I've caught something," Susannah said.

"Well, deploy your illnesses strategically, that's what I always say." Her mother nibbled the end of an asparagus spear. "If it's a cold, try not to let anyone know. Or if you must retire, infect as many other young ladies as possible first. You're not yet engaged, my darling, so wiping out the competition is still vital."

"You'd have me level the debutantes of London with bubonic plague so the duke can safely propose to me?"

"Lord, such drama. It's merely a cold, isn't it?" Her mother tsked. "And if it *were* the plague, well, we'd at least need to lay out the Bainbridge girls and the Redding heiress before your confinement."

Such a shame Julia wasn't here to mock Susannah's mother. But Lady Beaumont had a point; Susannah couldn't draw too much attention to her exhaustion. She couldn't have the gossips of the *ton* asking too many questions.

She took a bite of salmon, wishing she could enjoy the lunch more. It was truly a gorgeous day, with bright blue skies and warm breezes.

They were lunching at the Countess of Samswick's, one of the most fashionable hostesses in London. Even though Susannah didn't know the woman well, Constance snatched up every invitation they received. The countess had ordered the meal laid out in the garden to take advantage of the perfect weather. Henry and Annabelle were also here, of course, though they handled being sleep-deprived far better than Susannah. They'd had so much more practice.

And, of course, the Duke of Huntington had come as well. He was seated near the hostess, chatting amiably with her, but would look at Susannah now and again with a meaningful smile.

She clutched her fork so hard that her fingers hurt. It really felt like living two lives, didn't it? In the daylight hours, she was Miss Susannah Fletcher, almost-intended of a duke, with a life of society parties and lunches and balls. After dark, she donned a costume and descended to an underworld of tawdriness and art, a wolf's den indeed.

She thought again of Rafe Winters glowering at her, that wolf's cane of his snarling in her face. The memory caused

Susannah to shiver involuntarily. It also reminded her that this luncheon was a prime opportunity to advertise.

She caught Annabelle's eye across the table and made a significant hand gesture, alerting her friend it was time to begin their ruse.

Unfortunately, Annabelle was not the most skilled of deceivers, and smiled in perfect ignorance. For the moment, she appeared to have forgotten their plan.

"What is it, Zan? What's the matter?"

Susannah widened her eyes as everyone at the table turned to look at her. Wonderful. Bloody perfect.

"I wanted to say…" Susannah smiled. "How lovely that frock is on you, Lady Henry."

"Indeed. Sky-blue is such a fetching color on a young bride." The countess nodded, then continued with her discussion of the recent additions to Vauxhall gardens. Susannah bit her lip and tried gesturing to Annabelle again, hoping to trigger her memory.

"Whatever are you doing?" her mother hissed in Susannah's ear.

"I'm trying to tell Annabelle how much…I admire…her bonnet. It's, uh, trimmed very prettily." Susannah was about to lose her mind.

"Well, stop it! You're not schoolgirls anymore. How does this sort of behavior appear in front of the duke, for heaven's sake?"

Susannah bit back a scream, but to her immense relief, Annabelle finally remembered what the devil Susannah was trying to tell her. She whispered to her husband, who also recalled his duty and sent Susannah a reassuring nod. The message was clear: he would take care of everything. Thank goodness.

"Now, as to the gazebo," Lady Samswick said, "I'd never seen—"

"Speaking of gazebos," Lord Henry said, "is everyone here fond of nightclubs?"

Susannah wanted to crawl beneath the table. Then at least she could get some sleep away from prying eyes.

"I think that's hardly an appropriate question to put to a group of ladies, Douglass. Wouldn't you agree?" the Duke of Huntington asked, looking less than amused. Ashworth had once told Susannah that Huntington might have been something of a rake in their university days, but he was the pinnacle of honor when it came to defending women from scandal.

"Erm. Perhaps." Lord Henry blushed far too easily. "But that's rather the point. I was at the Wolf's Den last night and saw the most incredible musician. You wouldn't think that a place with the Den's reputation would hire anyone who had a taste for Vivaldi and Mozart, but she's the most astonishing talent I've seen in a while. Better than anyone we've listened to in a concert hall, I'd say."

"Have you such a discerning taste in music, Lord Henry?" the countess asked. *Ouch*.

"Henry told me about her," Annabelle said. "Apparently they're calling this girl the Red Duchess."

"An intriguing name! Though why in heavens would she choose that title?" Lady Beaumont asked.

"No one knows. She performs only masked and cloaked to hide her identity. No one knows where she came from!"

"A good idea to hide her identity." Susannah's mother made a disapproving noise. "Any woman caught performing at such a seedy club would be ruined on the spot."

Susannah's gut clenched.

"The Wolf's Den is hardly seedy, Lady Beaumont," the duke said. "I don't make a habit of going there myself, but I know the proprietor has expensive taste."

"He does," Susannah said.

The entire table stared at her as one. Annabelle had frozen with a forkful of asparagus half raised to her mouth, which was quite open. Oh, damn it! Susannah should know better than to talk when she was this tired. Anything was liable to come tumbling out!

"However do you know that, Miss Fletcher?" the countess asked.

"Oh. The Duke of Ashworth told me once. He says they have the finest of everything there." To Susannah's relief, everyone accepted that explanation without question. It was useful to have a former rake as a brother-in-law.

"Ashworth shouldn't speak of such things to a young lady," the duke said, shaking his head in disapproval.

"He only said it was a luxurious club, Your Grace. My brother-in-law never tells me anything too indiscreet." Susannah didn't mean her reply to sound so tart, but she resented the suggestion that men had to treat her like a glass doll because of her age and sex. She wasn't as outspoken as Julia, but Susannah had learned much from her stepsister, including how ridiculous their society's double standards for men and women could be. "Besides, you don't even know if the Wolf's Den is such a tawdry place. You said yourself that you don't go there."

"Susannah!" Her mother hissed while dabbing her lips with a napkin. "Watch your tone."

But she needn't have worried because the duke seemed only charmed by Susannah's spirited opinion.

"Indeed, Miss Fletcher. You're right, I shouldn't talk about something I haven't experienced." The duke took a sip of iced tea, and an idea seemed to light up his eyes. "I say, Douglass. Why don't you take me to the Wolf's Den tonight and show me this musical duchess of yours. Perhaps I'll change my opinion of the place."

Two radically different sensations coursed through

Susannah at the same time.

On the one hand, the duke was one of the most influential men in all English society. If he declared something good, a single word from him at a *ton* event and Susannah's success would be assured, not to mention Rafe's.

In one single night, their fortunes could turn around. Tingles of delight rushed up and down her spine.

On the other hand, the duke knew her far better than the casual drunks of the *ton*, and he'd be paying close attention to her as she played. If he realized who Susannah was, then it was all over. Not just her deal with Rafe, but her engagement and her reputation. Her life, and her family's lives, would be ruined.

Susannah dropped her fork with a clatter. Across the table, Annabelle had experienced the same realization at the same instant, for she squeaked in horror. Everyone was shocked by both the young ladies' strange and simultaneous behavior.

"Miss Fletcher! Lady Henry! Is everything all right?" the countess asked.

"There was a bee," they said in unison. Susannah shut her eyes. Damn everything.

"A single bee scared both of you at the same time?" The countess glanced about. "I don't see anything."

"It was under the table," Annabelle said badly.

"It was very fast," Susannah added. "Almost invisible, really."

"A most silent and deadly bee."

"But we're safe now."

Annabelle swallowed a whole glass of lemonade in one gulp. "I think we scared it off," she said, visibly sweating. They'd have to blame her perspiration on the sun's heat.

"How courageous of you." The countess sounded mystified.

Susannah could feel her mother's bewildered displeasure but had no time to worry about that. She and Annabelle struggled to contain their horror, but the outlook was bleak indeed. Susannah had to talk to Rafe as soon as possible.

...

Rafe paced outside of the dancers' dressing area, which was currently empty.

It was fifteen minutes till Miss Fletcher had to be onstage, and she'd not yet arrived. Fear was an unusual visitor in his life, but tonight it had its icy hands on his throat. Perhaps she wasn't coming at all.

Perhaps after the disappointment of last night, and after the way he'd snapped when his blasted knee hurt him, the young lady had thought better of their agreement and run from him.

The thought he wouldn't see Susannah again was a pain as shattering as the constant agony in his knee. He didn't want her last memory of him to be of a snarling, furious man stumping around with a cane. A weak, foolish man.

He should be more worried about his damn club and his plans for Sackville-Chambers, but somehow, he couldn't stop fixating on Susannah.

When she'd started talking him through their little strategy last night Rafe had felt, for one strange moment, less alone than he'd ever been. They needed each other.

No one, not even Jacks, had ever needed Rafe in such a manner before. To be truly needed by such a girl as Susannah Fletcher would be the pinnacle of his whole damn life, wouldn't it?

Idiot! He had to control himself. On the streets, if you let your mind slip away into fancy for one moment, you could end up broken or dead.

"Mr. Winters!" Susannah rushed over to him, breathing heavily as if she'd come for him at a run. She started pulling off her bonnet with shaking hands. "I need to speak with you."

Rafe had to clench his jaw to keep from grinning. She looked fresh and beautiful as ever, prettier even with her rosy cheeks and bits of flyaway hair.

Then he frowned. She sounded upset about something, and Rafe hated to think of anything upsetting her.

"Are you all right?"

"The Duke of Huntington is going to be in the audience tonight." The girl looked panicked. "He's coming specifically to watch the Red Duchess perform. I heard him talking about it at lunch today."

Rafe wasn't given to showing his emotions too freely, but he almost let out a delighted cackle. Even he knew that the bloody Duke of Huntington was a top mover in the world of London toffs. If the duke loved Susannah's playing, a few words from him here and there and all the genteel folk would show up out of obligation if nothing else. They'd do whatever that duke told them to; Rafe was friendly with the Duke of Ashworth, who was one of the few members of the aristocracy Rafe could stomach. Ashworth had once been a regular customer at the Den, before his marriage, and had told Rafe all about Huntington and his influence.

"Duchess, this is good work." He had to keep from showing her how delighted he truly was, but it was hard. He wanted to wrap her in his arms, hold her close against him. "You're more than keeping up your end of the bargain."

"You don't understand." Susannah appeared horrified, her shining copper curls in disarray about her face. "He's the man who wants to marry me. I know him very well. If he recognizes me, it's all over."

Rafe knew that his face had fallen. On some instinctive

level, he hadn't really believed Susannah's story about running from marriage to a duke. It'd seemed like the feverish daydreams of a naïve girl, but she looked deadly serious. That meant this girl wasn't being chased by a mere duke; she was being chased by *the* most influential and eligible bachelor in the whole bloody country.

And even though Rafe hadn't laid eyes on this man before, he suddenly hated him worse than he could remember hating anyone else.

"So. What are you going to do?" Rafe asked.

"What?" She seemed surprised.

"Were you waiting for me to make the decision for you, Duchess?" He smirked, trying to wrestle down the anger at this Duke of Huntington. "That doesn't seem like you, does it?"

"I want us to think up a plan."

"All right. But I don't think it's up to us at all. This is about you." Susannah worried her lip as he spoke. "If the duke recognizes you tonight, it'll go worse for you than it will for me. What are you willing to risk?"

"I'm afraid for my family." She meant it, he could tell. "I can't do anything to hurt them."

"You'll hurt them if you leave England and don't marry the duke. Isn't that right?"

Her eyebrows lifted. "Well…yes. That's true."

"If you want to be safe, leave here tonight and marry His Graciousness. Pretend you never met me before." The thought was a knife to his chest, but Rafe wasn't going to snarl or bully this girl into anything. She wouldn't let him, anyway. They were partners, like she said, equals in this. He was going to treat her like an equal. "If you want that life you've been dreaming of, put on your costume and play. Make sure the duke can't see your face or figure you out."

"Those are my only two options?" she whispered.

"It seems like they are."

Susannah's brow wrinkled. She looked at him with pleading amber eyes. "I'm scared."

It was such a naked, vulnerable admission that it caused Rafe's blood to thunder. He wanted to cradle her face in his hands and catch her lips with his. He wanted to hold her close against him, escort her upstairs and lock her away with all his other treasures. He wanted to take her in his arms, feel the patter of her heart beneath his hand, touch every secret place on her body. Lock her away in his fantasy world, safe from prying eyes.

But Susannah was more substantial than some gauzy dream. She needed to live an actual life. Even if she would not live it with him.

"I won't force you onto the stage. Decide your own fate, Duchess."

"What would you do if you were me?"

Run away with a club owner did not seem like the proper statement just now. "I've been afraid before, believe it or not. But you never get what you truly want in this life by playing it safe. Trust me."

"I do." She looked surprised by the admission. "I believe you."

"So. I wouldn't have the Den without taking a few monumental risks. What about you, Duchess? What's your freedom worth?"

She nodded. "I think the life you truly want is worth almost anything."

"So do I."

Bit of a lie, that. While Rafe didn't know much about this girl, he was a man who trusted his gut. He'd already seen her spirit, her courage, her talent, and her good sense, and Rafe felt that he might give anything he possessed in order to keep this girl with him. He wouldn't do a thing like that, of course. He'd never try to claim her. But when this was over, he'd be rich and accepted. That would have to be enough for one lifetime.

At least he wouldn't have to think of this Duke of Huntington sweeping Susannah into his arms, taking her to his castle, siring dozens of heirs upon her, and living in bliss the rest of his pampered, privileged life. Disappointing a damned duke would be some compensation for the loss of Rafe's own heart.

"I've made up my mind, Mr. Winters. You should go find your seat. I'll be on the stage shortly."

She was brave, the bravest girl he'd ever met in some ways. She knew everything she stood to lose, and still she dared. Susannah wasn't asking Rafe or anyone else to protect her. She would handle herself. He'd never met anyone as gentle and as strong before, and the contradiction made him almost wild with desire.

Rafe nodded at her.

"Play well, Duchess. Play for your life." And he walked away.

Chapter Ten

Rafe spotted the Duke of Huntington right away.

He was seated at a table in the center of the room with that Lord Henry boy, who looked dewy with perspiration. The little toff had every reason to be scared. If Susannah were caught, he and his lady would be in a right amount of shit.

Rafe went to take his seat at the table beside the duke's.

As he sat, he couldn't help looking at the man again. Tall, blond, handsome as some old god out of Greek mythology, wealthy, influential, and titled; the perfect embodiment of everything Susannah Fletcher should want.

Again, Rafe thought of the girl in this duke's arms, her lips soft upon his, and it made him so furious, he squeezed the head of his cane. The wolf's snout dug into his palm.

"May we help you, sir?" the duke asked coolly. He had noticed Rafe's stare and looked less than pleased. Lord Henry made a horrified face at Rafe over the duke's shoulder, then put a finger to his lips in a flailing gesture. He had all the survival instinct of a shaved miniature poodle.

"You're the Duke of Huntington, aren't you?" Rafe

asked.

"Indeed." The handsome man was polite but a bit distant. Probably had loads of people trying to cozy up to him for favors all day long. He had to be reserved on meeting folks, it seemed. "And who might you be?"

"Rafe Winters." He made a small, almost mocking bow with his head. "At your service, Your Grace. This is my club."

"Ah. A pleasure." Huntington relaxed. "You run a fine establishment. It's very luxurious."

Kind words, but Rafe thought of Sackville-Chambers.

Rafe wondered if this duke was saying the same thing to himself as the lord had: expensive taste, but no class. Certainly nothing up to *their* level.

Maybe this duke wasn't thinking any such thing, of course. Maybe he was an all right sort of toff. But the fact that Susannah wanted to get away from a man like this, the most powerful duke in all England, made Rafe respect her more than ever. She was a girl of substance and originality as much as beauty. God, he shouldn't like her this bloody much.

"I don't recall seeing you here before, Your Grace."

"No, I rarely frequent nightclubs. But Lord Henry has told me about the little prodigy who's about to take the stage. The Red Duchess, yes?"

"Yes. She's the finest musician in London."

The duke smiled. "I look forward to her performance, then. Mr. Winters."

"Your Grace."

The men nodded and the duke returned to Lord Henry, who looked like he was about to faint.

Rafe left the rich gents to their discussions and stared at the stage. It was a few minutes past, and Susannah had not been announced. If she'd changed her mind and left him, he was going to take an ax to that bloody pianoforte.

He wouldn't be able to bear looking at the thing that

she'd touched and abandoned, that hadn't been good enough for her.

He almost sighed in relief when Murray took the stage and bowed to muted applause. "Gentlemen, if you have come to be enchanted tonight, then the Wolf's Den has just the woman to cast her spell. May I present, the most illustrious and mysterious musician from here to the Russian steppes, the Red Duchess!"

It was a brief introduction, but classier than the last one. Rafe had made sure of it. Then Murray bowed out, and Susannah took the stage.

This time, Rafe couldn't even see her face. She curtsied with her red hood pulled all the way up, and her face lowered to the ground. You couldn't tell it was Susannah, but you also couldn't see a damn bit of her. There were some cross rumblings around them, as these blokes had come to see a pretty girl as much as to hear her play.

Susannah sat upon the bench and kept her body tilted slightly to the left, once again preventing any bit of her face from being seen. Would she even be able to play for an hour at that angle? Rafe thought about the Duke of Huntington seated there, ever so certain of his own worth. The duke was watching a woman who was risking everything to escape him, and he had no idea. Rafe felt proud and protective all at once, angry on Susannah's behalf. He forgot even his own concerns as he leaned forward a bit.

"Come on, Duchess," Rafe whispered. "You can do this."

Susannah didn't speak or introduce anything, only began to play.

Something was different tonight. She'd played well last time; her mastery over her art was always apparent. But this time her body moved fluidly with the music, as though she and the instrument were each a part of the other.

Rafe almost dropped his cane in his astonishment; it felt

as though the rest of the room had faded away, and it was only him sitting here in this darkened theater listening to Miss Susannah Fletcher.

Even though she hadn't looked at him for fear of revealing any bit of her face, Susannah's music made him feel alone. No, not alone, but private.

Rafe had never heard music like this before, wrapping around him like a caress, transporting him to some place fine and beautiful. Her playing made him feel like an aristocrat, or even royalty.

His pulse quickened as she thundered along the gorgeous passages; he wanted her. He wanted to take her gloves off and kiss the palms of her hands, the inside of her delicate wrists. He wanted to tear away that mask and cape, that gown she wore, and have his way with her on the stage with that music playing all around them, constant and sweet and intoxicating.

Halfway through the performance, Rafe realized he recognized the tune she was crafting. It was Susannah's own music, the piece she'd played for him during her rehearsal a few days earlier. Her own composition sounded to his ears as splendid and unearthly as anything by Mozart.

Susannah Fletcher had announced herself to the world tonight, even as she was hidden behind a mask and cloak. Only Rafe could see her for the incomparable jewel she was, with all her many facets and glittering secrets.

He almost forgot to breathe a few times as the girl went through her routine, and when she struck the final keys and the last golden note disappeared into the air, the audience was silent. Rafe didn't know if they were as stunned as he, or as uninterested as they had been last night. It'd better be the former.

But then, the Duke of Huntington pushed his chair back, stood, and applauded loudly. "Bravo!" he shouted, his face animated. "Magnificent!"

That was all it took. Almost as one, the theater rose to its feet.

Lord Henry was now mopping his face with a handkerchief from all the stress. Though it pained his knee, Rafe rose as well. He didn't applaud, only stared at the cloaked figure as she stood, curtsied with her head bowed again, and then rushed from the stage.

Seeing the duke's astonishment, Rafe couldn't resist a little jab. "Think she's as good as advertised, Your Grace?"

The duke only laughed.

"You have found a true artist." He seemed delighted. "Mr. Winters, she is astonishing. You must tell me who she is."

"She's the Red Duchess. I can't give you any more information on her, not even her age or her hair color. She likes to be a mystery."

"Well, if I had my way, she'd mystify all of London society. In fact, I may just see to it she shall."

"Really, Your Grace?" Rafe feigned nonchalance.

"Indeed. I think that this Duchess is precisely what Mayfair needs. She represents artistry and grace instead of meaningless self-indulgence."

"Meaningless self-indulgence pays better than artistry," Rafe muttered. The duke didn't hear, of course. Huntington shook his head.

"It's a damned shame you don't allow ladies here. There's a young woman I know who'd adore this."

Susannah, of course. Rafe almost laughed, while Lord Henry erupted into a spluttering coughing fit borne out of nerves.

"You should tell your young lady how much you enjoyed the performance," Rafe said. "You should tell her every detail." Susannah deserved to know how magnificent she truly was, even if she couldn't take credit. "Is she a music lover?"

"Yes. Until tonight, in fact, I didn't know another woman in London who could match her playing. I might have discovered the one opponent who could overtake her."

Rafe loved it.

"I hope we'll see you back here, Your Grace, if you enjoyed yourself so much." Rafe gave a lower bow this time.

"I should count on it if I were you." Huntington laughed. "Though as a word of advice? The audience might like to see *something* of the young lady's features. Even if she's homely, her playing more than makes up in terms of sheer beauty."

She's bloody gorgeous, you rich nitwit.

"We'll keep that in mind," Rafe said.

The duke and an almost hyperventilating Lord Henry left the theater. The men filed out, many of the regulars congratulating Rafe in a way they had not last night.

There was talk about bringing a friend tomorrow, or questions posed to Rafe if they could perhaps bring wives along, only to the theater, of course. He agreed to think it over, and then slowly made his way out of the room.

He ambled down the hall with ease, almost bursting with excitement. When he got to the dressing room door, he didn't bother to knock but flung it open. Rafe liked every inch of his club to be luxurious, even the bits that paying customers didn't see.

The dancers' dressing areas were furnished like a Parisian salon with gilded mirrors, lush Persian rugs, and satin-backed furniture. A few dressing tables and chairs were set up with mirrors and candles before them.

Pots of cosmetics lay messy upon the tables, while brightly colored costumes hung upon tacks on the wall, or on a dressmaker's dummy in the corner. Bouquets of roses, gifts from the women's many admirers, made the space smaller and fragrant. Susannah sat upon the edge of a settee, her mask in her lap.

"I say!" Susannah shrieked and slapped the mask over her face. When she realized who it was, she relaxed with a beleaguered sigh. "You could jolly well knock, you know."

Rafe shut the door. His entire body vibrated with ecstasy.

His whole life, men like the duke had looked down on him for his low birth and his dirty business, but tonight he had seen more than enjoyment in the man's face. He had seen admiration. Not just admiration for Susannah, but admiration for Rafe as the man who'd discovered her.

"You were a damn sensation." His voice was hoarse with excitement as he approached her. "The duke didn't recognize you, but he loved your playing. He said he's going to talk the show up to the whole of London society."

"You're joking." Her face paled, and then her cheeks bloomed with color. Susannah squealed into her hands. "He didn't."

"Man's a stiff, but he's got deep pockets and connections. With a fellow like him praising the club, Sackville-Chambers will have to be impressed."

It was going to happen. He was going to succeed. That long-ago little boy lying on a cold, dirty floor was going to have all his plans come to fruition.

"Oh, Mr. Winters!" Susannah, giddy as a child, leaped up and wrapped her arms around his neck.

He forgot how to breathe at the sensation of her body against him, her soft cheek pressed to his, the pleasing aroma of her perfume. He felt his cock stir, even strain against the front of his trousers.

Unfortunately, Susannah's enthusiasm set him off-kilter. With a curse, Rafe dropped the cane and fell forward.

"Oof!" Susannah cried as she landed upon the settee, and Rafe fell on top of her. At least it hadn't been the floor. "Oh, sorry."

He was lying directly atop her, and she was blushing. He felt the patter of her heart against his chest. When Rafe lowered a hand to steady himself on the settee, he clasped her satin-clad thigh by mistake.

A glorious, wonderful mistake.

Susannah's lips parted as she lay beneath him, those amber eyes now liquid with desire. Rafe saw it, plain as anything. She wanted him to kiss her, to touch her, perhaps to do more. To take and taste all of her.

"You really were glorious," he whispered. Oh, he ought to get off this girl right now, but his body was starved for this. Rafe's affairs were few and far between, and it had been months since he'd had a woman. Not that Susannah was any other woman, just some girl to lift her skirt and give him a few nights of pleasure. She was a Rembrandt, a Ming vase, a French antique, another of the costly treasures Rafe hoarded in his flat. No. She was even more than those baubles. She was priceless, wasn't she? "I liked that you played your own piece."

"Oh. That. I was so afraid I went blank on an actual piece to perform. I won't make such a mistake tomorrow."

"I want to keep it in the show. It's you. It's brilliant and gorgeous."

Susannah's blush deepened. Rafe held his breath, feeling how she trembled against him.

"It's no Mozart," she whispered.

"No. It's better than that." The world was only this moment, only this girl looking up at him with hope and exhilaration. "Like I said. It's you."

"Thank you for believing in me." Her lips quivered as Rafe lowered his face to hers. A little sigh of contentment let him know how badly she wanted this.

"It's like I told Sackville-Chambers the other night. I hire only the best. The rarest." He pressed his lips to her neck and luxuriated in the ecstatic cry she gave. "The most beautiful."

He kissed her neck down to her collarbone, all the while hitching the girl's leg around his waist. Susannah didn't stop this, only gave a breathy moan as Rafe rucked up her skirt and ran his hand along that shapely calf of hers.

God, she was put together like a bloody masterpiece. He'd never touched any woman like her before.

His fingers traveled up her thigh to the tops of her stockings and played lightly upon the silken flesh beyond. Susannah shivered in ecstasy. No one had ever touched her like this before. Rafe didn't want anyone else to have this, ever. Especially not that damned, cursed duke.

"Rafe," she murmured.

When she used his name, he was truly lost. He kissed her, devoured her mouth. She kissed back with equal passion, straining to press herself against him, to feel every inch of him. The animal inside of Rafe, the wolf that was ever close to the surface, seemed to howl in triumph as he tasted this girl. Her legs parted for him as though by magic, and he aligned his throbbing cock against her core.

"Oh my God!" she gasped, her eyes widening as she felt his clothed but erect manhood against her.

"You posh girls don't know what men and women do together?" He kissed the little hollow at the base of her throat, kissed the tops of her breasts that were pushed out the top of her gown's neckline. "You don't know what it feels like, to be had by a man?"

"Of course not." She didn't sound frightened. "Is it always like…this? Between men and women?"

No, he wanted to tell her. This was special. This was a passion he'd never known before. Rafe didn't answer with words, only traced his hand over the swell of her breasts. Susannah's chest rose and fell with her excited breathing, and she cooed as Rafe touched her all the way along her body until he lifted her skirts higher.

She tensed, but he kissed her.

"I won't violate you, Duchess. You've my word."

Susannah relaxed, though she still appeared nervous as Rafe's fingers played at the tops of her stockings.

"Do you want me to stop?" he asked.

Susannah looked conflicted, and then the crease in her forehead disappeared. "No," she whispered. "I want you to continue."

Rafe didn't need another word. He touched the fleecy hair that covered her mound, reveling in the astonished gasps that Susannah made. He kissed her on the mouth and deepened that kiss as his finger parted her and found her so silken and so wet for him.

He caught her muffled cry of delight.

"You ever touched yourself before?" he whispered in her ear.

"I don't know how you mean."

"Like this."

Rafe found that little bud in an instant and began to stroke it. At first, Susannah sounded almost horrified. Then, within seconds, the pleasure obliterated any concern as she wrapped her arms around his neck and buried her face in his hair. Rafe worked her, his fingers trailing up and down the seam of her, lavishing attention on that perfect spot between her thighs.

"Rafe, Rafe. Oh God, Rafe!"

Her hips lifted as the orgasm carried her away, and Susannah gave a cry of delight. Her cheeks darkened, her lips reddened, and the skin upon her neck and throat grew blotchy as she rode out her ecstasy against his fingers. While Susannah panted and relaxed against the settee, Rafe slid one finger inside of her. *God, so tight.* He wanted her the way he wanted to eat and to sleep and to fucking breathe.

"You're a good girl, aren't you?" he growled, kissing her. "Far too good for the likes of me."

"I'm not too good for you." Susannah kissed him, her eyes half-lidded with contentedness. "I want more. Please. I want you."

All Rafe had to do was undress her and have her, make love to her again and again upon this settee while she screamed her climaxes. He could take her upstairs to his flat and show her how good a silk-sheeted bed could feel beneath her naked and sensitive skin. He could think of nothing else he wanted to do, ever again, besides this.

But she beamed up at him with those pink lips and soft amber eyes. She was so trusting. She was so good. She deserved so much better.

Rafe shoved himself off her and sat at the foot of the settee.

She pushed down her skirts. "Rafe, what is it?"

"I'm sorry." He refused to look at her now. "I got carried away."

"But I wanted you to."

"This isn't good for you. I was weak. It won't happen again."

Susannah was a genius, a true artist. Meanwhile, Rafe had struggled at twenty-five to learn to bloody read. Though he'd eventually mastered it, he had been ashamed it took so long.

Rafe had been a thief and a scoundrel, but he would not be a monster. He wouldn't let her sully herself with him more than she already had. He had to protect her from himself, and from her own foolishness. Whatever it took.

He took his cane and got up, headed for the dressing room door.

"You can't just walk away," Susannah cried. "Not after that!"

"Believe me, if we'd gone any further, you'd have hated

yourself and me. I don't want you to have regrets." He mixed lies with the truth. "The business has to come first. We've got to stay away from each other."

Susannah stewed in wounded silence for a moment.

"Fine," she said stiffly. "Good evening, Mr. Winters."

Call me Rafe again. Let me hear you say my name.

"Good night, Duchess."

All the euphoria had burned away. Rafe left her behind with heaviness weighing him down.

Chapter Eleven

"Darling, I really am worried about you. Are you certain I can't send for a doctor?" Julia put down her teacup and sat beside Susannah on the couch. "These early summer colds can be dangerous."

"I'm just a little tired," Susannah said, stifling a yawn. "I haven't slept that well the last few nights."

No, last night she'd come home and snuck up to bed with help from one of the maidservants, then lain flat on her back staring up at the darkened ceiling.

She'd thought of Rafe's lips, his hands, the way he'd touched the most intimate place on her body and the way she'd just let him. Susannah hated him as much as she burned for him to touch her again. She was such a fool. He was like all disreputable men; he'd use her for his pleasure and then discard her when she bored him. She had to be smarter than this.

But it was difficult to be smart when her heart beat so bloody fast every time he was near.

"I think you should tell Constance to let you stay home for a night. You don't need to attend every single ball and gala. Honestly, you have a splendid conquest already."

Susannah hid her flinch. When she thought of Huntington, her thoughts became hopelessly tangled and she felt a heavy sense of dread. She'd betrayed his trust in her own way, and now that she knew how it felt to lie with Rafe atop her, she didn't know how she'd manage it with any other man.

Fortunately, two children bounded into the room and put all Susannah's self-pitying thoughts away. Well, they didn't quite bound. One child toddled, and the other sort of...rolled.

"Felicity! What are you doing with those things on in the house?" Julia sounded exasperated, though she smiled.

"Sorry, Your Grace. I was just showing Arthur how these foot-wheels work! I think that's what I'll call them, anyway. Aren't they the cleverest thing?"

Felicity had strapped what appeared to be small wooden planks to her feet and attached four miniature wheels to the bottom of each. She rolled about, flailing her arms to keep balance as she sped faster and faster, heading for the wall... and a priceless antique clock.

"No!" Both Susannah and Julia yelled at the same time and jumped up, but Felicity had the good sense to fling herself out of the way and roll across the carpet. The girl laughed when she'd finished her adventure and sat up, her curly black hair in a tangle around her face.

"It's all right! I saved the clock. I ought to show Arthur my new flying machine. I do believe it shall work, and even if it doesn't, I shan't die if I jump from only the second story window."

"You will do no such thing," Julia said, picking up a toddling, giggling Arthur. Lord Arthur Carter, Marquess of Kerrick and heir to the Ashworth estate, blew a spit bubble at his mother. Julia fussed over him and kissed his cheek. He was a small, sweet child with his father's sable hair and Julia's blue eyes. Susannah adored him, and she adored Felicity as well.

Felicity Berridge was Ashworth's thirteen-year-old ward, the illegitimate child of an earl. The duke had taken charge of her as a baby, and while they had to be discreet about her parentage until Felicity came of age, Julia had insisted on bringing the girl to town with them for the Season, so she could enjoy the delights of London. Felicity was the most talkative, jubilant child Susannah had ever met, and Julia petted and fussed over her as she would her own children. Indeed, Susannah believed the Ashworth family to be among the happiest she had ever seen. Theirs was a home filled with love and laughter.

Proving her point, Julia went and helped Felicity remove wheeled shoes while Arthur hugged his older sister. The duchess laughed as she assisted Felicity in getting off the ground.

"Now where on earth is your governess?" she asked.

As if taking a cue, the salon door flung open again and a breathless Miss Winslow appeared.

The governess was normally serene and smiling, but right now she looked as if she were about to faint. She put a hand to her heart and bent over. "Forgive me, Your Grace… She ran off… Arthur… On wheels… The vase in the east wing… With the pink flowers…"

"Calm yourself. It's all right." Julia soothed Miss Winslow as Arthur toddled over and clung to the governess's skirt. "The children are fine, and I always hated that vase. It was a gift from Gregory's great aunt or something. Tasteless. Ashworth will give you a rise in pay for destroying it, I know he will."

Miss Winslow laughed a bit as Julia ordered her to sit down and have some tea. After having spent much of her life as little more than Constance's maid, Julia insisted on caring for the servants in her household as people rather than employees. Miss Winslow, having raised Felicity, was practically a member of the family. Susannah smiled at the governess as she took her seat opposite.

"How are you?" she asked.

"I'm well, Miss Fletcher. Thank you for inquiring." Miss Winslow gave a small smile and sipped her tea.

There was something strange between Susannah and the governess these days, and Susannah didn't know why.

For years after Julia's marriage, she and Miss Winslow had been fast friends. While the governess was eternally quiet and reserved, she had a warm manner of speaking and many interesting things to say. These days, however, it seemed they scarcely spoke two words to each other. It made Susannah sad, though she'd never bring it up to Julia. She just wished she knew what she'd done to wound Miss Winslow.

The salon door opened again as Julia had sat Felicity down and was warning her not to spill tea and crumbs on her new frock.

The Duke of Ashworth entered, with the Duke of Huntington not far behind. Susannah felt her heart in her throat, and her cheeks began to burn.

She looked away quickly, ashamed now to speak to Huntington. If he knew what she'd done last night, he'd refuse to ever meet her again. But he ought to know, yes? It wasn't right to keep this sort of a secret from a man who wanted to marry her. A man whom she'd become increasingly certain she did not want to marry.

But whenever Susannah felt like being bold, making a statement the way Julia would, her courage abandoned her. It was so difficult to make herself heard, or to voice what she wanted. That wasn't the way "nice" women behaved, after all. Though that was bloody ridiculous.

"I want to know who broke the cherry blossom vase in the east wing," Ashworth said, his deep, rich voice booming.

He glared at the assembled women and children. "And then I want to offer a handsome reward, because I've been desperate to get rid of that eyesore for the last five years."

"Me! It was I!" Felicity jumped up and waved her arms so that her guardian could not miss her.

"Hmm. Well, I *was* going to give the heroine a thousand pounds." Ashworth dug a bag of boiled sweets from his coat pocket. "But these spice drops should be even more appreciated."

Felicity cheered and ran over to claim her prize, almost tripping over one of her wheeled shoes and sprawling out at the duke's feet.

With a groan, Julia carried Arthur over to his father. "You can't spoil her supper like this! She's had a bit of cake and tea already."

"My darling wife, you must know that children thrive upon a diet of sugar. They're like hummingbirds in that way."

As the duke and duchess continued to argue playfully, Huntington approached Susannah. He was carrying a bouquet of roses and bowed over her hand with a smile. "You look lovely as ever, Miss Fletcher."

"Thank you, Your Grace."

Miss Winslow made a soft noise that only Susannah heard. *Oh dear.* The governess's cheeks had more color than Susannah had ever seen before. Her hazel eyes brightened when she beheld the duke, but when he offered his roses to Susannah the color withered in the governess's cheeks. She cast down her eyes and seemed to shrink away. When the duke politely greeted Miss Winslow as well, she feigned a smile, but then folded back in on herself.

"I must see to my charge. If you'll excuse me, Your Grace. Miss Fletcher." Miss Winslow curtsied and went to collect Felicity.

Susannah's heart broke for the governess; now she

understood. She'd been oblivious to it before, how deeply in love with Huntington Miss Winslow was.

Why did the world have to be this way? Miss Winslow loved the duke, but the duke loved Susannah, and Susannah loved—

No one. I don't love anyone. And even if I did, he wouldn't love me. He couldn't.

That thought was like a blade twisted in her heart.

"You look so sad, Miss Fletcher." The duke appeared concerned.

"Oh, I'm only tired. Beg pardon, Your Grace."

"I suppose that's natural. You young ladies are run so ragged during the Season."

"I suppose I'll be able to sleep in July." Susannah laughed.

"Perhaps even sooner. After all, once a lady is publicly engaged to be married, she needn't make such an exhibition of herself before the *ton*."

Susannah bit her tongue to keep from making a rude noise. She glimpsed Miss Winslow over the duke's shoulder. The governess had listened to his words and drooped further.

"Oh, but I don't think anyone would want to be engaged this early in the Season." Susannah almost dropped her teacup. Her nerves were shredded. "There's still so much to do."

"Oh?" He smiled but seemed puzzled.

"Yes. Ah. That is..." Her mind revealed nothing. Her mind had given up and gone to sleep to avoid the embarrassment. "The, er, anticipation of things makes them sweeter when they arrive. Don't you find?"

The duke appeared to find that notion much to his liking. "Indeed. You're very wise, my dear. One must always savor the moments leading up to pleasure."

Susannah wanted to throw the bouquet to the floor and ask in a loud voice why on earth he wanted to marry her. Was it because of her youth? Her looks? Her family connection with Ashworth? All those things? Why did people fall in love with one another, anyway?

Why did people desire those who were no good for them?

Again, she thought of Rafe's hands upon her body and between her legs, and it took everything she had not to blush.

"I came to see you to mention something," the duke said. "I may have discovered the greatest musician in all of London, and in the most peculiar spot."

"Oh?" A little jolt of excitement rushed through her veins. Now *this* Susannah was happy to talk about. "What spot is that?"

"The club in Mayfair that Lord Henry Douglass mentioned at Lady Samswick's luncheon. The Wolf's Den. This Red Duchess of theirs is sensational. I've finally found playing to rival your own," he teased, his eyes sparkling with pleasure. "Though I'll wager the Duchess isn't half so fair as you."

Susannah almost burst into peals of riotous laughter; her nerves were liable to snap soon. "How kind of you to say."

"I wish they allowed ladies into the club. It would be my great honor to escort you there to hear this woman's music."

Susannah was relieved that Rafe hadn't changed that rule yet. Hopefully he never would; she couldn't imagine a more awkward situation than sitting at a table with the duke, waiting for herself to come onto the bloody stage. "Oh, I'm not certain my mother would like me to be in such a place, Your Grace."

"Of course. How thoughtless of me. It's my duty to safeguard you against all indecent exposure."

He was a noble man, but Susannah wished he didn't sound so stuffy. Rafe didn't treat her as some porcelain doll, but almost as an equal. Even when he was brusque with her, Susannah knew he believed she could take it. He thought her strong and competent.

The duke stayed a bit longer, then took his leave. Ashworth saw him out, while Miss Winslow followed his departure with longing, secretive eyes.

Meanwhile, Susannah was counting down the hours until she could sneak away to the club. She wanted to belong to a world of vibrancy and decadence again…even if it meant pretending that nothing had happened between Rafe and herself.

. . .

Tonight, Susannah shared her changing room with several other women.

She'd never spoken with people like them before, women who smoked openly and laughed loudly. They had adopted French names as those sounded far more "elegant" than English ones. Celine, Sophie, and Antoinette walked around in their stays and undergarments without a thought for modesty. Susannah sat in quiet awe of them.

"You're that Red Duchess, aren't you?" Celine raised an eyebrow as she puffed a perfect smoke ring into the air. "I hear the crowds went wild for your playing."

"You managed to get 'em all on their feet without taking any clothes off?" Sophie was stretching for a dance later, one foot high upon the wall as she bent over it. It was the most risqué move Susannah had ever seen a woman make. "You must be talented."

"I suppose I am." Susannah toyed with her mask shyly. "How long have you all worked here?"

"Three years." Antoinette put on her dressing gown and tossed her curls over her shoulder. "I won't leave until I'm too old to do a back flip. You can't beat the pay." The woman selected a candied almond from a little silver dish beside her. "Plus, I've never met another employer who understands the importance of keeping his dancers well fed."

It was true. Rafe let his staff have the run of the kitchens and as much champagne as they desired.

"This place was a godsend," Celine said. "After my husband walked out on us, the Wolf's Den was like a dream come true. I don't know how I'd feed and clothe my daughter if it weren't for Rafe. Well, I imagine I *do* know how. Only it'd be flat on my back instead of light on my feet."

"Oh!" Susannah could not believe how informal and brazen these women were. She adored it.

"We're fortunate," Celine added. "Mr. Winters treats his girls well."

"I'd like to get treated well by Mr. Winters." Sophie chuckled before snatching Celine's cigarette and taking a drag. "Lord, even if he's a beast, he's a gorgeous one."

"Pity he never fools around with his employees. I don't generally like club owners getting handsy with their dancers, but I'd welcome *his* hands anywhere he wanted to put them." Antoinette giggled as she applied rouge to the apple of her cheeks.

Susannah grew stiff with embarrassment, and she also flushed with a little excitement. So, Rafe never kissed his employees? Then perhaps Susannah was a little special to him. Even though she shouldn't want to be...

The dressing room door opened, and Susannah threw her mask over her face quickly. She sighed in relief when it was Rafe. Her heart picked up its pace when she noted how sinful he looked this evening. His black hair had been pomaded to curl devilishly over one eye, and a sapphire winked at her in the pristine silk folds of his cravat.

"Good shows tonight, ladies. Antoinette, don't forget you're in the ballroom this evening. Soph, get your costume on. Oi, you know I don't like smoking in the dressing rooms."

Sophie crushed the cigarette out and crossed her eyes at Susannah in mockery of her boss. Susannah smiled. Celine, meanwhile, stood and threw on her dressing gown in haste.

"Rafe, can I talk to you?" she murmured. The woman

looked strangely shy as Rafe jerked his head for her to follow him. They left, shutting the door behind them.

"Is everything all right?" Susannah asked. The way Celine had looked almost fearful didn't sit well with her.

"Hope so." Antoinette frowned as she painted her lips. "Rafe's a good employer, but he can be moody."

Susannah couldn't help her curiosity. She tied on her mask and snuck out the door, ignoring Sophie's and Antoinette's questions. Susannah crept down the hall until she heard the murmur of voices coming out of the men's dressing room. One of the voices was Celine's.

Susannah paused outside and listened intently.

"…sick." Celine sounded like she fought against tears. "The doctor thinks it's curable, but she needs constant attention. I know I got to earn money for the remedies, but if I'm not there to give them to her, I can't see how she'll get better. All I'm asking's to skip the second show tonight so's I can go home and check in on her."

"You'll do no such thing," Rafe said, gruff as ever. "That's not how things work around here."

Susannah screwed up her mouth in indignation. That bastard! Celine had to be speaking of her daughter, who was probably home all by herself. All she wanted was a measly hour or two to look in on the girl! And after the women had been speaking so fondly of Rafe and all he'd done for them.

"Here," Rafe said. "Take this."

Susannah paused and grabbed one peek around the corner. Rafe was counting out a wad of bills while Celine blushed and stammered.

"Rafe, I can't."

"Here's thirty pounds. Go home and stay with her until she's well again."

"Please don't fire me."

"I'm not firing you. This is for medicine, the doctor, and

anything else she'll need. I see you around the club before she's healthy, there'll be hell to pay." But he didn't sound so ferocious now, and Celine laughed. It sounded like she was crying as well.

"I'll pay you back."

"It's a gift. It's not coming out of your wages. No mother should have to choose work over nursing her sick child." Rafe sounded so serious. Almost pained. "Now get out of here. Go on."

Celine thanked him over and over as Susannah rushed away and flung herself back into the ladies' dressing area. She now felt almost ashamed for listening in on something so noble.

"So? Did he chew her ear off?" Antoinette was adjusting a golden wig on her head as she looked at Susannah in the mirror.

"No." She felt almost dizzy as she flopped onto the settee. "He was very kind."

"That's our Rafe. A right bastard, but a soft touch where it counts." Sophie giggled as she added something about how she hoped his touch wasn't *too* soft. While the women continued to joke, Susannah could think only of what she'd overheard. She doubted an earl or a duke would give a servant thirty pounds and time off just to care for a child. Susannah had never seen such decent behavior.

When she thought of Rafe now, Susannah's pulse didn't merely race. She wanted more than to feel his hands on all sorts of indecent places on her body. She wanted to kiss his lips with tenderness, stroke a hand through his hair, look deep into his eyes as she held him.

She'd have to be careful from now on. Nothing would ruin her future happiness so much as falling in love.

Chapter Twelve

Two nights later, Susannah finished her show and returned to the dressing room. She could move slower tonight, since she was technically staying with Lord and Lady Henry. Susannah didn't need to hurry home and pray she wouldn't be caught by her mother. Annabelle had told her before dropping Susannah at the club that she ought to enjoy herself. *Don't worry about rushing straight home, Zan. Stay and have a drink! Do something bold and exciting for yourself.*

A few more weeks of this, and Susannah would live in such a manner all the time. She'd be out until the early hours of the morning, dining whenever and with whomever she pleased. She grinned to think of it.

A knock came at the door. Susannah put on her mask. "Come in."

Jacks entered, a letter in hand. "Miss Fletcher. Rafe wanted me to give this to you."

"Oh?" Susannah wrestled with her own excitement. These last few nights she and Rafe had been virtual strangers. Susannah opened the note. The handwriting was strong and precise, almost rigid.

My carriage is outside. Join me for supper?
R

Now this was odd. For days the man pretended like he didn't know her, and now he wanted to have dinner with her? She could never be certain what Rafe would do next, which was part of the excitement. Susannah didn't want to live a life preplanned and coordinated. One might as well not live at all if that were the case.

Why not? It was only dinner, after all.

Susannah walked out the back door of the club, her red hood pulled over her face. At the corner of the street waited a black-lacquered coach trimmed in silver leaf, one of the handsomest conveyances she'd ever seen. A wolf's head was painted in silver upon the door. A footman opened it and helped her up the red velvet steps. Susannah found herself alone in the velvet and satin quiet of the carriage. A small box was waiting beside her on the plush bench. Opening it, she found an ivory-colored mask.

Yes, she must be careful to conceal her identity still. Susannah tied the mask on, imagining what it would feel like to move through the world entirely as herself. She wondered if everyone wasn't masked in their own way, concealing some important part of themselves to blend in. Susannah hated that idea.

Rafe didn't conceal himself at all, did he? He didn't apologize for who he was.

After a short drive, they stopped outside a large brick building.

Susannah was fascinated as she stepped onto the street. The people were dressed fashionably, sometimes riotously so, yet also moved with greater speed and ease than anyone in the *ton* ever did. Energetic laughter and shouted comments sounded here and there about the street. Susannah giggled, feeling buoyed by the energy all around her as she climbed the steps.

A man in livery opened the door and bowed her through. "Welcome to the Bracewood Club, ma'am."

Susannah gasped. She'd heard stories of the Bracewood Club, a place where artists and musicians mingled alongside badly behaved royalty. This was where the Prince Regent often took his favorite mistress. Susannah had always yearned to see this place, but of course could never ask to be taken by Huntington. Somehow, Rafe had known exactly what she would like.

I mustn't like him too much. He was still temperamental, after all, even if he was a generous employer.

"Um. I believe I'm expected by a Mr. Winters?" she asked the man.

The fellow grinned. "Don't worry, love. He's a member here. You'll be well looked after."

Susannah found a server in a powdered wig waiting for her when she entered. He recognized her, probably by the mask, and bowed. "This way, madame. Mr. Winters has arranged a private room."

She tried not to look too amazed as they walked along the Bracewood Club's halls. As they passed open doorways, Susannah caught sight of dancing couples, heard a few silvery notes as an opera singer performed. A man chased a woman down the hallway, both laughing with abandon. Everyone here was high-spirited, everything from the velvet wallpaper to the crystal chandeliers was beautiful and opulent.

Susannah had never been so excited.

The server bowed to her. They stood before a pair of gauzy curtains, no doorway in sight.

"Through there, madame. Mr. Winters has already ordered champagne."

Heart pounding, Susannah slipped through the curtains.

Her mouth fell open when she saw what awaited her.

This wasn't a private dining room so much as it was an intimate chamber one might find in a Persian palace. Lush silk wall hangings warmed the space, and long, low tables ran along every side of the room. A lavish supper had been laid out already with every kind of dish available.

There was roast duck and a braised shank of wild boar in a burgundy wine sauce; a whole pineapple set upon a silver dish, clusters of dark red cherries encircling it; meringue and marzipan and a silver pot of bubbling chocolate.

And seated at a table set for two in the center of the room was Rafe, a bottle of champagne uncorked beside him. He poured the fizzing drink into a glass and offered it to Susannah.

"Here, Miss Fletcher. You look like you could do with a bit of refreshment." His grin was wicked, and he was well-pleased with himself.

The man was dressed in a coat of midnight blue satin, a diamond winking in the pristine white of his cravat. His black hair was artfully pomaded, his squared jaw clean-shaven. He looked like sin itself, a painted image of a fallen angel.

Susannah sipped the champagne, relishing the way it thrilled through her body. She took her seat opposite the Wolf of Mayfair. "I must say, I believe you've outdone yourself."

"I think anything that's worth doing is worth overdoing. Don't you agree?" he asked.

"I do, as a matter of fact."

"What would you like, to start?" Rafe waved a hand over the cornucopia of delicacies that waited on the tables. "I had the kitchens prepare as many dishes from as many countries as they could think up."

"What?" Susannah gasped as she realized that he spoke the truth.

Rafe lifted a silver lid off a bowl that contained a strange-looking food that smelled heavenly. "The chef's Italian, so he made certain to include tastes from his home in particular. This is pappardelle, though I don't know if I'm saying it right." Rafe looked a bit nervous as Susannah took some of the pasta onto her plate. She'd been desperate to try this kind of cooking for years, but as it was "foreign" food, her mother had a deep distrust of it. Susannah took a bite and closed her eyes in bliss.

"When I leave England, Italy shall be the first place I visit," she said.

"You think that stuff's good, wait for dessert. There's something called a tiramisu here," Rafe said. "They tell me it's layers of cream, coffee, and cake."

Susannah was about to cry. "That sounds wonderful."

"The chef said it was invented in Treviso years ago. They served it right next to a brothel in the town." Rafe smiled as he took a bite of the pasta dish for himself. "Apparently, men would enjoy it after a night with the ladies to 'restore' themselves."

Heat crept up Susannah's cheeks. This was the kind of talk that ought to horrify her, but instead it made her feel alive and giddy. With Rafe watching her across the candlelit table, obviously enjoying her as she enjoyed herself, it also felt sinful. Deliciously so.

"Maybe I ought to be careful how much I partake," she whispered.

"It's wise to be careful, I suppose," he replied. "But don't forget, Duchess, that life's meant to be lived. If you're too careful, you'll miss the best parts of it."

She could not have agreed more. Susannah wanted to try everything available tonight, from the Moroccan lamb dish to the French pastry...to the man sitting across from her. From the way he regarded her, a ravenous light in his eyes, the wolf seemed to have the same notion.

"Thank you for doing this for me," Susannah murmured.

"But I must ask why."

"It's simple. Soon I'll have my property and you'll have your freedom. When you set sail across the world, you ought to know some of what's waiting for you. There's so much you're going to experience, Susannah."

The sound of her name on his lips made her feel hot and strange all over her body, in between her thighs especially.

"Then thank you. Rafe." She loved how his name felt on her lips. His jaw clenched a bit in appreciation of the sound. "I must say, you're not at all like I initially took you to be."

"That a fact? What did you think of me?" He didn't sound angry or anxious, only curious. She found it was hard to tear her eyes from his as she took more champagne.

"At first I thought you were a brute."

"And now I'm not?"

"I think you can be hard when you have to survive." Indeed, he could be intensely masculine when he needed to be. "But you also have an artistic soul. And…a kind heart."

"You think I'm kind, Duchess?"

"I think you're helping me to achieve the life I want. I don't just mean paying me the money. I mean listening to my ideas, supporting my music." She gestured at the dishes. "Encouraging my tastes. No one has ever seen me before, not really. I adore my stepsister, and I know she wants me to be happy, but she doesn't understand the way you do."

"Understand what?" His voice was hoarse, almost a growl.

"What it is to want something other than a life of duty and tradition. To want your own life on your own terms."

"And that's what you want, is it?"

"It's what I need." Susannah knew those words were true. She needed a life of exploration and art, and she needed…

Him.

The thought made her almost shudder. No, she couldn't mean that.

But when she shut her eyes at night, he was one of the last thoughts that floated through her mind as she sank into sleep. And he often pursued her through her dreams, making Susannah yearn to remain asleep for years. Forever.

This won't last. I can't be too foolish now.

Rafe was careful as he stood and moved his chair over to sit directly alongside her. He winced a bit as he made to sit again, then relaxed. He took up his champagne glass and held it in a toast.

"Then here's to our business partnership." His eyes fixed on her mouth. "To getting what we both want. To you, for having the nerve to go through with all this." They clinked their glasses. "I doubt there's another girl like you in the whole of the *ton*."

"Well. I doubt there's another man like you in England." Susannah drank, feeling weightless and wicked. A drop of champagne slipped from the corner of her mouth, and he quickly brushed the pad of his thumb along her lower lip to catch it.

Susannah held her breath, the barest sensation of his skin making her burn. They remained close, as if waiting for the other to make the first move.

"We don't want to be fools," Rafe said at last.

"No. But…can we be friends?"

Even if she wanted more than friendship, Susannah didn't want to ruin this partnership. She didn't want to fumble both of their dreams right as they seemed about to be born.

"I like that idea. More than I should," he murmured.

"As do I. But I'm tired of being eternally safe."

"Then you're wiser than most people in this world." He grinned. "All right, Duchess. To friendship." He proposed another toast. Their glasses rang, and they drank.

To friendship, Susannah thought. And freedom. And fire.

Chapter Thirteen

Rafe couldn't believe it'd been almost three bloody weeks since they'd started this ridiculous ruse, and he couldn't believe how well they'd been doing.

The Rose Room was packed nightly with the fanciest toffs and social climbers in all of London. He'd even established a rule that permitted gentlewomen into the theater, though they weren't allowed elsewhere on the premises. He had also begun charging admission solely for the Red Duchess's nightly shows, and the income from that alone was sweet as honey.

But nothing was sweeter than Susannah Fletcher.

The highlight of Rafe's entire day was when he could sit at his table in the Rose Room and let her heavenly playing envelop him. They'd adjusted her costume a bit so that she wore a full-faced mask, not allowing anyone even the slightest glimpse of her features. Rafe had worried that the look would be too strange, but it worked. The utter mystery of the Red Duchess's identity had the upper classes enthralled.

After Susannah's show, Rafe would see out all the fancy folk and then hurry to speak with Susannah before she had to rush home. Some nights she made the show with only seconds to spare, having faked flu or a stubbed toe or death or whatever was necessary to get her out of going to a party. The girl looked exhausted, but also triumphant whenever they met for him to congratulate her.

Sometimes, Susannah would be staying with Lord and Lady Henry for the night, and those were the evenings Rafe liked best. The lord and lady allowed Susannah to come home at whatever hour pleased her, so there was no need to run out after her show.

That meant Rafe had time to spend with the duchess in private.

The first time he'd asked Susannah to have supper with him, he'd been convinced she'd turn him down. Now it was a little ritual with them, the after-show champagne and dinner. Tonight, as the applause died and the rich folks began exiting the theater, Susannah would be staying later. The thought of it made Rafe almost giddy with pleasure.

He'd taken her to the Bracewood Club a couple more times, which she'd adored. He'd wanted to escort her to the ballet when she yearned to see what was onstage, but that had been too risky. Even masked, it was likely someone would recognize Susannah. Sometimes Rafe would even escort Miss Fletcher back to Lady Henry's in his coach, the two of them chatting as they rumbled through the London night. Rafe hated how short the drive was; once Susannah had asked to be taken through the park, and he'd quickly obliged. It had given them almost twenty more minutes to be alone together.

Every second he could spend with her was precious as a gem.

Tonight, they'd be staying at the Wolf's Den. Rafe had his people ready a private chamber for him and Miss Fletcher, one of the smaller rooms with a locked door and plenty of iced champagne. For supper, he ordered oysters and turtle soup, only the finest. He'd never give Susannah anything less than his best.

He took care of some business on his way to the room and found Susannah waiting for him by the time he arrived. She was seated on a velvet sofa with a glass of fizzing champagne before her on the table. The bottle was on ice, with a second glass awaiting him.

"I think that was the best show yet." Susannah giggled, the candlelight painting her face in gold and shadow.

Rafe could have stared at that face for hours. She had such a youthful, almost impish beauty about her. Susannah was fresh as spring rain. God, Rafe had such an urge to taste the champagne on her lips. They hadn't kissed or done anything improper since the night the Duke of Huntington had first come to the show, but every moment between them vibrated with the tension of such a possibility. Rafe didn't know how much longer he could withstand the desire.

"You're a bloody sensation." He seated himself beside the girl and topped up her glass before filling his own. Rafe's body buzzed with erotic excitement.

Here she was, this woman of whom he couldn't stop dreaming, smiling at him over a glass of champagne in a private room. Rafe felt like one of those gentlemen out there with family money to burn and a title to burnish. Susannah made him feel like a king, or a god.

How the hell was he ever supposed to let her go?

"To a successful partnership." Susannah clinked her glass with his. "I rather like being in business with you, Mr. Winters."

I'd rather like to be in bed with you, Miss Fletcher.

He didn't say it, of course. Rafe drank the toast, devouring Susannah with his eyes. He felt the need to touch her pulsating through him, and Rafe could swear the girl looked as though she wanted him, too.

She sighed, her cheeks darkening with what Rafe hoped

was a blush of longing. He allowed himself to move closer to her, to let his knee brush her own. Susannah didn't back off. She smiled in contentment.

He could kiss her, make love to her on this sofa, and she would enjoy it. He could see to it she didn't get with child; the tryst wouldn't ruin her life. His balls ached with how badly he wanted her. Rafe gazed at the swell of her bosom, and wondered how she would feel entirely naked beneath him.

If he made his move, there was a chance she'd let him and welcome it.

You can't do this to her, you bastard. Stay in control. Rafe wanted Susannah to have everything in the world that she craved, and he wanted her to have it without regret. As much as he needed her, he needed her happiness more. When she'd thanked him at the Bracewood Club during their first supper, thanked him for helping her and supporting her, Rafe had felt like a truly good man for the first time. He always wanted to be good to her, no matter what it cost him.

"Here." Susannah put down her glass and took up a handful of pages. "I did as you asked."

It was the song she'd first played for him during their rehearsal before they'd kissed. Rafe had requested the music be written down and smiled as he looked over the pages.

"I hope you're not planning to steal my melodies," she teased.

"I'm a collector of beautiful things. This music is exquisite." He looked into Susannah's bright eyes. *As is the musician,* he thought.

"So. You want to collect my music, then?"

"Something like that." That wasn't the whole truth behind his interest in having a copy of her work, but she'd find out the full scope of his plans in time. He placed the pages off to the side and drank his champagne.

"We're close to triumphing. I can sense it," Susannah

murmured.

"So can I. Sackville-Chambers should be coming round to talk business next week. I've got that feeling in my gut that says it's going to go my way. *Our* way." Susannah was more a partner in this than any other person he'd ever had in his life, including Jacks.

"After we succeed, what do you plan to do with your Corner Castle?" Susannah asked. "For some reason, we never get around to talking about your future plans."

True. If they spoke of the future, they spoke of hers. Of the places she'd go, the music she'd create. Rafe wanted to hoard as many images of her enjoying her life as he could, like a dragon curled around its treasure.

"The Corner Castle? I'll see that it's the grandest hotel in all of England or the Continent." Rafe spoke of his vision with near reverence.

He could picture it, a building lit with candles in every room, with fancy carriages pulling up outside, servants in crisp uniforms handling luggage for all the wealthiest and most blue-blooded men and women in Europe.

Crystal chandeliers in the dining room, silk sheets on every bed. A world of beauty, a world in which he'd never have to see ugliness or poverty ever again. "My fortunes will be set. I'll be able to move through society as an equal, and no one will ever look down on me again."

"I see." Susannah frowned as she studied him.

Rafe cleared his throat. "And you, Duchess. What are your immediate plans for my money?"

"Oh, I've arranged almost everything in my head. I'll leave a letter for my mother and Julia on my pillow, then sneak out of the house with a packed valise just after midnight."

"Only one valise?"

"There are plenty of dressmakers on the Continent. Besides, I want to purchase my own clothes to my own tastes." She seemed lost in her imaginings. "The first stop will be Spain, I think. I want to head right for Madrid and see the opera and the bullfights. From there, I'll take a ship across the Mediterranean to Italy. I want to see Venice in the summer and Rome in the autumn. Come the spring, I'll head even farther east. I want to play with the greatest musicians in Vienna and perform my compositions for the Czar in Russia."

"For a woman who hates to plan anything, you've got a real schedule worked out." They both chuckled at that, and Rafe thought how everything she wanted in this world was so beautiful and fine. It was a shame she wanted to do all this traveling on her own, of course, but he'd rather she be alone than shackled to that duke.

If she couldn't be with Rafe, he would like to think of her free...and alone. Not lonely, of course, but not bogged down with love for any other man. He couldn't bear that one thought, that she would come to care for someone. Someone who wasn't Rafe.

"More than anything, I want to feel free to *not* make a schedule. I want to make all my own decisions." Susannah laid her cheek upon her hand and stared dreamily into the air. In that moment, her beauty was beyond anything Rafe had ever seen. No painting he owned could match that wistful expression. "I don't want to have to beg anyone for money, or to be allowed to go where I please. I don't want to marry for position; I don't want to be defined by the man who makes me his wife." She blushed and turned down her eyes. "This has to seem very foolish to you."

"No." He meant it, too.

"Really? Not so long ago, you called me a fool for not wanting to marry a duke."

"That was before I got to know you. You'd be wasted trapped in a castle, looking out a window your whole life. Men like me see things only in terms of security. Maybe it's smart, but it's not particularly wise."

Susannah blushed. "Well. It helps to understand the reality of what you're getting yourself into, doesn't it? Thank you for that."

Susannah looked at him with those amber eyes, eyes like whiskey or autumn leaves. The girl could make Rafe into a poet or something else ridiculous if he wasn't careful. Again, he glanced at her lips and recalled their sweetness.

"May I ask you something else?" Susannah murmured.

Yes, you can kiss me. Yes, I'll kiss you back. Anywhere you like.

"Perhaps," Rafe growled. He forced the thought of kisses from his mind.

"Where do you come from?"

"The rookery. It's a collection of streets around St. Giles, down near Camden Town." His answer was short, his tone firm.

She wouldn't let it go, though. "I mean who are your family? Do you have brothers or sisters?"

"No family. No brothers, no sisters. Jacks is the closest thing I have in this world to family." Rafe poured himself another glass of champagne, hoping she'd leave off this line of questioning. No such luck.

"What was your mother like?"

Rafe set the bottle back into the ice with a firm hand. "Look at me and ask yourself: do I seem the sort of man who had a happy childhood?" Rafe let the grimace and the busted knee answer for him.

Susannah looked away. "I'm sorry, I don't mean to pry. I want to know more about you, that's all."

"I think you know plenty. More than most people ever find out."

"Is that so? Even if I know nothing about your past?"

"People like me don't have beautiful pasts or noble

families. Most of the time, we don't want to look back. The future's the only thing we've got."

"You're right," Susannah whispered. "All we have is the future." She cleared her throat. "And the present, of course."

"Well. Yes."

He noticed then that she had turned herself to face him fully.

Susannah pulled the fingertips of her kid glove, sliding it from her arm. Her delicate hand was bare. The mere sight of an extra inch of her flesh set Rafe on the edge of becoming truly bestial. He wanted those silken arms twined about his neck. He wanted those fingers sliding through his hair.

"I've been thinking of the future." Susannah inched nearer to him, the whisper of her silk-clad body against the velvet cushion its own sort of music. "I'm going to explore the whole world and meet all sorts of people but, well…" She looked shy. "I know absolutely nothing of men."

"I don't think nothing's the right word," Rafe croaked. He thought of touching her between her legs, the glorious sound she made as she climaxed.

She seemed to recall the same scene, and blushed. "But there's more I want to understand about desire. About what it is to be with a man."

"What are you saying, Duchess?"

"Susannah. Call me Susannah, please." She quivered as she settled nearer to him, and he breathed in the honeysuckle of her perfume.

He wanted to bury his face against her neck, trace his lips along the line of her pulse. Rafe dreamed of sinking inside her, finding a refuge for the first time in this world. A true haven. His heart pounded as she laid her soft hand against his cheek.

"Susannah. What is this?"

"I wanted to say that I think of that night in the dressing

room," she replied. "I think of it often. I want…more."

It sounded like it cost her much to say that word. A young woman asking a man to take her was unheard of in her world. Asking it outside of marriage made her the worst sort of girl.

At least, the snobby class would see her as bad. To Rafe, she was a goddess in the flesh. He scarce drew breath as she came closer, her lips just above his. She was giving herself to him, wanting him. Wanting all of him. All he needed to do was take her.

"You know what I am," he muttered.

"I do. I know what I want, too." She sighed, tilting her head. Presenting herself to be kissed. "This is a partnership, isn't it? We should both be satisfied."

She was willing to give herself to him and expect nothing in return. She'd ruin herself with him if he let her. She had the same appetites and passions as any gentleman. Combined with a rare spirit and a brilliant soul, she was the finest gift Rafe could ever receive.

His cock strained, his whole body ached for her touch. Rafe could have her, have her several times over. But it wouldn't be enough. Once he tasted her, he'd hunger for nothing and for no one else the rest of his life.

She wouldn't stay. She wanted the fantasy, the Wolf of Mayfair. Not Rafe Winters the gutter snipe, the businessman, not a life spent in Mayfair looking over accounts and keeping ahead of creditors.

Rafe could have had the Red Duchess, the mysterious genius, the toast of London. But he wanted Susannah Fletcher, the debutante.

He knew he'd never recover from her loss. Not if he had all of her for even one moment.

When Susannah leaned forward as if to kiss him, he pushed her away. It wasn't a hard shove, but it was firm. She blinked in astonishment.

"We're partners, like you said. In business, not pleasure," he grunted.

"I thought you liked to mix business with pleasure." She looked hurt. *Good*. She needed to get these thoughts of him out of her head.

"Not when the stakes are this high. You said you wanted friendship? That's what I can offer. Nothing else, Duchess."

"Susannah."

"Miss Fletcher." The way he said it was a door closed between them. "I wouldn't be good for you, and I know you wouldn't be good for me. It's not personal." His stomach clenched. "Just business."

Just business. Those were the words that defined his life, that clarified his future. In his own way, Rafe was a cautious man. He never took a bet with impossible odds. He never gambled with anything he could not afford to lose, like his pride. Or his heart.

"I see." Tears gathered in her eyes. Susannah got to her feet and swept on her red cloak. "I'm sorry to have inconvenienced you, Mr. Winters. Good night."

She left him there, alone.

Rafe's body burned to go after her, but his knee was in too much pain. Besides, there was nothing he could offer her, while she offered him the world. And he could never bear to lose the world itself.

...

Susannah wiped tears from her cheeks, ordering herself to stop crying.

She pulled the hood over her head, ready to hurry outside and find Henry and Annabelle's coach that had been left for her. All she desired now was a few hours of sobbing into a pillow, her friend petting her hair and asking what was wrong.

Rafe must truly have no feelings for her.

She'd thought he yearned for her as she did for him, but he must have meant it when he said he wanted only business between them. Only friendship. How conceited was Susannah to believe that any man she wanted would feel exactly the same way about her? Perhaps when he'd stopped himself after touching her on the settee in the dressing room that night, he'd done it because he truly wasn't interested in her. Not in the way she was interested in him.

Oh, she was such a fool.

Susannah normally went out the club's front entrance, but tonight there were too many people she knew hanging about. Better to be safe. She ducked past servers and crept around the main bar, headed for the side entrance into an alleyway.

Susannah opened the door to the alley but paused on top of the stairs. She heard men's drunken, loud voices a little farther ahead, echoing in the darkness. It sounded like they were laughing hard at something. Or someone.

"You've been a delight, gentlemen." That was Celine's voice, and Susannah knew that exact tone. Celine sounded confident and implacable, but inside she'd suffered a wound. "But if you don't mind, I need to get back to work."

"Is work the proper word for what women like you do?"

Lord, Susannah knew that voice. The Honorable Jacob Wembley, son of Baron Wembley and heir to his estate. Jacob sounded as though he'd drunk his weight in ale tonight. Keeping her hood up, she crept nearer and found Celine surrounded by Jacob and a couple of other drunken louts. They were all well dressed and coiffed, all respected members of the *ton*.

"I'm certain I know more about real work than men like you ever could." Celine tried to walk past them, but two blocked her way. Her hands balled into fists at her sides.

"Better making honest money on a stage than drinking away cash that others sweat to provide you."

"Did you hear that?" Thomas Paltrem, heir to an earldom, hiccuped as he swayed on his feet. "This bitch thinks she's clevererer, uh, cleverinst, um, *hic*, more smart than us!"

She certainly is, and much better mannered. Susannah should turn and go, but the rage clouded her vision. How dare they speak this way to Celine? How dare they!

"I think, therefore I am," Celine grumbled, and shoved past the two blocking her path. One of them grabbed her by the arm and threw her against the brick wall with awful force. Susannah gasped.

"Ow!" Celine cried out as Jacob started yanking at her gown.

"Thinks she can talk to her betters that way." Paltrem chuckled.

Celine slapped his jaw, sending his head snapping backward. While the bastard teetered about, trying to get his equilibrium back, Celine attempted to leave once more. Unfortunately, she couldn't outpace three drunk men.

Paltrem laughed as Celine struggled against the other two, and he began to close in. "If she likes earning money, let's show her how to truly service a man."

For Susannah, that was past what could be endured.

"How dare you?" she shouted, keeping the hood over her face as she marched up to them. The sound of a young woman's voice startled the bastards.

Celine seized her opportunity and ran back inside, glancing at Susannah as she passed. Susannah ought to follow suit, but rage blinded her. Never in her life had she seen such dishonorable behavior. "The three of you are despicable! You aren't gentlemen. You deserve to be shut out of good society. When the other members of the *ton* hear of your disgraceful behavior, they'll turn their backs on you!"

"And who are you, exactly?" Jacob slurred, squinting at her. "Push back the hood an' let us see your face."

"You don't know me. But I know you, Mr. Wembley." Susannah made certain to remain on the edge of a shadow, ready to flee if fleeing was required. "I doubt that the Honorable Miss Amelia Glossip will appreciate the knowledge that her fiancé is a violent wretch."

Jacob's eyes widened. Thomas and the other fellow snickered.

"Don't laugh, Mr. Paltrem." She glared at Thomas next. "While your uncle draws breath, you're not the Earl of Darrow just yet. You wouldn't have a penny if your aunt decided to cut off her support, and Lady Darrow dislikes nightclubs and debauchery. If she learns you were found drunk at the Wolf's Den, I shudder to think what that could do to your finances."

"W-Wait." The men realized they were not as covered by their wealth and privilege as they had previously believed. They still couldn't see Susannah's face, but she'd made it abundantly clear the damage she could do them if she wished. The third fellow, whom Susannah didn't recognize, lurched forward.

"What are you all standing here for? We need to shut the little bitch up!"

That was Susannah's cue to flee. She whirled around, prepared to race back into the club and hide until the gentlemen were gone.

But as she turned, a figure came at her out of the night. The tall man surged past her, and out toward the three bastards at Susannah's heels.

Rafe swung his walking stick. Susannah cried out as the silver wolf's head collided with the side of Thomas Paltrem's face. The man collapsed to the ground, moaning with his eyes shut, blood gushing from his mouth.

"You lot." Rafe sounded like a malevolent creature now,

something out of a dark wood in a ghostly tale. He stepped before Susannah, brandishing his stick. "Get away from my place. Don't let me see your faces here again."

"Mr. Winters, please," Susannah hissed. She appreciated him wanting to strike a blow for Celine and to protect her, but the matter had been dealt with. Violence would lead only to trouble. Unfortunately, it seemed violence was all that Rafe wanted right now.

"Y-You struck him!" Jacob sounded like a frightened child now that a full-grown man with a weapon had appeared. "You…you piece of filth! Who are you to raise a hand to men like us?"

"You're using the word 'men' very loosely, boy."

"How dare you call me boy!" Jacob charged at Rafe, and Rafe delivered a devastating blow to the bastard's midsection. As Jacob fell to his knees, gasping for air, the third member of their party helped Thomas to his feet. The three backed away down the alley. Rafe didn't move from Susannah, blocking her from their eyes.

"Come here again, and I'll break your skulls open." Rafe's threat landed because every one of them believed he could do it. "And don't think that we haven't kept all your gambling debts recorded nice and clean in our ledger. Your grace period's up. I'll expect payment in full by tomorrow afternoon, or I'll have some of my associates start paying calls on you. They're much nastier than me. You don't want that."

"You are no gentleman." Paltrem slurred it like it was the greatest insult of all time.

"If you lot are anything to go by, I'm damn proud not to be one." Rafe raised his cane. "Get out of here!"

And they went, Jacob shouting something about how Rafe would regret this. Susannah rushed over to him.

"It was good of you, but very foolish!" Susannah gripped

his arm. "I had the situation under control."

"I gotta protect what's mine, Duchess. You and Celine work for me. I look out for my people."

But the panic and the fury she'd heard in his voice hadn't sounded like a businessman protecting a mere asset. "Please. Come inside."

"I'll get them." Rafe was being carried away by his fury. He took a powerful step forward, making as if to go after the fleeing men. "They don't know who they threatened."

But he had overestimated his own resilience. With a cry, Rafe grabbed at his bad knee and collapsed to the ground. His cane fell beside him with a clatter. His face was twisted in pain as he gripped his knee, cursing softly under his breath while he massaged it.

"Rafe," Susannah whispered. She knelt beside him, touched his shoulder and his face, and he looked at her. For the first time, she felt he truly looked at her. "Let me help you. Please."

This time, he didn't argue, only let her take his cane and guide him back into the club.

Chapter Fourteen

Susannah was stunned by the beauty of Rafe's flat. She'd expected something ostentatious, with plush velvet drapes and overstuffed seats, ornate antiques littering the walls without thought or care to how it all looked. She'd expected him to have expensive rather than good taste, a bit reminiscent of his club downstairs.

She'd been so bloody wrong.

His taste was impeccable, better than any member of the *ton* she'd ever met.

Jacks had come outside as well and helped Rafe back up the stairs. She'd laid him out on a chaise longue of midnight blue satin, which went beautifully with the other pieces of furniture he'd settled about the room.

His artwork had been painted by masters and could have proudly hung in the king's own chambers. Lord, there was even a fine pianoforte here, placed against the far wall of the parlor.

"I can't play," Rafe said when she looked at it. "But I like how it looks. It makes the place feel more dignified. Ah, shit!" He yowled some more as Jacks tried dabbing cold water on his knee.

"Amazing. The man can take on three drunk monsters but can't endure a little water." Jacks shook her head, but it was only teasing. She smiled at Susannah and got up. "I'm going downstairs for some liniment and bandages. This clod keeps none in his house. I suppose such things aren't 'fancy' enough for such a grand location."

"Keep talking that way and I'll toss you out the window." But Rafe's threat rang hollow. Jacks laughed.

"Look after him until I'm back, if you can stomach it," she said to Susannah. Then it was only Rafe and she, alone together. A stately grandfather clock ticked in the foyer, the only sound besides Susannah's rather loud breathing. She could even hear the beat of her heart. She knelt beside Rafe and studied the knee once more.

She could have wept at the sight. She'd heard that someone had wounded Rafe there, but wound was not grisly enough of a word. They'd shattered him.

The entire knee was a red ball of scar tissue. The scars lay across his flesh like thick, ugly stripes in chaotic zigzag patterns. When Susannah touched the cool, wet cloth to the knee, Rafe flinched and hissed in pain.

"You trying to kill me, Duchess?"

"Death doesn't seem like the proper reward for rushing to protect me, now does it?" Even if Susannah had handled those bastards, they'd wanted to hurt her. She knew they'd have done dreadful things if they'd caught her. "Thank you." She felt shy suddenly. "I'm glad they never learned who I was. They might have if they'd nabbed me."

"Worrying about your reputation? They'd have done a lot worse than spread gossip, you know."

"Worrying over reputations isn't for me, so much as for my family." Susannah dipped the cloth and wrung it. "Even though my stepsister's a duchess, if people found out who I was, her standing in society would plummet."

"I don't understand why she or you care about those bastards." Rafe lay back upon the chaise, half his shirt unbuttoned and his sleeves rolled. He'd splashed water on himself earlier to wipe the sweat away.

Susannah had never seen anything like that hard, masculine chest before, the perfectly defined ridges of his stomach, or the faint trail of dark hair that began at his navel and disappeared beneath his clothes. His arms could have been fashioned from steel, or marble. The pain in his knee only made Rafe's eyes blaze brighter. He was furious at his own pain, struggling to overcome it. No matter what, he would not succumb to anything that opposed him.

God, he was the most extraordinary thing she'd ever seen.

"What did you say?" Susannah had been too distracted by his beauty to hear his words.

"If your stepsister's a duchess, she's got money enough to last her a lifetime. Why should you all worry about pleasing people you don't like or respect?"

Susannah sighed and dabbed at his knee. This time, Rafe didn't wince so much.

"I suppose that's one of those big questions that philosophers ponder all the time. Why do we hurt people we care about for the approval of those we hate?" She dipped the cloth once more. "I don't have the patience to think about those sorts of things, I suppose. It makes me a frivolous girl, I know. But I just want to live and find my own happiness." She couldn't believe that they were put on this earth only to suffer and never to have what they wanted.

"Living's a good thing to want," Rafe said. To her surprise, he held one of her copper ringlets between his fingers. He smiled as he touched her hair. "I think you're smarter than any of those other society misses. Or any of their gentlemen, for that matter."

Susannah's heart beat faster as his fingers stroked her cheek, as his rough hand cupped her face. She left the basin and the cloth and allowed Rafe to lure her closer.

His icy eyes were half-lidded, his sumptuous lips parted. Susannah wanted to kiss him more than she'd ever wanted anything before, food or shelter or even air. If she couldn't kiss this man, she didn't think she could ever be happy.

"I thought we didn't mix business and pleasure," she murmured.

"I'm starting to think that's not possible with you." He gazed into her eyes. "I get pleasure whenever you walk into the room. Whenever I hear you laugh. No, I can't separate you and the business at all."

"Rafe," she whispered.

"Susannah." He had called her by name before, but had it ever sounded so sweet? She couldn't recall, only knew that she wanted to hear her name on his lips again. And again.

And as she thought of lips, Susannah held her breath as he touched his to hers for the first of, hopefully, many kisses—

"Got the liniment," Jacks said, reentering the room.

Susannah fell backward in surprise, her foot accidentally knocking over the basin.

Rafe swore and leaned over the side of the chaise. "You all right?"

"Yes. But your rug's a bit soaked. I'm sorry."

Rafe grumbled about that as Jacks knelt beside him, righting the basin. She winked at Susannah.

"No harm done. Why don't you head off home now, miss? I can handle it from here. Thank you for helping to get him up those stairs." Jacks lightly whacked Rafe's shoulder. "This one's got it into his head he's invincible and don't need nobody's help."

"*Any*body's help," Rafe murmured.

Susannah saw so much of him in that one moment. The

man who wore his toughness and low birth like a badge of honor, a shield against the jabs of the *ton*, but inside he was also a man who wanted to be proper. He wanted to be seen as a gentleman.

It broke her heart to think he didn't know how much better than those so-called gentlemen he already was.

"Jacks is right," Rafe said. "Go on home. You've a night off tomorrow; you've earned it. But be ready for Wednesday night."

"I shall." Susannah left with all those unsaid words still hanging on her lips, and as she climbed into Henry and Annabelle's carriage, she thought of how she'd longed to stay with Rafe. How she wished Jacks hadn't come back into the room.

How, if she had even half the chance, she would give all of herself to Rafe Winters and never regret a moment of it.

• • •

Rafe could scarcely feel the pain of his knee any longer. He could think only of Susannah's face and her lips, the mere touch of them, before Jacks had spoiled it.

"You and the Duchess seem to get on quite well." Jacks cocked a brow as she finished rolling a bandage about his knee. "Maybe she could be a permanent fixture 'round the Den."

"Don't count on it." Rafe felt surly now; he always felt surly, but this was worse. He didn't think he'd have the strength to stay away from Susannah much longer. "Once she has the cash, she's on her way to the Continent."

"Plans change, don't they?"

"Not for her lot."

"She don't, sorry, *doesn't* seem like their lot, though. Does she?" Jacks took a chair and leaned her elbows upon her knees. "I don't know another man or woman of her station who'd have come to Celine's rescue like that. No thought for herself, none at all."

God, that was true. When he'd learned the ridiculous and brave thing Susannah had done for Celine, his heart had ached. She was a pure soul.

How many times did he need to remind himself? She didn't belong here in shadows and the world of fantasy, did she? Susannah ought to be in the bright, sunlit world. She needed to choose the right path for her future, and Rafe needed to ensure that she did.

"She's a good girl, but she is what she is." Rafe sat up and rolled down his trouser leg. His knee did feel a great deal better. "We can't alter what we are, Jacks."

"Oh?" Jacks leaned back in her chair. "Y'know, I could've been like my mother or sisters and married some drunk, raised a pack of kids, and tried to pretend I was happy. That I didn't want to be what I wanted to be, that I didn't want to love who I wanted to love. I made a choice a long time ago to change, and I've never regretted a day. If I can do that and be happy, who's to say that little Duchess doesn't have the same strength?"

Rafe didn't want to listen to her. It gave him too much hope. "Good night, Jacks. Thanks."

She huffed and left the flat, knowing that there'd be no talking to him now.

Rafe hobbled over to the window and gazed out upon the streets of Mayfair.

He stared at the Corner Castle with its dark, boarded-up windows, and dreamed of lights and music, of satin and silk. He dreamed of being what the world told him he could never be: a gentleman. More than that, a gentleman who could entice a woman like Susannah to fall in love with him.

Most of all, a gentleman who could make her stay.

Lydia Drake

• • •

Rafe had waited every night for Sackville-Chambers to return.

He knew His Lordship had heard the buzz about town, the fantastic little Red Duchess Rafe Winters had dug up and put on display at his club.

But more than that, Rafe wanted Sackville-Chambers to see the alterations he'd made elsewhere on Susannah's advice.

There were gentlewomen as patrons now, at least in the club's front half, and that meant modifying the, er, more lascivious décor. The paintings of nude courtesans had been replaced by erotic-yet-tasteful images from Greek and Roman mythology.

The girls who served the front area wore slightly higher necklines and lower skirts. True, some of Rafe's longtime customers had abandoned him, annoyed by this new, more tasteful endeavor, but if it got him the Corner Castle, it would be worth a temporary dip in profits. And besides, the smaller theaters still entertained in their lurid, risqué fashion.

So, when the little lord arrived and moved through the redecorated Den, appraising everything he saw, Rafe could feel this was the moment. If he did not win now, then it would be never.

"Here for the show tonight, my lord?" He greeted Sackville-Chambers at the bar, where the man had ordered a dry sherry.

"I've come to see the crowds you're attracting and their reactions to the girl. Though I must admit, I'd have returned if only to hear her beautiful playing."

"She's improved since last you were here. Sounds impossible, but it's true."

He had Jacks seat Sackville-Chambers at Rafe's table and bring out a bottle of their finest wine, which the lord liked a great deal.

As Murray came on to introduce the Red Duchess with an air of mystery and almost religious solemnity, Rafe noticed Sackville-Chambers nodding in appreciation.

Of course, Susannah's playing was impossible to dislike.

Rafe could even forget his nerves when he listened to her create the most heavenly sounds upon that one, small instrument. He watched her gloved hands and imagined kissing her palms, her fingertips. He wanted to feel that rosy little hand around his cock, squeezing him until he was hard. He wanted her so badly he almost went wild sitting there, feet from her and unable to touch her.

When the show ended, Rafe scarce heard the enthusiastic applause and cheers as the audience rose to its feet. Sackville-Chambers was among them and seemed pleased as he surveyed the room.

After the people had filed out, Sackville-Chambers touched Rafe's arm. "I believe I'm prepared to give you my decision," he said.

Rafe took them to the office and ordered Jacks to come, trying to pretend ease when all he felt was nerves. He hadn't been this nervous since he was a kid, the time he'd been apprehended by the law for picking a pocket. Only quick thinking and agile leaping had saved him from facing a judge and jail, or the workhouse, or perhaps even hanging. If he could see this through, he would never have to feel like that scared little boy ever, ever again.

He was almost there. Almost there.

"I like the changes you've made to the atmosphere of the club. At least, for the most part." His Lordship enjoyed a sip of Rafe's finest port, drawing out the moment. Rafe might explode or whack the man with his cane.

"And? What've you decided, sir?" Jacks, too, was ready to burst out of her skin.

"I approve of your tasteful change in furnishings, as well as how you've staged and marketed that sublime Red Duchess. You've rethought the seediness of your organization, which I appreciate. Therefore, I think you might be the man to transform the Corner Castle into something worthy of its illustrious past. So, I have decided I'll sell to you."

Rafe wanted to get up and dance around the room, laughing and whacking objects off the shelves and walls with his cane. That snarling silver wolf's head seemed to be grinning tonight, merriment glinting in those ruby-chip eyes.

"You won't regret this, my lord." Rafe stood with the help of his cane. "You have made a great decision tonight."

"However, I need assurance on two things before we can proceed." Sackville-Chambers settled comfortably in his seat, looking in total control. "First, your initial offer was too low. I want an extra fifty thousand pounds for the place. In addition, I want ten percent of your hotel's future earnings."

Rafe almost burst out laughing, but mercifully stopped himself. He also nearly smacked the lord with his cane, but wisely resisted that as well.

"Our initial offer was more than generous," Jacks said, shooting a look at Rafe to signal that he needed to keep silent. When it came to careful negotiations, Rafe was as useful as a military cannon in a flower shop.

"Indeed, but it's also apparent to me that you're in desperate want of my property. So, I've upped the price, and I want future earnings. Of course, if you'd prefer, I could take fifty percent of all future earnings and nothing further up front now. That's the offer. You may, as the merchants say, take it or leave it."

Rafe could do what he usually did with the other thugs and lowlifes he did business with: he could growl, threaten this man, and beat him into the floor. But that sort of thing didn't work with Sackville-Chambers's lot. The high society thugs were worse than those from the gutter; the ones with class and breeding had the law on their side, no matter how they bent the rules.

If he took the second option, Rafe would be a lot safer in the short-term, but that hotel was his. His own vision, his dream. He would not give someone like this poncy lord half of it. A taste he could bear to part with, but not half. 10 percent he could endure. So, that meant the fifty thousand up front. Rafe could spare it. He'd be placing his own solvency and that of the Den in jeopardy, but once the hotel opened, his worries would be gone forever. He knew by looking in the lord's oily little eyes that the man wasn't going to negotiate. He had no reason to, since he held all the power in this room. Not only the power of owning the property Rafe wanted, but the power society gave him.

"All right," Rafe growled. "You have your extra cash."

"Rafe," Jacks whispered.

"And what's the second thing?" What more could this greedy bastard want?

"The sale is final. Once money has changed hands, I'm done with the place. There will be no reneging on our agreement."

"You're going out of your way to make this sound suspicious, aren't you?" Rafe narrowed his eyes.

"I simply don't wish to deal with you any more than is necessary, Mr. Winters."

"The feeling's mutual, believe me."

Sackville-Chambers sipped the last of his port as Jacks pondered.

"I expect you'll allow us to inspect the premises before we sign?" she asked. "Get our own people to make certain Rafe's not purchasing a firetrap or something that needs rebuilding from the ground up?"

"Naturally." The lord stood, and Rafe and Jacks rose

with him. "Gentlemen, this has been a most interesting opportunity for me. Do your inspection, and I'll have my solicitor draw up the necessary papers in the meantime. Good luck."

"Don't say things you don't mean," Rafe muttered.

"Why shouldn't I wish you luck? I've my own investment in the place, after all." His Lordship put on his hat and tipped it. "I'll reach out in a day or so."

This time, Rafe didn't walk the bastard out. He sank back into his chair and thought and thought, staring that silver wolf right in his jeweled eyes.

This had now become a bigger gamble than he'd anticipated. If one thing went wrong with the renovation of the hotel, he'd be ruined. Lose everything he'd worked his whole lifetime to build. But if he succeeded, he'd become what he'd always dreamed of being. A gentleman. A man of legitimate business.

And more than that, someone with the kind of wealth, influence, and station who might entice Susannah into his arms. The girl was a pure soul, but she could never resist freedom *and* money. Rafe could give her both in spades, and she could give him her love. Her presence. Her laughter and her brilliance. Susannah Fletcher could only be his, through the realization of this one dream. And ridiculous as it was to think about, Rafe could concentrate on nothing else.

"I don't think we should do this," Jacks said. She kicked the leg of his chair. "Oi, do you hear me? This'll cut into the last of our liquid funds. If we slip up, the club's finished and so are we."

"I need this, Jacks." Rafe poured himself a glass of port and swallowed it in one go. "And you know I don't need anything. We got where we are today through massive risk." He climbed to his feet. "If this comes through, we'll never have to risk anything again."

"But Rafe," she said.

He didn't listen to however that sentence ended, only left his office and stalked through the halls of his club.

The Wolf's Den had become more than his business; it was his home, his sanctuary. The buffer he put up between himself and the rest of the ugly, uncaring world.

But he was almost there. And then Susannah might fall into his arms, sigh as he undressed her and entered her, be his in body and spirit and…

Shit. He stopped walking as the realization weighed him down. He'd accomplished their mission. The Corner Castle was going to be his. Which meant it was time to give Susannah her share of the money.

It was time for her to leave him behind.

Chapter Fifteen

After the show on Thursday night, Susannah waited eagerly for Rafe to knock on the door and invite her to a private room for champagne or perhaps a light supper.

It was another of her nights with Annabelle, which meant she didn't have to be back until the early morning hours. She hadn't seen him Tuesday, and last night he'd ducked out immediately after the show with Lord Sackville-Chambers. Tonight, perhaps they could discuss that almost-kiss of theirs.

Or perhaps they might do it again.

She bade farewell to Celine and Antoinette and turned on her stool, waiting for his knock. But five and then ten minutes passed, and the knock never came.

Flustered, Susannah put on her hood and ducked into the corridor. Fortunately, Jacks was hurrying past on business of one sort or another.

"Jacks! Have you seen Rafe?"

"Oh. He should be across the street, at the Corner Castle." Jacks looked hesitant as she spoke. "He's having it inspected to make sure he's paying the right price for it."

"Oh. Oh!" Susannah bounced up and down on her toes.

"That means he convinced Lord Sackville-Chambers?"

"Indeed. I think we're overpaying, but it's not my decision in the end."

Susannah couldn't concentrate on Jacks's complaints or concerned grumblings as she walked away. Rafe had won! They both had! She was going to have her money, and then she'd be off for that life of adventure. She'd leave for Italy, for Greece, perhaps head into Turkey and even beyond. She'd see everything, do everything, meet everyone…

But Rafe would not be there.

That realization soured her joy, and she felt a leaden weight in her gut.

This success with Sackville-Chambers meant the fulfillment of her dream, but it also meant there was nothing to hold Rafe and her together any longer.

It shouldn't have mattered, but Susannah felt hollowed out on the inside just picturing their goodbye. She'd never see him again, would she? Not unless she came to London for a visit and looked in on him. By that time, he'd have forgotten her and surrounded himself with beautiful women. It would be easy for him to move on and cast her aside in his memory.

Could she do the same?

Susannah felt confused as she hurried across the street to the Corner Castle. She saw a light flickering inside the easternmost window on the first level. Two figures were talking together inside. She could see only silhouettes, but one appeared to be Rafe's. She could tell by his height and the way he had of standing, rigid against the world and prepared for any danger.

Feeling foolish, Susannah climbed the front steps and found the door unlocked. She poked her head inside and gazed about the place. The foyer itself was massive and at least twelve feet high, perhaps more. In the murky distance, Susannah saw cloth-covered pieces of furniture and a shaded chandelier. Two staircases twisted on opposite sides of the grand room, headed toward a magnificent landing on the second floor.

Already, she could imagine the fancy crowds milling about the lobby, liveried footmen rushing to and fro with luggage. Rafe's hotel would be grand.

He'd be happy without her. Susannah told herself that the tears pricking the corners of her eyes were because of the dust in here.

"You won't get the kind of renovation you're wanting for less than ten, maybe twenty thousand." A male voice echoed along the hallway, approaching Susannah. She heard the rhythmic tapping of Rafe's cane. "It's got good bones, and the space is adequate. But are you certain? It'll be a large undertaking, and with the cash you're already spending it could end up floundering."

"I get what I want, Corkus. Always do."

The men stopped in surprise when they beheld Susannah. All thought of what to say flew out of her head.

"What the hell are you doing here?" Rafe snapped. Not the most romantic opening.

"I came looking for you. I wished to speak with you."

"Yeah. I've needed to talk with you as well." He didn't sound pleased by the prospect as he shook hands with the other man, Corkus, a short, balding fellow with a pleasant demeanor. "Say hello to Betsy and the kids. And don't worry; I know what I'm doing."

"I've never seen you be wrong yet, it's true." Corkus tipped his hat to Susannah and left.

She and Rafe now stood in the dusty, dimly lit foyer in utter silence. She could only appraise the figure of the man standing before her, the glorious, furious beauty of him. Susannah's heart seemed to ache at the mere thought of leaving him. But perhaps he wanted her gone.

As if in answer to her fearful thought, Rafe shook his head. "You posh girls are damned nosy. It'll be a delight to finally be shut of you."

"Yes." Susannah dug her fingernails into her palms. "Jacks told me Sackville-Chambers was selling to you. Congratulations."

"We ought to discuss your payment." Rafe cleared his throat and sauntered past her. "Come on. We'll do it in a place with bloody light."

Susannah felt numb as she followed him to the club, then climbed up the stairs and walked into his flat. Already it felt like he was ready to get rid of her. She couldn't decide between anger and sadness; at the moment both roiled behind her breast. They moved into the front parlor, where he sank into a chair and gestured for her to take a seat as well. Susannah obeyed and tried to think of what to do as they lapsed into painful silence.

"Why the hell are we sulking?" Rafe said. "We ought to celebrate our success."

"Indeed." Susannah bit her lip and fought against tears. He didn't seem to care that this was the end of their partnership. Susannah was alone in her unhappiness, and that made the unhappiness even worse. "Perhaps we might have some champagne?"

"Are you crying, Duchess?" Rafe looked befuddled. "Is this because your time as my headlining act is coming to an end? You'll find an audience across the water, don't worry about that."

"How can you possibly think that's why I'm upset?" Susannah snapped. Her passion surprised even herself. Oh, this was impossible.

Susannah wanted to kick over the chair and scream, break all the antique mirrors in the place, roll up the priceless Persian rugs and set them on fire. Anything to escape this hideous unhappiness. She turned away from Rafe, so angry with herself for appearing weak in front of him. She wanted him to see her as a woman of the world, not some whining little girl.

"Is it the money? I'm not going to shortchange you. I may be paying more for the Corner Castle than I initially thought, but I'm good for the cash I promised," Rafe said. "Don't worry about that. Just tell all the people you meet on your travels about the Den and my hotel. That'll be good publicity for us. Perhaps you'll think fondly of us from time to time."

"Yes, I'll send you a letter from wherever I land." Susannah wanted to scream and shout. For the first time in her life, she wanted to throw a proper fit. She wanted to let every feeling trapped inside her find expression through her voice, not her music.

"I'm sure the girls'll like reading of your exploits. I'm sure they'll miss you." He didn't mention himself.

"Must you be such an insufferable ass?" Susannah said. Damn, now she really was crying.

"What's wrong? You've got what you wanted, and so have I. Our business relationship is done." Susannah realized that Rafe himself was struggling against some painful emotion; she'd missed that earlier. Jaw clenched, he climbed to his feet and went to a handsome desk of polished mahogany in the corner. He opened and closed drawers with quick, harsh bangs, looking for something. "I'll have a note written for my banker and sent to him for the money. I don't keep five thousand in cash on me, but you'll be paid and on your way out of London by the end of the week. Will that suit you, Miss Fletcher?"

He was breaking under the strain of some overwhelming emotion just as she was. He slammed one of the drawers so hard that the desk rattled. Rafe stopped moving and rubbed his eyes. He looked wearied by something.

Susannah got up, marched over to Rafe, and grabbed him by his arms. Even though he wasn't moving away from her, she felt the irresistible urge to force him to be still and look at her. She wanted him to understand what she was feeling, even if she barely understood it herself.

"The hell do you think you're doing?" He looked amazed. Susannah clung as tightly to him as she could.

"That will not suit me at all. I don't want to leave you, you incorrigible ass!" Susannah had never spoken to anyone like that before. She'd never known this part of herself existed beneath the well-bred, proper young lady. But she found that she liked this uninhibited side of herself.

"What do you mean?" Rafe continued to regard her with wariness, like nothing so much as a wild animal listening for the hunter's footstep. "What do you mean you don't want to leave?"

"I mean what I say. I don't care about the bloody money. I don't care about the Continent, or the great stages of Europe, or the duke or my family or anything else. All I care about now is you." The words tumbled out, and with every new one she watched as Rafe loosened his guard more and more. He looked at her with pure surprise as she continued.

"I told you already that I've thought of you ever since that night in the dressing room." She let the tears come now; she didn't give a damn if she embarrassed herself. "No, since the first time you kissed me. Bloody hell, perhaps I've been thinking of you over and over since the first time we met when I was up on the stage of your club. I don't want to leave the Den. I love it here. I love the girls, and Jacks, and the audience, and I love…"

"What?" He sounded choked. "What do you love?"

It went against every instinct in Susannah's breeding and common sense, but she no longer cared. Instead, she wrapped her arms around his neck and kissed him.

Susannah felt like she was coming home the instant their lips met.

He held her tight with one arm and lifted her off the ground so that only the toes of her slippers made contact with the rug. This time, there was no hesitation. Susannah moaned as she kissed him as hard as she could, and she felt her whole body quiver as he growled his passion in response. When Rafe's hand traveled along her body and squeezed her bottom, Susannah felt how badly she wanted him inside her.

It would be her ruin, but she didn't care. Tonight, all she wanted was him. She wanted every perfect inch of him.

"So soft," Rafe whispered. He kissed her neck, his stubble scratching her delightfully. "So sweet."

"Yes, Rafe. Yes."

"You want this, then?" His words were hot and wicked in her ear. "All of it?"

"Yes. I want you. Please."

"A good man would send you away, worried about your virtue." He claimed her mouth in another searing, ferocious kiss. "But I'm not a good man."

He was wrong, he was the best man she knew, but Susannah didn't want to argue with him. She wanted only to give him all of herself.

Rafe herded her backward, through a doorway that led off the main parlor. Susannah found a chamber with candles lit around a massive bed covered in the finest French satin bedclothes. Her nipples hardened as Rafe kissed and sucked at her neck, moaning with how heavenly it felt. It was difficult to manage kissing while Rafe used his cane to position himself. He stumbled and, with a muttered curse, sat down hard upon the edge of the bed.

"Are you all right?" Susannah passed her hands through his luxuriant black hair and groaned when he kissed the hollow of her throat, as his tongue traced along the tops of her breasts.

"I'll be better when I've seen all of you."

Susannah wanted this more than she'd ever wanted anything, but her hands still trembled as she turned to let him unbutton the back of her gown.

She was still in costume from being the Duchess, and her outfit was scarlet all over. Red gown, red shoes, red stockings. She shrugged off the dress and let it crumple to the ground. Her heart beat against the cage of her ribs as she turned and listened to Rafe's bestial, guttural moan of approval.

"You're a vision," he rasped.

They kissed, and Susannah melted as his tongue stroked against hers. She kissed the hard, masculine line of his jaw, loving the little growls of pleasure she wrung from his lips. Susannah shoved at his coat, happy when he helped her in taking it off. She undid the buttons of his shirt and tugged off the cravat.

Rafe obliged, and soon he was naked from the waist up. Susannah shivered at the sight of his godlike physique. In the candlelight, every muscled inch of him was defined in breathtaking detail. The broad planes of his hard chest, the lean, taut line of his stomach, the muscles of his arms all made her grow even heavier between her thighs. Rafe pulled her against him, pulled her onto his lap. Susannah gasped as she sat down and felt the hard, almost rock-like bulge at the front of his trousers.

"You never seen a man before, have you?" he whispered between hard, hot kisses. God, he smelled sensational as ever, soap and tobacco and cold London nights.

"No. I haven't." They both knew what he meant by that.

Rafe slid her off his lap and undid his belt before unbuttoning his trousers. Within seconds, Susannah saw the full length of his manhood, and gasped. She'd never imagined anything could be so long, or so large. His cock was rigid with desire for her, almost an angry red. Susannah, without thinking, touched it.

Rafe groaned as she slid her hand along the shaft, astonished at the sensation, like steel wrapped in velvet. When she touched the swollen head, Rafe took her hand away.

"I think we need to take it a bit slower. I'll spend too early if we keep going like this."

If she wanted to run, she needed to do it now. This was far more serious than playing music in a gentlemen's club. If she went any further, Susannah would be lost forever. But if this was lost, she never wanted to be found.

She stepped out of her slippers, unlaced her stays, and then shrugged out of her chemise. She was now entirely bare except for her red silk stockings. Those she kept on; there was something scandalous about it that she relished.

"Oh fuck," Rafe whispered. All the hardness fled his face as he took her in. "You're perfection."

Susannah felt a bit shy to be standing naked in front of a man. Her nipples beaded from her arousal and from the cool air, and she was so embarrassed she almost covered her breasts with her hands. But Rafe pulled her to him by the waist and had her straddle him once more. Susannah felt his member positioned at the mouth of her wet, slick opening.

She dug her fingers into Rafe's hair as he kissed and licked at her nipples, one after the other. A deep, urgent tickling had begun inside of Susannah's core, and she started to whimper as she felt like a bird lifting into the sky. Rafe stopped lavishing attention on her sensitive nipples and kissed her mouth once more.

"Here, Duchess. I'll show you how to pleasure yourself in safety. You'll still be a virgin for any future husband."

Susannah couldn't think or speak any longer. Rafe took his manhood and stroked it against the wet, velvet seam of her body. Susannah whimpered as he placed the underside of his cock against her slick folds.

"Now move your hips. Up and down. Like you're riding me," he whispered.

Susannah did as he instructed, moving up and down while the hard, hot part of him pressed against the most sensitive spot on her body. He watched her greedily as she moved. She locked her fingers together behind his neck and pistoned her hips faster, her cheeks heating up as that divine tension began in her core and her legs yet again.

Rafe bared his teeth, breathing in rough, tight gasps as she rode him nearer to the climax of her pleasure.

"You're such a beautiful girl," he hissed. "So good."

It was as if every point of sensation in her body came together in a glorious burst of light. She'd never known such excitement, the surge of such ecstasy, and it almost brought tears to her eyes. Susannah screamed as the climax erupted all through her body, every bit of her spent and warm and languid in an instant. Rafe suckled at her breasts and neck, his hardened cock still pressed against her.

Susannah knew he'd kept her technically pure to protect any future marriage she might make. But she didn't want purity any longer.

She grabbed his velvet cock and positioned it at the opening between her legs.

"Susannah." He sounded shocked.

"I want all of you inside me."

"You do this, there's no taking it back." But the yearning in his voice was unmistakable.

"Let me, Rafe. Please. I want you so much."

He dug his fingernails into the blanket beneath him as she began to sink around him, inch by tight, wet inch.

Susannah felt sweat along her hairline as he began to open her. She flinched as she felt her body stretch to accept him.

Rafe placed his hands upon her hips, his thumbs stroking her pelvis and touching the curls above her sex.

"If you want it," he said, "then allow me to help."

Oh, she wanted it. Susannah took a deep breath and then cried out as she sank down hard upon him, as Rafe pulled her hips down to meet his. Susannah gasped as she felt his body slide deep inside hers.

She shivered and wrapped her arms tight around his neck, trying to get used to the torn sensation. But even at the worst of the agony, he felt so damn right inside her. Rafe gave soft, joyous moans as his hands traced up and down her back, as they cupped her breasts.

"You're spectacular," he said, and kissed her. "There's no other woman like you in the world."

Even though Susannah didn't know technically what to do, nature guided her movements. She began to ride him, moving up and down, slowly at first before picking up speed. He twisted his hips and angled his thrusts to meet hers, and soon the bed was creaking in rhythm with their union.

The movements became easier as the pain faded a bit, and soon Susannah was going as fast as she could. She looked down the hard and perfect line of his body, where it met and merged with her soft, white flesh. She watched his cock as it pumped in and out of her, and felt another climax begin to build. Her breasts were flushed with passion, and his chiseled body gleamed with a light sheen of sweat as their union grew more frenzied.

"You're a goddess." Rafe gripped her by the waist and helped guide her up and down him, harder and harder. "Susannah, you're a miracle."

"Yes, Rafe." She moaned his name over and over again, "Rafe, Rafe," and as she did, heat bloomed throughout her body as she achieved her climax. Her body squeezed his, pulsating as she milked every last golden sensation that she could from him. Climaxing when he was inside her was even more wild and thrilling than before; it made her feel uprooted, entirely free and alive. Susannah threw her head back and screamed out her ecstasy, not giving a damn who heard.

The next thing she knew, Susannah was on her back upon the bed, with Rafe hovering over her, a lustful haze in his eyes.

"You sound so gorgeous when you come," he said. Susannah gasped as he gripped her thighs and slung her knees over his shoulders. She was so tight and vulnerable in this position as he kissed her greedily. "I want you like this. At my mercy. My pleasure."

"Yes," Susannah groaned as he slid deep inside her, stretching her and spearing her to the very hilt. He rode her roughly, her legs still hooked over his shoulders, her opening so taut now that every movement of his gave the most glorious friction.

"This is mine." His blue eyes were ice and fire now, shimmering with greed as he beheld her underneath him. "Only mine. Your cunny is my prize."

She moaned, loving the way his words increased her pleasure. Susannah thrust her hips against his as, with a crescendo of noise and light, she exploded in another climax. She called Rafe's name over and over as he pumped faster, until finally with a strangled cry he pulled out of her, rolled over, and spilled his seed upon the bed.

Susannah lay there with a hand across her stomach, trying to catch her breath. She was slick with sweat, and the space between her legs felt raw, but she had never felt better in her life. This had been more than even Julia's old Gothic novels had described. She felt like she was made of sunlight and music.

This was the happiest she had ever been, perhaps the happiest she would ever be.

"That was incredible," she whispered.

Rafe, having finished, rolled back atop her and pressed her into the mattress with the strength of his body. They kissed, and he ran his tongue along her lower lip, tasting her in the way an animal might.

"I never had a virgin before." He sounded almost shy and uncertain. So unlike the brash Rafe she knew. "I didn't hurt you, did I?"

"The pain was worth the pleasure." Susannah kissed him. "I doubt any lady in the *ton* has ever experienced a wedding night this sensational."

"That's because those women marry blue-blooded imbeciles." His tongue entered her mouth as he kissed her deeply. Susannah's body heated with the rapture he inspired. "But you're smarter than any of them, Your Grace."

"Susannah. Please, just call me Susannah from now on." She petted his cheek and smiled as his eyes softened. Rafe kissed her lips once more.

"Very well, then. Susannah." He kissed her neck. "God, it's a beautiful name, isn't it? Susannah. Susannah." He kissed her chest, and her breasts, and all the way along her stomach, whispering her name over and over.

Rafe didn't finish kissing and licking between her legs until Susannah had screamed his name in return.

Chapter Sixteen

The next morning, Susannah could not force herself to stop smiling, not even as Annabelle drove her home and pestered her with questions the entire time.

"You must tell me what went on." Annabelle clapped her gloved hands and bounced up and down in her seat. "Oh, you came back so late! It rather shocked Felps, but we needn't worry. He's loyal and spreads no gossip. It's a great reason to pay butlers handsome salaries, particularly in town. Oh, but you must at least give me a hint! Did you kiss? Embrace?" Annabelle tittered over the next idea. "Have you seen him *undraped*?"

"Really, Annie! You should have a care for my delicate, unmarried sensibilities." But Susannah couldn't even pretend to be stern.

"Oh? Are they still so delicate?" Annabelle chewed at her full lower lip, utterly delighted. "I noticed you winced as you took your seat in the carriage. Don't pretend you didn't!"

"For your information, sitting on a wooden bench and playing for an hour straight every night takes its toll on the body. It's a physical challenge, mastering an instrument."

"Indeed. Mastering *his* instrument would provide a challenge most women would happily accept!"

"You're indecent!" But Susannah laughed to the point of tears, delighted to at least have Annabelle to talk to. "Oh, you really can't say anything to anyone. You know that, of course, but I must beg for your discretion again."

"My angel, no one shall hear a word from my lips. Besides, I spend most of my time with Henry, and he usually keeps my lips engaged in other, even more pleasurable activities."

"Yes. Kissing is wonderful." Susannah could have swooned thinking of Rafe's deep, masterful kisses of the night before.

"Yes, darling. But kissing which part of him? That's the question."

The girls shrieked and laughed as the carriage pulled up to Beaumont House. Susannah hugged Annabelle, promising to see her at Mrs. Tarkington's garden party later that afternoon. Even though she'd gotten barely a wink of sleep, Susannah felt full of energy as she hurried up the path to her front door. Nothing and no one could spoil this day or this feeling.

"Beg pardon, Miss Fletcher," Hodge said as he let her in. "Lady Beaumont wishes to speak with you in the morning room."

Well. Except for her mother.

Susannah hoped that her mother would be in good spirits, but that was, sadly, not to be. Constance stitched at her sampler with restrained fury and looked as though a thundercloud had taken up permanent residence directly above her head.

"Hello, Mamma. I'm back," Susannah said.

"So I see." Lady Beaumont stabbed her needle through the sampler and tossed it aside. "And how is Lady Henry Douglass this morning?"

"Annabelle is fine. We had such a good time last night."

"Yes, at the Parkhurst ball. You *did* attend the ball, did you not?"

"Oh. Um." Susannah knew that answering yes would probably be met with accusations of lying. "We decided to, well, not attend?"

She made it a question, wincing as Constance glowered at her. Pip, Constance's small, yappy miniature poodle, woke from his place on the floor at his mistress's feet, yawned, and yapped at Susannah. Constance petted his head, as if thanking him for a job well done.

"I was most irritated when I decided to attend myself and found neither of you had turned up. His Grace the Duke of Huntington was also there, you know. I'd mentioned you'd be in attendance with Lady Henry, and he came specifically to see you." Her mother drew herself up, chest swelling with indignation. "I looked a proper fool in front of a duke. Like I didn't know where my own daughter was keeping herself!"

"Please, Mamma, we didn't mean to not attend." Susannah was grateful she and Annabelle had come up with a mutual excuse to explain their absence. "Annie was struck with a headache earlier in the evening, so we stayed in."

Susannah's mother resembled a morose ice sculpture. She always insisted on dressing in the height of fashion, and in wearing ice blues and pale purples she claimed suited her complexion. In reality, the sight of her managed to lower the temperature in any room by several degrees. But her mother's chilly appearance and demeanor aside, Susannah had never, ever before felt as bitten with cold as she did while Lady Beaumont glared at her from the sofa.

"If I were to ask Lady Henry, would she tell me the same story?"

Susannah's stomach constricted painfully.

"Oh, why must you treat me like a child always?" She

hoped to get off the topic of last night as quickly as possible. "You never treated Julia as one, even when she was a child herself."

"Julia has many bad qualities, but a lack of maturity was never one of them. She was always a sly little thing, but you? You have all the sweetness and tenderness and feminine grace she lacked. But those virtues come with an accompanying set of vices, which includes flightiness and lack of common sense!"

"I am not flighty." Susannah was about to say that she had plenty of common sense, too, but stopped herself. Any woman with common sense would never have given her chastity to a rakish club owner, nor would she be sneaking about behind all the backs of the *ton* to play music nightly under an alias.

That realization drove all the joy from her and replaced it with leaden feelings of concern.

"If it seems as though I'm worrying over you constantly, it's because I know what an important time this is in your life!" Susannah's mother thawed a bit and came to embrace her. Lady Beaumont petted her hair as she spoke. "You're about to become a duchess! Married to one of the few men in all of England whose wealth eclipses even the Duke of Ashworth's."

"That's what this has always been about, hasn't it?" Susannah snapped. She broke out of her mother's embrace, a bold action she'd never taken before. "You don't care about my happiness. You just want me to marry better than Julia did."

"I want for you to have the best!"

"Well, what if your idea of the best isn't the same as mine?" Susannah shocked herself by saying those words, but it was too late to take them back. Her mother blinked in incredulity.

"What, pray tell, is *your* version of the best?"

Susannah's nerve became fired up, but then abruptly died when her mother pushed back. She knew she ought to stand her ground the way Julia might, but it was unthinkable.

"Um." Susannah swallowed; her throat was so dry. "Perhaps I don't wish to marry the Duke of Huntington."

Lady Beaumont was still and silent, so much so that Susannah feared she might have killed her mother, or perhaps cast a freezing spell upon her. Perhaps Lady Beaumont would languish here in this fixed, frozen place for the rest of the London Season without another word to speak. Lord, wouldn't that be wonderful?

"You are a spoiled, conceited little girl." Her mother's chin quivered with suppressed anger. "You ask why I treat you like a child? This is the exact reason! What kind of little fool claims she doesn't want to marry a duke? Have you lost your head?"

Susannah winced, retreating inside herself at once. "I only said perhaps," she whispered. "You and everyone else seem to take it for granted that it's what I want."

Pip began to yap and growl at Susannah, bowing with his front legs and wagging his fluffy tail in the air. Perhaps he was speaking for Constance now, calling Susannah every ugly dog-name in the book.

"I did not spend decades of my life strategically climbing up society's ladder for you to turn down a duke's proposal! Do you think I married Sir Arthur because I loved him? Do you think I married your father for love?"

"Don't talk about Papa like that!" Susannah had no memory of her father, but from what she'd gathered over the years, he'd been a kindly and good-tempered man.

"I did it for you, don't you understand? Everything I have ever done, every sacrifice I have ever made has been so you could have the best! And now here we are, with you about to become one of the most esteemed women in English society, and you tell me that you don't want it?" Her mother nabbed Pip, who'd been clawing at her skirt, and held the poodle to her chest. Two sets of eyes reproached Susannah, one ice blue and the other round and, well, doggy-like.

"I just said perhaps I don't want it." But Susannah's voice was already failing her.

"Susannah, I love you. But if you refuse to marry the duke, I will have nothing to do with you ever again."

"You can't be serious." It was as if she'd been struck in the stomach. Susannah's eyes filled with tears. This was her mother, after all, the woman who had given birth to her. Who had raised her and, supposedly, loved her. How could any mother mean such words to her own daughter? "You wouldn't do that."

"I blame myself for having spoiled you all these years. Regardless, I won't stand by and watch you ruin your life, and I can't bear to have all my hard work undone because of some fantasy you wish to live. If you do anything to insult the duke or ruin his proposal, you will leave this house!"

Susannah realized that her mother meant every word. Her love, or at least her acceptance, was purely conditional. It was such a shocking, miserable moment and it scared Susannah badly.

"I just said perhaps." Susannah let the tears course down her cheeks now, a crushing weight upon her chest. She could be angry with her mother sometimes, particularly when Lady Beaumont was mean about Julia, but Susannah loved her. The thought that her mother would no longer love her if Susannah didn't marry the right person threatened to break her heart. "I was only angry. I didn't mean it, Mamma."

Lady Beaumont put one arm around Susannah and kissed the top of her head. Pip was smushed directly against Susannah and growled at her.

"I know how nervous you must be. So, no more nights spent with Annabelle until we get this bloody proposal business settled. I don't need to be worrying about you every hour of the day."

Seeing Rafe would be almost impossible now. Susannah didn't care about performing as the Red Duchess any longer. All she cared about was seeing Rafe again...

But the choice was Rafe or her mother, Rafe and her entire future in the only society she'd ever known. Julia would always love Susannah, but she'd be so bitterly disappointed if Susannah went through with her plans.

What had she done? How could she have been so foolish? She was damaged goods now; she couldn't possibly accept the duke's proposal without telling him everything, and once she did, he'd spurn her. She was trapped between two devastating choices. She cried harder than ever.

"There, there. It's all right." Her mother kissed her cheek. "Go upstairs and have a lie down. You'll give yourself a headache with this much crying. Besides, we have Mrs. Tarkington's garden party later this afternoon, and I wish for you to be fresh-faced and smiling. The duke will be there, you know."

"Yes." Susannah's voice sounded lifeless. "I'm just tired."

She dragged herself upstairs and lay down on her bed.

Every time Susannah thought of facing Rafe and telling him it was over, that she would never see him again, it felt like she was stabbing herself in the chest with a rusty penknife. But how could she choose him over her mother, Julia, and every part of her life? Susannah had been a fool to think she could have everything she wanted. Her family's love, her freedom, Rafe; she could never have it all. Something had to be lost.

Even as it killed her, Susannah knew she had to break it off with him.

Chapter Seventeen

He couldn't stop thinking of her.

Rafe sat through the meeting with Sackville-Chambers, Jacks, and the solicitors, and could barely hear a word any of them spoke.

This should be the most important transaction of his life, but even plans for the Corner Castle had been eclipsed by Susannah Fletcher. The fearlessness with which she'd given herself to him was admirable and erotic all on its own, but coupled with her tenderness, her loving and gentle spirit, it created the most amazing whole.

She was fiery and brilliant, soft and sweet. His whole body ached to be without her, his heart especially.

He had to make Susannah want to stay with him. Now that he was becoming a great hotelier, a posh businessman, he could afford to give her all the little luxuries and standing in society that she deserved.

Perhaps he'd never be a duke, but he could be richer than one in a short amount of time. He could become one of the richest men in England and purchase those stately country manors and enormous London townhomes for her.

Give Susannah emeralds and diamonds to wear, a barouche with velvet-lined seats, anything and everything she desired. Travel, too, of course, he could send her around the globe three times together if that's what she wished. She could have the world *and* English society; she didn't have to choose.

He just had to complete this deal. *Almost there.*

"Well, Mr. Winters?" Sackville-Chambers's solicitor looked at Rafe as though he were some form of very clever insect. "Are you prepared to sign?"

"I still say we should think this through a bit longer," Jacks whispered in his ear. "We've given ourselves no room to maneuver if something goes wrong."

"No. I'm ready." Rafe had not worked hard and risked everything over and over just to stumble three feet from the finish line. He took up his pen and signed where the solicitors told him to sign.

"Excellent. Pleasure doing business with you, Mr. Winters." Lord Sackville-Chambers seemed pleased with himself in an oily way. *Prick*.

"The pleasure's entirely yours, then." Rafe couldn't resist poking the snobbish lord, especially as he now had what he wanted. The lord's face fell, as did those of his prim solicitors.

"I certainly hope you know what you're doing," His Lordship said in a sniffy tone. He stormed out of the office.

Rafe's legal team left with the others, and soon it was Jacks and he alone together. She sat on the edge of his desk, kicking her booted heel back and forth. It made a rhythmic knocking sound that began to drive Rafe wild.

"If I don't give you enough to do, be sure to tell me. I can always think of something," he grumbled.

"Far be it for me to ever agree with Sackville-Chambers, but he's right." She shook her head. "I hope you know what you're doing, Rafe."

Jacks stormed out and slammed the office door before he

had a chance to argue. *Damn.* Rafe leaned back in his chair and shut his eyes, luxuriating in the quiet.

The club at midday was one of the slowest, most silent places in the capitol, and Rafe loved that. He needed the quiet and the rest. He'd been deprived of both for so much of his life.

Almost there.

Then he'd have a penthouse on top of his new hotel, or a mansion in Hyde Park. He'd have space and greenery and plenty of quiet. It would be a secluded little paradise, a forest in a fairy tale. Only he'd be the one enchanted, waiting until Susannah walked in the door one day and declared that she'd seen Rome and Venice and that now she wanted only to be home with her music…and him.

Rafe imagined her composing, her playing wafting through the halls of his house like perfume. He'd be alone with her, be with the only other person in this world who could ever truly understand him. He'd be her servant, make this world whatever she wanted it to be. God, his cock ached at the thought of the tight, sweet space between her thighs, how she fit about him marvelously. His heart pounded to imagine her laughter. He wanted to hear that bell-like voice whispering his name.

"Rafe?"

Ah, shit. Rafe opened his eyes to find Susannah standing before his desk. She was dressed like the proper miss she was, in a light muslin gown with a bonnet and a pelisse, gloves on her hands, a reticule strung about her wrist. She looked like any other wealthy virgin in this city, but she wasn't like them now. She wasn't a virgin, for one, not after his attentions the other night, and she was far too bold of spirit to ever be thought an ordinary girl of the *ton*.

"Well. Your timing's perfect." He rose to meet her. "I was just thinking of you."

"I…" She shook her head, blushing in embarrassment. God, he loved how she blushed. "I haven't been able to stop thinking of you for two days now."

"You don't have to think any longer. I'm right here." He moved around the desk, ready to claim her in a kiss. Ready to invite her upstairs to his flat, to all the hours of pleasure they could enjoy together.

Ready, above all, to lose himself in her arms and press her close to his body, to talk with her about what she wanted, any and everything she desired.

"Please don't." Susannah shied away from him.

A pained frenzy began inside of Rafe; he'd already lost one precious, irreplaceable woman with no warning given. His mother had been there one day, gone the next. The slightest move toward rejection threatened him with misery. "What's wrong?"

"Nothing's wrong with you." Susannah gazed at him with such sweet longing. "You're perfect."

"Well. Nice to see you've still got sense." His heart continued to pound as he grabbed her about the waist and pulled her to him. Rafe leaned against the desk for balance. "We're two perfect people." He kissed her jaw, listened to her breathy sigh of pleasure. "Two people with insatiable appetites." He kissed her neck, tasted the faint violet of her perfume. The sweetness of her body was a drug all its own. "Two people who do so much better without clothes."

He tugged at the ribbons of her bonnet, but Susannah broke away and gave her back to him. She was rejecting him, then, wasn't she? She was weeping to think of what a monster he had been to rob her of her virginity when she was most vulnerable. When she had needed him to be a gentleman and refuse her advances.

But Rafe was not and never would be a fucking gentleman.

"You've come to say goodbye." He didn't make it a

question.

"Yes." The one word trembled.

Rafe shut his eyes. His happiness had been so overwhelming, he should have known it couldn't last. He stumbled around his desk to sit back in the chair.

All the bright promise of that deal with Sackville-Chambers seemed depleted now. There'd be no mansion in Hyde Park, no country estate, because she would not be with him. What was the point of anything without her?

"Very well, then. Goodbye." He started fussing with things, putting paper away, rearranging pens, anything to avoid looking at her. To avoid feeling.

"Is that all you can say?" Susannah faced him.

"Goodbye's a simple word and idea. This doesn't need to be dragged out." He forced himself not to snarl at her or throw her out of his office. He didn't want Susannah to feel relief as she walked out of his life.

"Do you have to be like this?" Her voice trembled, but she sounded angry. *Good.* He wanted her anger, her fire. "Why can't you see how hard this is for me?"

"I'm sure you never considered something could be hard for me, eh? Duchess?" He would not call her Susannah now, not if she begged him. "Well, I don't own you. Not even after that night. A woman's got the right to make up her own mind about things, and it's clear you've made up yours. Now if that's all you came here to say, you've said it and you can leave. I've business to attend."

"Would you just listen to me?" she cried. Susannah tore off her bonnet in frustration, leaving her coppery curls disheveled about her face. A gorgeous sight, that. "This isn't what I want. Not at all."

"Really?" Rafe forced his heart to slow down. Hope only ever disappointed him. "Then why are you doing it?"

"My mother has noticed all my absences in the evenings.

She's forbidden me from staying with Lady Henry until after the duke proposes and I accept."

"Ah." Rafe thought again of how he'd like to mash that Duke of Huntington's perfect face in. "So, the Red Duchess is no more? That what you're saying?"

"I can't see how I'll manage to get away with her watching my every movement. Can you?"

Rafe wished he could stick this mother of hers in a sack.

"I suppose the question now is, why do you need to trick her at all?" Rafe narrowed his eyes as he studied Susannah. "I'm ready to pay you the money you're owed. Five thousand pounds. With that kind of cash, you can leave your mother's house and set up where you like. You can leave the country. Why should you care anymore what your blasted mother knows or doesn't?"

"Haven't you had a mother yourself?" She sounded exasperated. "Don't you know how difficult it is to go against them?"

"No, I don't know." Rafe's knee hurt with a sudden vengeance. He rubbed it, wincing. "I don't know anything about that."

"Oh. I'm sorry." She looked on him with genuine sympathy.

Rafe couldn't let himself fall back under her spell. At least, not that easily. "If you can't bear to disappoint her at all, what was the idea behind everything you've done so far? Was it all for nothing?"

Susannah wavered, and then sat down hard in a chair before his desk. She worried at the fingers of her glove over and over, an evident sob building in her throat. God, she was so passionate and gorgeous…but Rafe could not play these games forever. Despite what most people thought, he did indeed have a heart, and it could break more easily than anyone knew.

"I meant to go through with it. I did. But now I don't think I can."

"Why?"

"My mother said that if I don't marry the duke, she'd never see me again."

"Then she's a real bitch."

Susannah frowned. "You mustn't speak of her like that."

"Any mother who'd say something like that's a bitch, and a real one at that." To Rafe, it was too incredible. He imagined having a daughter as fine and brilliant as Susannah, and then tossing her away if she didn't marry well enough in society. Some women didn't deserve to be mothers.

Susannah got up, marched around the desk, and tossed her reticule in his face.

"What the—?" Rafe was shocked. He'd dodged fists and clubs before, but a reticule was a new weapon.

"Why can't you understand? Even if she's being horrible, she's still my mother! I can't just throw something like that away." She whirled around and gave him her back again. Rafe watched her delicate shoulders tremble. "I don't want to marry the duke—"

"Then don't. It's bloody simple."

"But if I don't, my mother will never see me again."

"You'd waste the rest of your life and deny yourself happiness to keep that woman around?" Rafe stood and leaned on his desk for balance. "I knew you were sheltered, but I never thought you a coward."

"Don't call me a coward." She turned and shoved at him. Rafe didn't even totter an inch; she was a bold girl but had all the physical power of a twig. Susannah huffed in irritation, and shoved him again, and again, looking for a reaction. When she began to push against him, cheeks flushed with the effort as she attempted to topple him over, Rafe laughed until his gut hurt. "Oh, it's not funny!"

"It's bloody hysterical." Rafe took Susannah by her petite waist and lifted her onto the desk. She sat there, mouth agape, with Rafe wedged between her thighs, his body holding hers still. It was a heavenly place to be. "You're right; anyone who's done what you've done can't be called a coward. But you need to make a choice, Susannah."

"Why do I have to choose between you and the Den and my family?" She sounded indignant now, her amber eyes glinting with fury. "Why can't I have everything and everyone I love without sacrificing a bit of it?"

"That's not how our world works," he said, though Rafe's heart beat faster in triumph as he realized she'd included him in the category of those she loved. "Ask yourself what you'd regret giving up the most, and then act." He winced. "I'm not trying to make this decision harder. I understand if it'd be easier giving me up."

"It wouldn't." She clung to his shoulders, bringing her rosy mouth so close to his. "Don't you know that, you silly man?"

Rafe was a fellow who took advantage of every opportunity he was handed, and this was no exception. He kissed her, kissed her until she was cooing and breathless with it. Susannah wrapped her legs about his waist as he pressed her closer to him. He kissed her lips, her cheeks, kissed the sweet white line of her throat. Rafe's body needed her touch again. Two days without her had been a lifetime.

"Like this, then, love?" he whispered. He guided her hand to the fall of his trousers, luxuriating in the pleasured moans she gave as she felt how hard he'd become for her. "If you don't want it anymore, then tell me so now."

"I want it," she keened. "Rafe, I want you. Oh God."

They kissed as he slid her skirts around her knees, running his hands over the silken length of her stockinged legs until he found that perfect, velvety juncture of her thighs.

"You can have all this," he breathed, parting her folds with a finger and stroking that clever little bud between her legs. He loved how wet she was for him already. Susannah lifted her hips, desperate for his touch, for his cock. He stroked her, worshipping the sweet, slick sounds of her arousal. "Only say you want it, Susannah. Only say you want me."

"I want you more than anything in the world. *Oh*."

She shivered as the climax overcame her. Rafe tasted her lips, flushed with her passion, and as she languished in the aftereffects, he unbuttoned his trousers and took out the great length of himself.

"You want that duke to have you like this?" he whispered, sliding himself inside her, relishing every silken inch. "Want him to ride you?"

"No." She gasped as Rafe began to fuck her, his cock sliding in and out of her, in and out. "God, you're so good."

"You can have what you want, Susannah." Rafe lost himself in the pleasure of her body, of the slick little sanctuary between her legs. Already he could feel his end was upon him, that tug in his balls and his lower back, the urge to spill all his seed inside of her. He couldn't do it, he had to protect her…but it would be so nice to claim her with that last little act. To make his mark upon her forevermore. "All you need do is choose."

"Yes. Yes." She squeezed her eyes shut, pressing her body against his as the pleasure built once again.

"He wants to have you," Rafe snarled, grasping her hips and ramming himself into her over and over, harder and harder. The pens and papers upon his desk jumped with the motion, and the bloody thing creaked and groaned with their exertions. "He wants to put his gracious cock inside you, fill you with his heirs. But you don't want that, do you?"

"No, God, no." Susannah shrieked, moving her body faster and faster. "I can't live without this."

I can't live without you, Susannah.

The wolf inside him was howling with delight as he took possession of her, made her his own, utterly. They clung together now, each riding the other to their ecstatic pinnacle. As Rafe felt her ripple around his cock with her orgasm, he thrust once, twice more, then managed to take himself out of her in time to spill in his own hand.

His heart had never beat this fast before, and his pleasure had never been this good. While he cleaned himself, Susannah lowered her skirts and slid off the desk. She was still shy with him, but all her previous concern had fled. When he held her this time, she kissed him over and over.

"I'm sorry," she murmured. "I shouldn't be so afraid."

"Eh, you'd be a fool not to be." He felt so strong with this woman in his arms. As long as she was his, the world could not touch him. "And you're no fool."

"I'm going to find a way to tell my mother I'm not marrying the duke. And Julia as well, though Lord knows she'll be disappointed." That hurt Susannah, Rafe realized. Disappointing those she cared about hurt her worse than her own pain could.

"You're too sweet for this world." He kissed her eyelids with absolute tenderness. "Certainly too good for me."

"That's not true." She brushed her nose against his, such a soft and affectionate gesture that it undid Rafe even more than their sex had. "Will you give me time to sort things out?"

"I'm not afraid to hold out for the best." Rafe kissed a smile onto her lips. "How do you think I got where I am today?"

Chapter Eighteen

Susannah shouldn't have stayed the extra two hours with Rafe, but she'd been too relieved to simply go home.

The realization she would stay with him, that she would not and could not ever marry Huntington, had made her feel soft and cozy as the tension fled her body...and sleepy as well.

After their reunion in his office, Rafe had invited her upstairs to lunch with him in private. Perhaps he'd wanted something more—perhaps Susannah had as well—but she'd scarcely been through two bites of salmon before she'd felt her eyes starting to droop.

Rafe had chuckled. "I didn't realize I was so boring," he'd said.

"I might just shut my eyes a moment. If that's all right."

The next thing she knew, Susannah had been laid out on the settee, a throw rug draped across her lap. Rafe had kissed her forehead and her eyelids, had stroked the backs of his knuckles across the slope of her cheek. He'd murmured words about how brilliant she was, how brave and beautiful. Then he'd gone to his desk in the corner to write some letters and look over some books while she napped. Susannah had felt cocooned and safe, in precisely the right place.

For the first time in so long, she felt truly at home.

When she jolted awake a couple of hours later, she flinched as she listened to the clock chiming three in the hall. She couldn't afford to be careless just now. Not until she'd discussed everything with her mother and Julia.

Rafe wasn't there when Susannah rose. He'd left a lot of papers strewn about his desk—like her, he wasn't a believer in keeping everything neat and orderly. She had a feeling that was Jacks's contribution to the partnership.

Smiling, Susannah walked over and gazed down at the documents. She couldn't say what possessed her, except perhaps interest in Rafe's affairs. She expected to see blueprints of the hotel renovations, lists of material and costs. She was surprised when she found a set of plans, but not for a hotel. She was no skilled architect, but Susannah recognized that these drawings displayed a series of flats.

Why would Rafe want to build flats? Hadn't he enough to deal with just now?

"Oi." Rafe appeared in the doorway. Susannah squeaked and dropped one of the papers, which fluttered to the floor. "Snooping around, are you?" But he didn't sound angry.

"I see you plan to endlessly expand your empire." She meant it as a joke, but he frowned a bit. *Oh dear.* "Sorry. What are these, anyway?"

"Some future ideas. Something I've wanted to do for some time." He picked up the pages and neatened them.

"You're planning to let flats?"

"To rich toffs and second sons of nobility, yeah."

Susannah was puzzled. These plans looked simpler than the younger sons of most earls would fancy.

"But that's not what these are," Rafe continued. "These are more personal."

"Personal how?"

"You're a nosy thing, aren't you?"

"Well. I'm told I've an attractive nose."

Rafe chuckled; she noticed how it was easier to make him smile now. Easier to see warmth and life in his eyes. He slid an arm around her and kissed the tip of her nose.

"That's true," he murmured.

"You don't have to tell me your grand plans. But I'd like to know."

Susannah had never been one to look to the future too much, but nowadays she thought of the coming years and, increasingly, she saw Rafe in those fantasies. She wanted to know him; she wanted to know all of him. She wanted to be close to him, as close as he'd allow.

"My plan's to buy a row of houses on the western edge of Camden Town and break them up into flats. Good flats, mind you, with proper ventilation and light. Clean spaces that are healthy."

"For your renters of lesser nobility?" she teased.

"For women." Rafe shrugged, looking almost embarrassed as he turned his head from her. "Working girls and the like. I knew my share of them when Jacks and I were coming up, and they had it rough. Rougher than any man I knew. At least blokes like me could fight and scheme our way to a better life. In the rookery, if you're a girl who doesn't marry well, you'll never get out. And if you don't marry at all, or if he leaves you with the kids, you starve. Too many women had to turn to selling whatever parts of themselves they could to survive." Rafe's gaze hardened a bit. Susannah wondered if there was more to this story that he wasn't telling her but didn't dare ask. She would let him reveal himself in his own time. "There ought to be a place where they can find their feet if things have gone wrong. If they want to get out of a bad way of life, or if they need to try for something different. I feel like if I made it out, I should set something up for the others like me. Especially if they're starting out even further behind than I did."

She knew he was a kind man, kinder than most people would ever know. But the fact that Rafe cared so much, the fact that he understood other people so well, made her feel lit up with pride. Susannah slipped her arm through his. She leaned up and kissed his cheek.

"Mr. Winters. I do believe you might be a good man," she whispered.

"Well, don't tell anyone. I've a reputation to maintain." The wicked, slightly wild look he gave her sent warm tingles rushing up and down her arms. "I wanted to do something like this, but I always needed the extra security of more money. More members in my club. More everything. But the other day I had my mate Corkus begin drawing up the plans. Once the Corner Castle's restored and opened, this'll be the next thing we focus on."

"I'm glad you've given it your attention." Susannah felt pride glowing in her breast.

"Good." He tilted her chin and kissed her lips. "Because it was you who inspired me to do it at last."

"Me?" She was shocked.

"I want you to be proud of me, Susannah." He looked at her with those wary blue eyes, that burning, all-consuming hunger for her, for life, for everything simmering beneath their deceptively cold surface. "I want to amaze you."

Rafe had shown her tenderness, but this might have been the first moment he expressed true vulnerability. Her breath stopped in her throat; he valued her judgments. Her feelings. He valued *her*.

"Believe me, Mr. Winters." She kissed him gently. "You already amaze."

• • •

Over the next week, Susannah attempted to figure out how to approach Julia and her mother about all this.

She couldn't tell them of Rafe, at least, not until things with him were more settled. In the meantime, she needed to find a way to break things off with the duke before she could speak with her family.

But whenever she had a moment with Huntington, she decided she really ought to alert her mother and Julia first. And when she was about to speak with the women, she'd think she must explain matters to the duke. After going back and forth like this a bit, Susannah grew frustrated. She had to do something! She made her decision. The first person who had to know about Rafe and everything else was her mother.

Of course, the day Susannah had finally worked up the courage to discuss these difficult things was the same day that Lady Beaumont looked up from her teacup and said she was going to be out of town for two or three nights. She would leave at once.

"You remember Mrs. Ralston, in Surrey? She's taken to her bed, poor thing. The doctors aren't sure she'll last to the end of the month. I must see her and pay my respects one final time."

"How kind you are, Mamma." Susannah's mind spun, trying to work out what to do. There was no way she could shout this great secret to her mother on her way out the door.

"Well. That woman lorded it over me last summer when her daughter snagged an earl. I need to see the look on her face when I speak of you and the duke!"

Ah. Yes, that seemed more like her mother. Susannah was coming to realize that you could love someone without liking them very much.

"So may I stay with Annabelle while you are gone?" Susannah's heart beat faster.

"Heavens, no. You'll stay with Julia. It will be even

better, if you think of it. The duke and Ashworth are such close friends. I'm certain you'll see a great deal of him." Her mother huffed as she added a lump of sugar to her tea. "I do wish His Grace would hurry up and propose. The Season is nearly done!"

Yes, it was. Susannah was quickly running out of time.

She sent a letter to Annabelle, who managed to take the message to the Wolf's Den and let Rafe know Susannah was still working on the problem.

Annabelle handled being a go-between quite brilliantly. She returned Rafe's note to Susannah, asking if, due to her mother's absence, there could be one final engagement for the Red Duchess on the Den's stage. The ticket sales would be astronomical. It would also give him another opportunity of seeing Susannah while everything sorted itself out.

Yes, Susannah replied. This Saturday would be her final bow as the Duchess. She knew Julia would allow her and Annabelle to spend the evening together, which would provide the perfect cover. She'd play her music from behind the safety of her mask one last time and, even better, see Rafe again.

Every time Susannah thought of Rafe, she felt wonderfully indecent. She'd sit with society matrons and exchange idle gossip while burning inside with a secret. That she, Susannah Fletcher, was no mere debutante. She was a paid musician, a wanton lover, and soon to be freed of their petty games forever.

In the meantime, though, Susannah was happy to be with Julia, Gregory, and the children. The first night she came to stay, after she and Julia had seen the children to bed, Susannah accompanied the Ashworths to the opera. Susannah loved to go whenever possible, especially when they were staging anything by Mozart. As fate would have it, that night they were performing *The Marriage of Figaro*, Susannah's favorite opera. She adored the comedy and romance of it, and the music was heaven itself.

As they took their seats in the Duke of Ashworth's box, Susannah noticed that Ashworth and her stepsister exchanged knowing glances with each other.

"What are you both up to?" Susannah whispered.

"You make us sound as though we were conspirators in some great scandal." Julia fluttered her fan in pretend indignation.

"The lady doth protest too much. We both know the duchess would like nothing better than to be embroiled in a scandal." Gregory waggled his eyebrows at Susannah. He was a splendid brother-in-law. An only child of neglectful parents, he'd always wanted siblings and was happy to treat Susannah as the little sister he never had. "Really, courting scandal is a Carter family tradition."

Susannah gave a small, nervous laugh. Hopefully Gregory and Julia would forgive Susannah her own amount of scandal. Come to think of it, this might be the perfect opportunity to discuss Rafe and the duke with her stepsister.

"I need to speak to you both about something important," Susannah whispered.

But neither Julia nor Gregory had heard her; they were both smiling broadly at someone who'd only just entered the box.

"Huntington! What a splendid and not at all prearranged surprise." Ashworth chuckled as he shook hands with the Duke of Huntington.

"It's such a shame you were never able to pursue a career on the stage, my love," Julia drawled. "Your acting skills are incredible."

Susannah froze in horror, trying to will herself to pretend normalcy while Huntington kissed Julia's hand and took his seat beside Susannah. The Ashworths conspired together, heads close, fan fluttering, undoubtedly delighted with themselves for staging this scene.

"How are you this evening, Miss Fletcher?" Huntington asked.

Susannah couldn't meet his eyes. This was all a horrible muddle of confused emotions. First, she was ashamed of herself for cavorting with Rafe before properly breaking things off with the duke; second, it wounded her to know that she was to hurt him in any way, because she did *like* Huntington. You could, Susannah realized, like someone very much without loving them.

Then when she thought of the row this would start with her mother, how betrayed Julia and Gregory would feel, how society would gossip about her... Well, it was almost too much. Perhaps if she swooned right now, Julia would take her home and Susannah could avoid the duke.

"Miss Fletcher? Are you well?" Huntington sounded concerned.

"Yes." Even Susannah heard how strangled her reply sounded. "Um, I do love Mozart. Don't you?"

"Yes. Quite." He seemed perplexed.

The curtain had risen on the beginning of the opera.

Figaro, a lowly servant, was measuring space in his room for a wedding bed, singing about his happiness in marrying the maid, Susanna. But all the while, the rich and powerful count plotted to seduce young Susanna away from her devoted and decidedly lower-class lover.

Susannah believed that art should reflect life, but she sometimes wished it wasn't so bloody on the nose.

"You've been difficult to find these past few days," the duke said. "I've greatly missed the pleasure of your company."

It seemed Julia and Gregory were doing everything possible to eavesdrop, short of turning in their seats and watching the girl and the duke as if they were players on the stage. Gregory inched his seat back again and again, almost leaning into them. Susannah wondered if her stepsister and brother-in-law had placed bets upon when and where the duke would propose. She wondered how much they'd both wagered. She knew Julia would triumphantly collect if she won.

"Yes. As I have missed yours. Um." Susannah couldn't concentrate. Between the two dukes, her beloved and infuriating stepsister, and Mr. Mozart, there was no room to breathe. "I've been thinking, Your Grace," she began, uncertain where the devil she was headed with this.

"A worthy pastime."

"Have you ever considered what your life would have been if you could have made all your own decisions?" Susannah was trying to figure out the best angle at which to faint. She didn't want to hit her head too hard, but drawing a little blood would be useful to her escape.

"I can't imagine any life better than the one I have." His Grace smiled. "Especially not the life I expect to enjoy very shortly." He gave her meaningful glances.

Jump from the balcony! The women below you are wearing ostentatious feathered headdresses that will cushion your fall.

"Well, you're very fortunate there. But then again, you're a man. It's so much easier for a man in this world to steer his own ship, as it were. Even if you're expected to carry out a duty, there are still so many things you can become if you choose. I'm right, aren't I?"

"I should say." Huntington was being politely confused.

"What I mean is, it's hard being a woman for so many reasons. Uncomfortable slippers, vicious competition, and the pressure to always be appropriate would kill any ordinary man from the strain." Where was she going with this? "Because…because ladies have so little control over their own futures, don't you see? We must sit around waiting for other people, usually mothers or men, to decide our lives for us. It's exhausting, wouldn't you agree?"

"I suppose I would." Huntington studied her with great coolness and understanding.

Susannah's heart began to slow. Perhaps he truly did understand her meaning!

"I don't want other people to make up my own life for me. Such a thing doesn't suit at all. I can't sit around forever, waiting for other people to tell me where I'm to go or who I'm to become. Yes? You see what I'm saying, Your Grace, don't you?"

The duke reclined in his seat, a finger laid on his lips. He gave a wry, almost sad smile and nodded. Oh, he understood! Susannah could have collapsed with relief.

"Your meaning is plain to me, Miss Fletcher. Never worry." He was graciousness itself as he took her gloved hand and kissed it with great formality.

Susannah could have burst into tears of giddiness. Now her mother would not have to be told that Susannah didn't want to marry Huntington; the duke would merely take his attention away from Susannah.

Lady Beaumont would be peevish, but she couldn't blame her daughter for that, could she? It wouldn't be her fault if the duke changed his mind, after all. It was all going to be fine! She was saved, and Susannah could have cheered.

"Incidentally, Miss Fletcher, I have a proposal for you," Huntington said.

Susannah almost shot out of her skin, while Julia was so excited in her eavesdropping that she whapped Gregory in the face with her fan as she hastened to turn around.

"Oh?" the duchess said.

"Julia, my love, Hunt is speaking to Susannah." Gregory massaged the side of his face. "Also, remind me to purchase a lighter fan for you."

Huntington smiled. "I've heard news about town from the Wolf's Den. Apparently the mysterious Red Duchess is to play her last show on this coming Saturday."

"Oh, what a shame. I'd heard she was wonderful," Julia said. "Didn't you tell me she was excellent, Ashworth?"

"My love, since becoming ensconced in the coziness of married and family life, I no longer frequent spots such as the Wolf's Den." Gregory kissed his wife's hand. "Besides, their drinks are bloody overpriced."

"Anyway, Miss Fletcher," Huntington said, trying to get past the Ashworths, "I'd hoped that I might escort you to see her final performance this coming Saturday."

Susannah had never experienced the sensation of being crushed by a runaway boulder, but she believed now she could approximate the feeling.

Screaming would do her no good, nor would running away or acting as if she'd suddenly forgot how to speak English. She had to move quickly, think of something. Her reputation depended upon it, not to mention Rafe's.

Come on, she thought to her great, troubled brain. *You can still save this. Do something!* Alas, her brain had ceased all higher functioning.

"Oh, it sounds so wonderful." Susannah sought a way out. "But, well, I'm not certain how pleased Mamma would be to hear the news when she returns. After all, she doesn't approve of such places."

"Tweaking Constance's nose is the greatest reason to do anything." Julia patted Susannah's gloved hands. "Forgive me, darling, but you know I believe in enjoying life's simple pleasures."

Susannah laughed breathlessly. "I certainly do."

"Why don't Julia and I attend alongside you?" Gregory asked. "I've longed to see this cultural treasure myself."

He glanced at Julia. "Not to make you jealous, my love. Of course not."

"Why should I be jealous?" Julia asked, sweet as sugar. "I know that no other woman in London can ever eclipse me in your heart."

"Too true, my beauty."

"And I know too many devastating ways to prod the human body with a pencil for you to ever try anything."

"Indeed. Your pencil-torture skills are beyond compare."

While the Ashworths and Huntington laughed together, Susannah stared directly onto the stage, watching Susanna and Figaro come up with several cunning tricks to outwit the dastardly count. If life were an opera, she could come up with an ingenious plan to save herself in all the five minutes it would take to sing an aria.

But life was not an opera. It was more like a lowbrow comedy filled with pratfalls, where no one remembered their lines and the scenery kept falling down.

In two days' time, Susannah's final performance would be the end of her.

Chapter Nineteen

Rafe was pleased to see the high turnout for the Red Duchess's final performance.

He was far less pleased, however, when it was fifteen minutes till curtain and his star arrived to her own concert as a guest. When Susannah entered the Rose Room on the Duke of Huntington's arm, she looked ready to faint, or otherwise spew her guts all over the carpeting.

The Duke of Ashworth was also there, accompanied by his duchess.

Seeing Ashworth would normally have made Rafe feel more at ease, since this duke was one of the few toffs who still had a sense of humor about him. But Rafe also knew that Ashworth was brother-in-law to Susannah, and an observant man.

Even if Susannah managed to break away from Huntington and perform, she'd never be able to keep her secret from the sharp, watchful eyes of her brother-in-law. Nor from her stepsister, the duchess, for that matter.

Rafe had heard about the Ashworth fairy tale romance years before. He knew they were utterly devoted to each other. He also knew that the duke and duchess were regarded as two of the cleverest people in London.

Why did smart people insist on coming to his club? They made everything more difficult.

"Evening, Your Graces," Rafe muttered, refusing to meet Susannah's eyes. It took all his will.

"Hello, Winters." Ashworth clapped him on the shoulder, a gesture full of friendly affection.

Rafe liked the man, certainly liked him better than he did this Huntington ponce. Not that there was anything really wrong with Huntington other than the fact that he wanted Susannah. But that was reason enough to hate the fellow.

"Come to hear the Red Duchess's final act, Your Graces?" Rafe tried to feign indifference. Susannah, meanwhile, looked as though she were ready to collapse. That beautiful, reckless girl; how the devil had things got this complicated?

"I'm only glad Miss Fletcher will have one chance, at least." Huntington beamed at the small, copper-haired girl on his arm. "She's an especially talented musician, you know."

"I don't doubt that." Rafe didn't know whether this was hilarious or horrifying. "Please sit where you'd like, Your Graces." An idea struck Rafe. To Huntington, he said, "As a matter of fact, Your Grace, I'd be honored if you and your young lady would join me at my personal table as a gesture of thanks. You're the man who made the Duchess's success possible."

"Please, I merely spoke the truth."

"Thank you. I should like that very much." Susannah smiled, a good little actress.

Rafe saw the Ashworths to prime seating on the balcony level, then returned to Huntington and Susannah at his own table. He ordered a bottle of his best champagne, ready to drink it all himself to escape the tension. What the fuck were they to do? It was five minutes until the curtain was supposed to go up!

"Oh! Your Grace, I seem to have dropped one of my gloves." Susannah sounded distressed as she noted only the one cream-colored kid glove in her hand. "Would it be a terrible bother to ask you to check in the vestibule?"

"Of course not, my dear." Huntington got up, though he turned a wary eye onto Rafe. "Please have a care to your language, sir. Miss Fletcher is a lady."

"Oh, she is," Rafe drawled.

When the duke had left, Susannah appeared quite grumpy.

"Oh, fuck all these patronizing men," she muttered. It so caught Rafe off guard that he had to cough to disguise a laughing fit.

"How the devil did this happen?" he whispered, returning to the matter at hand.

"His Grace asked to escort me here, and my stepsister and Ashworth made it impossible for me to decline the invitation."

Rafe seethed. Why did the English upper classes live to ruin his plans? He glanced at the doorway, hoping the duke would not find Susannah's glove too quickly.

"Don't worry." She'd intuited his concern and produced the second glove as if by magic. "He's a diligent man. He should be occupied for a few minutes."

Cunning little minx. Even in the middle of a bloody catastrophe, Rafe wanted to kiss this woman until he stole all the breath from her body. But he couldn't let his heart lead him around right now. His head was on the chopping block.

"I don't suppose there's any way you can excuse yourself to go powder your nose, do your turn as the Duchess, and then come back?"

"I've never met the woman who took an entire hour to powder her nose," Susannah said, sounding cross. "And I doubt your audience would appreciate a five-minute show."

Rafe could have screamed his frustration.

"You need to think of something," Susannah hissed.

"Well, I'm not setting fire to the club to get these wankers out. And I doubt I'd fool anyone if I put on that Red Duchess kit and tried banging at the instrument myself."

Rafe stood up as a thought bloomed.

"Where are you going?" Susannah asked.

"I need to measure some girls," Rafe replied, and strode off.

...

"Where did Winters go?" Huntington asked as he retook his seat, after apologizing that he could not find her glove to save his life.

"He said something about speaking with the Duchess before she went on." Susannah's heart thumped louder in her ears as the minutes crawled by. She stared at the stage that was supposed to be hers, the pianoforte that she should be playing now.

All around her, the crowd began to grow restless. It was almost ten minutes past, and the Red Duchess was never late.

"Perhaps after the show I can find a way to introduce you both." The duke smiled and kissed Susannah's hand. "One great lady musician ought to meet another."

Susannah laughed politely while inside she screamed. The audience began to grow louder with its rambunctious disappointment as the minutes ticked by and no Red Duchess appeared.

"Is she always this late?" Susannah's throat was parched.

"Not when I've been to see her." The duke seemed puzzled.

Finally, Susannah watched as Murray was led, or rather

shoved onto the stage. Rafe hovered in the wings, motioning with his hand while making angry faces. Murray appeared dizzy as he faced the crowd.

"Ladies and gentlemen, the Wolf's Den is proud to present, for the final time, the mysterious and melodious Red Duchess!" Murray bowed, left the stage to scattered applause, and then the crowd applauded more rigorously when the Red Duchess appeared.

It was the most surreal moment of Susannah's life, watching *herself* as she curtsied to the audience. It was the Red Duchess, with that ostentatious red velvet cape, the crimson hood, and the full red mask that hid even the tiniest hint of features. The Duchess sat on the bench and laid her hands on the keys.

Susannah swore she could taste her own heart as the "Duchess" began to play. But the woman hadn't gotten more than two wobbly notes out before she began to cough violently.

The crowd gasped as the Red Duchess stood up from the instrument, knocking the bench over as she staggered backward. People began to get to their feet in panic as the poor woman wobbled back and forth, choking and coughing, until finally she collapsed to the stage and was laid out on the floor. It seemed she'd passed out, or even worse, died. Susannah watched it all with an open mouth.

"Oh no!" Murray came onto the stage, head in his hands. He gave a cry of mock horror, a very bad performance indeed. "It must be the plague!"

Susannah noted Rafe in the wings cursing wildly, looking ready to throttle Murray as the theater began to empty at an alarming rate.

"Please everyone, do not panic," Rafe called as he strode onstage, shouldering Murray out of the way before he knelt and lifted the Duchess's head. "There's no plague. I think it must be nervous exhaustion. This is why the Duchess is retiring from the stage."

There were cries of horror, irritated shouts asking where they could get a refund, and a few drink orders as well.

Susannah heard, from up in the highest reaches of the balcony, someone cry out that never, not once, had the Red Duchess played "Little Mary Beth Lost Her Spoon." This statement was followed by weeping.

"I can't believe this." The Duke of Huntington shook his golden head while Susannah bit her tongue to keep from giggling. What a strange yet fitting end to the Red Duchess's tenure as one of London's leading stage acts. "I'm so sorry, Miss Fletcher. Truly. I'd wanted you to hear the woman play ever so much."

"It is the thought that matters most, Your Grace."

Huntington smiled ruefully. "You know, at least this evening cleared one matter up for me. I'd begun to half suspect that you, Miss Fletcher, were the Red Duchess all along."

"Me?" Susannah thankfully did not squeak.

"I couldn't imagine two such brilliant women could dwell in the same city and not be the same person." He was teasing her, thank God. "At least I now know that you were not the lady in question. Though I suppose we'll never know her identity."

They watched as Rafe and Murray dragged the Duchess off the stage. Susannah suspected it might have been Celine, or perhaps Antoinette. They were both near to her height.

"I suppose every woman ought to be allowed a bit of mystery," she said.

"Too true. Well, let's find Ashworth and your stepsister. I believe this calls for a late supper, wouldn't you agree?"

"Oh yes. I do." Though Susannah could have done with a stiff drink more than food.

Chapter Twenty

The next day, Rafe and Jacks were sharing a drink in his flat.

Though it was only the early afternoon, they both needed a good sip of whiskey. The rather memorable debacle of last night required it.

"A true shame we had to refund all the tickets." Jacks sighed as she poured herself another glass. "We could've used the money, particularly now."

"I think Celine overdid it on the coughing a bit." Rafe gazed out his window onto the bustle of Mayfair below. "But she managed quite well otherwise."

"So the Red Duchess is no more, and right when we could really use her." Jacks sighed and ran a hand through her short crop of hair. "You heard about the restoration? It's going to cost more than we expected already. Over a thousand pounds more."

"We can get by," Rafe said firmly. "Besides, it's not like we have a choice to back out now."

"Yes, thank you for that." Jacks stared into the dregs of her glass, moody as hell. "I keep telling myself we could offload the Castle onto another buyer if we really needed to, but we'd never recoup the money we put into the place. Not even half of it. It's too big to be a private home and too dilapidated for most businessmen to want to take on."

"Which is why we'll be heralded as geniuses when the hotel opens and we've proved ourselves." Rafe swallowed the last of his whiskey, then stoppered the crystal decanter. "We're one step ahead of the rest of them, Jacks."

"I've looked over the books." His partner gave him a meaningful glance. "We'd be much more in the black if you didn't pay five thousand to Susannah."

"She earned the money. It's hers. I've been a thief, Jacks, but you know I've never been crooked like that. I pay folks what I agreed, especially women."

Rafe thought of mothers like Celine, struggling to scrape by with a child to feed. He recalled his own mother, and all she'd done in her short time on earth to provide for him. No, Rafe didn't back out on an agreement like this.

"Miss Fletcher?" Jacks rose to her feet. "What brings you 'round these parts in the middle of the day?"

Rafe gripped his cane tight as he stood, hoping to quiet the pounding of his heart. Susannah had appeared in the foyer, beautiful as ever in a pelisse of white and a day dress of apple green. It brought out the bloom in her cheeks, that color. Her large, doe-like eyes gleamed like two polished topazes in the afternoon light.

"I'm sorry to intrude. I wanted to speak with Mr. Winters, privately."

"That'll be all, Jacks." Rafe almost shoved his friend out of the flat. Jacks sighed as she went and bowed quickly over Susannah's hand.

"It was a pleasure doing business with you, Your Grace. Don't worry. If you're here on account of collecting your payment, Rafe's not going to back out."

"Oh, I wasn't worried about that." Susannah was in such

earnestness, too. She drove Rafe half-wild with her sincerity. Her honesty. Her generous heart. And, of course, that sweet, delicately curving body hidden beneath her garments.

"Oi, Jacks. Lock the door on your way out."

Rafe finally heard his muttering partner leave, and then it was Susannah and he all alone together in this world. This luxurious world, a sanctuary high above the hubbub of the crowd. Rafe had often liked being up here on his own, but no more. Now he wanted to share its treasures, share all of it, but only with one specific person.

"Well." Susannah sat in Jacks's place and picked up a cut-crystal glass. "Might I have a drop as well?"

"You sure your duchess sister won't notice you smashed in the middle of the day?" But Rafe grinned as he poured. Susannah took a sip and made a satisfied noise. He liked a woman who appreciated good whiskey.

"Julia and Ashworth are spending the day at the races with the Duke of Huntington. I managed to bow out due to tiredness. Annabelle picked me up for a 'restorative' day at her home and dropped me here."

"Remind me to purchase this friend of yours a disgustingly large jewel as thanks for all her assistance."

"I think Annie would prefer a lifetime membership to the Wolf's Den. She rather enjoys gentlemen's clubs. She says they're ever so much more fun than ladies' salons."

"She's an original girl." Rafe took the glass when Susannah finished her whiskey, set it down, and pulled the girl onto his lap with one elegant gesture. "You both are."

Susannah kissed him and kissed him again, giggling when she felt him rise to the occasion.

"I like to know that you like me so much," she whispered, the teasing little minx. She kissed his jaw and whispered in his ear, "I like to think you want me as much as I want you."

"Believe me," he growled, "there's no limit to how I want

you, Susannah."

"I like it when you say my name." She peppered light, sweet kisses along his jaw and upon his lips. "It sounds like, I don't know, like summer air in a meadow."

He laughed. "You've an original way of seeing the world."

"I *do* still want to see the world." She twined her arms around his neck. "But I was thinking that it wouldn't be much fun to do so alone. Wouldn't you agree?"

She appeared so shy, so nervous, so unlike the radiant, fearless girl he knew.

"I suppose I would. Of course, I haven't found many in this world I trust enough to have fun with." He nibbled her chin. "Though you might be an exception."

"I hope you mean that." She put a hand to his cheek and looked deep into his eyes, as if trying to discern something in their depths.

"I do." He frowned. "Don't dance about things, Susannah. Tell me what you're thinking."

She bit her lip. He'd never seen her this shy before. Not even when she was standing in the lobby of his club, trying to ask for a job.

"Well, my mother returns from her trip tomorrow. I'm dining with her and the Ashworths, which is when I plan to tell them that I'm not marrying the duke. I'm also going to tell them that I've been the Red Duchess, and that I've made enough money to go out on my own. Nothing will be held back."

She was taking a step into a brave new world, then. She truly was the most courageous woman he'd ever known.

"I see. Doubt that'll be received as nicely as you want it to."

"Yes, I expect my mother will make good on her threat never to see me again." Susannah smiled, but he saw her struggling against a deeper, sadder emotion. Somehow, she could find it in her heart to love even the most disgraceful wretches. It was yet another quality of hers that Rafe adored. "But I must be honest, mustn't I? If I don't want to live a life that makes me unhappy, that is."

"Too true."

"Then..." She took a deep breath, as if preparing herself to dive into an icy pond. "Then it might be even nicer if I could tell them about us."

It was as if a whole field of fireworks had gone off inside him, Roman candles whizzing in place of his thoughts. Rafe's world became a celebration for a moment.

She wanted to speak of their relationship. Hell, maybe even of love. He knew she'd never love him as he loved her, but he could keep her happy enough, couldn't he? Enough that she'd never think of all she'd missed out on, being a duchess.

"You could do that," he said roughly.

But then he recalled his conversation with Jacks just now, the thoughts about his mother. Rafe considered how he'd been born, where he'd been born. Rafe had taken his first breaths in a debtor's prison, emitted his first cries on a freezing winter morning with only criminals for company. Even if he could give Susannah a life worthy of a princess, he himself would never be anyone's idea of a prince.

"But maybe you shouldn't." Rafe ordered his heart to stop hurting as he said the words.

"Why?" Susannah took her arms away from him. She got off his lap, fear dawning in her eyes. "Because you don't wish to be with me." She made a soft, hurt sound. "At least, not officially?"

"Officially?" Rafe could scarce believe the words she'd spoken. "You can't think of wanting to marry me. Or me to marry you."

"They're rather the same thing, aren't they?" Susannah

sat down hard upon the sofa, her arms wrapped about her stomach. She seemed as though she'd be sick. "Oh, I should have known."

"Known what?"

"How could I be such a little fool?" She put her face into her gloved hands. "I thought you loved me."

The words lit too much of a fire inside of Rafe. Too much hope. He couldn't hope like this. He knew she'd liked him, enjoyed him as a lover, but to think she could… To think a young lady like this could ever have tenderness toward Rafe, or love him, was too extraordinary for words.

Unless she wanted only to gauge *his* love as a way of making sure he married her and kept her honest. Rafe felt too dizzy, too uprooted. This was all too much to hope for. "We've never spoken of feelings, Duchess."

"Susannah! I'm not the Red Duchess anymore. I'm Susannah bloody Fletcher." She was struggling not to weep now, dashing tears from her cheeks. "I knew you could never love me the way I loved you, but—"

"*What?*"

She mistook his astonishment for anger. "Well, don't yell at me. I suppose it was a childish mistake."

"Are you saying you love me, then?" He spoke as he would during a business transaction, gruff and to the point. He was too excited to be poetic. He was rough, common, coal instead of a diamond.

But she didn't seem to mind that, did she?

"Yes. Of course. Why would I ever give you my virtue if I didn't love you, you bloody fool?"

She was ready to start arguing with him, but Rafe wanted to laugh with delight and relief. She loved him. By some fucking miracle, she'd said that she loved him. And God, but he loved her as well. Rafe loved Miss Susannah Fletcher in a way he'd never imagined he could.

But…

"You wouldn't feel this way if you knew what I was." Rafe looked away from her, unable to bear seeing the light of love as it fled her eyes when she heard what he had to say.

"I know you to be a brilliant, good man who cares for those around him. How could I possibly not fall in love with someone like you?" Susannah gasped, as if she'd been struck. "But if you don't want me to love you, if you can't love me, then just say so. I don't need you to 'warn' me away from you."

"Of course I love you! How could I not?" Rafe snapped. Fuck, not the most romantic declaration in the world. "Forgive me. I'm not much good at speaking about things like this."

"About love?" Susannah's voice quavered as she slowly got up and went to him. She touched his face, and he snatched her wrist and kissed her palm.

God, the rose and honeysuckle scent of hers was a balm to his frayed nerves.

"I've never admitted this to anyone before in my life, but I'm scared." He held her close, his eyes squeezed shut as he felt her reassuring touch on his cheek. "I'm scared that I have you now, and in a few more moments I won't have you ever again."

"That's impossible," she whispered. He felt her fingers slide through his hair, felt her soothe every battered inch of his soul. "Nothing could change my feelings."

Pretty to think something like that, but Rafe knew the truth could do a lot of damage. If he wanted her, if he wanted to be worthy of all of her, then he needed to let her see the man she thought she loved. She had to make her own decision with all the facts available.

"I want to tell you about myself. Once you know everything, then you can say if you love me or not."

She took his face in her hands and lifted his eyes to hers. It was like being caressed by sunlight itself. His whole body relaxed and felt warm, even as his heart pounded in fear.

"Tell me, then," she whispered.

"I'm no gentleman, Susannah. I never have been." Rafe didn't want to do this, but he couldn't look into those clear, amber eyes and not confess. "I'm the son of a whore, fathered by one of her clients."

Susannah frowned. "Why should that matter to me in the slightest?"

She was amazing, this one. "Most in society look down upon men of my birth."

She did not react further. "I see. Go on, then."

"My mother was a good woman, but an unlucky one. She plied her trade for seven years in order to feed and clothe us both, bringing me up in the brothel where she worked. When I was seven, she caught some disease from a John and withered away. When she got too sick to work, the bastard who ran the brothel kicked us out into the street. We got sent to the workhouse, where she died."

It felt like releasing a horrible pressure in his chest as he spoke the words. Susannah slowly knelt by his feet, holding his large, rough hand in both of her small, delicate ones. "Go on," she whispered.

"I ran away. Begged on the streets until a man took me in, trained me up to be one of his crew of little pickpockets. I stole, did whatever he asked, and eventually moved my way up to burglary. I was a good thief; it was the only thing I was ever any good at." She must be disgusted with him by now, but Rafe pressed on. "Breaking into houses and taking jewels and fine clothes was like a puzzle to be solved. It entertained me. I got better and better at my so-called profession. Over time I came to have my own crew, including Jacks. We were one of the gangs to be reckoned with, until some bloody bastard looking to move in on our territory jumped us and bashed up my knee."

All these years later, Rafe could still feel the blinding pain as his kneecap shattered. Susannah squeezed his hand, pressed her lips to his knuckles.

"It's all right," she whispered. There was no judgment or disgust in her sweet amber eyes. Only acceptance. Rafe had never known anything like it before.

"Everyone expected that'd be the end of us, but I hated him too much. Hate was how I powered my way through everything. Every blow I received, every night I went hungry, that hate just burned inside me like a damn torch. So I found my way back to strength, hunted him down, destroyed his gang, and bashed *both* his legs. When I was finished, I left and let him crawl his way home. I don't know what happened to him or his people. Chances are they're dead by now."

A tear slid down Susannah's cheek as she listened. But Rafe got the awful, beautiful feeling that she was weeping *for* him, not *because of* him.

"And?"

"And that's when I got smarter. Started thinking of the future. I knew that if I stayed in that underworld, I'd be dead before I was forty. Despite how shit life could be, I wanted to stay alive. So I moved my business from picking pockets to gambling, which is just a fancier way of picking pockets if you think about it. Turns out I was good at that, too. Soon I had money, and success, and then I had the Wolf's Den. Now I've got one more leap to make, and then I'll have my hotel and my blocks of swank flats and everything else in this world that I want. But it won't never, sorry, *ever* change what I am and where I come from. I'm just a bastard and a criminal. I've ruined people's lives. No matter how successful I am, I won't be anything else than a thug. Ever. And I don't know that a young lady like you ought to be with a piece of scum like me."

"That's not true, though." Susannah wrapped her arms around him and kissed him. Rafe could feel her tears against his cheek. "All you've done is prove to me how strong you are. You could have let all this misery turn you into a hard, cruel man, but I've seen how you are with Jacks and Celine, and all the others who work in your club. I've seen the good you want to do for women like your mother, who have no one else to protect them. You didn't let what happened to you turn you cruel. You've made something beautiful out of nothing at all." She kissed his lips over and over, sweet, gentle kisses the likes of which Rafe had never known. "You're more of a gentleman than any member of the *ton* I've ever met."

That was the moment Rafe knew he was lost forever.

Charming this girl with his wealth and success had been one thing, but she knew all of him now. His low birth, his criminal past, the pain he'd suffered and inflicted on others, she knew all of his secrets and she not only still loved him, she admired him.

"You're the finest lady of them all, Susannah," he breathed. His cock ached, and so did his heart. He held her closer than he'd ever dared, allowed himself to kiss every inch of her face with tenderness as well as passion. "I can hardly believe you're real."

"I am real," she whispered. They held each other close. "And my love is real, too, Rafe."

He had more than her body; he had her heart as well. It was chaos, sheer incredible chaos, but it was also the great joy of his life.

Their kissing turned from soft to heated, and soon he had Susannah in his bedroom. She unbuckled him and he unbuttoned her, and within moments there was nothing between them save air.

He had never known a more exquisite woman. Her breasts were pert, all rose and cream, and the soft curves of her body felt like heaven in his arms.

Rafe laid her out upon his bed and kissed a path down

her naked body, between her legs. When he parted her folds, kissed and licked that one intimate spot at the center of her thighs, he loved to listen to her gasps, her moans of pleasure.

It took no time at all to speed her to a climax, and then she was groaning that she wanted him, all of him. Rafe settled his hips between her parted thighs and slid himself inside of her. It was like coming home, this union, and he rode her soft and slow at first just to experience every perfect inch of her.

Susannah dug her fingernails into the flesh of his back, moaning with bliss as he made love to her. Rafe kissed her lips, her passion-flushed cheeks. As he rode her harder, he listened to her cries of ecstasy in his ear.

"Oh, Rafe. It's so good," Susannah whispered, wrapping her legs around his waist as he pumped in and out of her. She was giving him everything she was and had. He wasn't going to last much longer.

"You're perfect." He made love to her until he couldn't control himself, until the world around him began to break apart. "Susannah, I'm going to spend."

She kissed him, moved her hips in rhythm with his, groaned as another orgasm took her and keened breathlessly when, at the last possible second, Rafe pulled out of her and spilled his seed upon the bedclothes.

She was a goddess of love and desire, this one, with her sweet body and her pink lips swollen from kissing. Susannah watched him with half-lidded eyes and smiled as she gathered him into her arms.

"I love you," she said. "I love you so much."

Rafe kissed her, tasted the prospect of heaven in her lips.

"I'd die for you," he said. And he meant it.

Chapter Twenty-One

Susannah returned to Carter House with everything right in the world.

He loved her; he'd said so, and she believed him. God, she loved Rafe. It was the easiest thing in the world to love somebody. Susannah had always thought the process to falling in love would be fraught and difficult, like picking your way over rough terrain in the countryside. How wrong she'd been. When nature simply brought two well-matched people together, nothing could be more straightforward.

She thanked Peele, the Ashworths' tall, graying butler, as he greeted her.

Susannah all but floated toward the western parlor, where she'd decided to wait for Julia to come home. She'd tell her stepsister tonight, come clean about Rafe and the Red Duchess and everything. Julia would be shocked, perhaps even angry, but Susannah knew she'd never hold a grudge. Besides, Julia would understand if anyone would.

For a while, Susannah had believed she must be defective. How could she fail to love the duke, after all? Any woman would love a rich, handsome, titled man if given half the chance, wasn't that right? Susannah had believed she must be incapable of love.

And then she'd come to love Rafe, and now everything made so much sense. It wasn't her fault she couldn't love Huntington, nor was it his. It simply wasn't meant to be.

Perhaps Susannah wouldn't need to have this conversation anyway. After all, the duke had seemed to understand her perfectly well that night at the opera. He'd been friendly when he took her to see the last Red Duchess performances, that was all it had been. Friendship. Perhaps he'd already explained this to Julia and Gregory. Wouldn't that be marvelous?

"Beg pardon, Miss Fletcher," Peele said as Susannah was wandering off. "Lady Beaumont arrived a half hour ago. She's waiting in the morning room."

Susannah froze, certain her heart stopped beating for a moment. Her mother was here? And a day early? "Oh. I didn't expect her today, Peele."

"She's aware, miss. She told me she'd be happy to wait for you and Their Graces."

Now Susannah's happiness curdled in her gut. She walked to the morning room, dread building inside her. Her mother rarely came home early from outings. Either Mrs. Ralston had died sooner than expected, or something was very wrong. Susannah almost hoped it was the former and was shocked at her own crudeness.

Lady Beaumont was sipping a cup of tea when Susannah entered. These days, she was never certain how her mother would behave when Susannah met with her. Fortunately, or perhaps unfortunately, Lady Beaumont was in tremendous spirits.

"There you are! Peele told me you didn't accompany Ashworth and Julia to the races." She clucked her tongue but didn't sound angry. "Well, no matter. They should be home soon, and they're bringing the duke with them!"

"How do you know that, Mamma?" Susannah felt liable to faint into the sugar bowl. "And why have you returned so early? Is Mrs. Ralston, that is, has she passed on?"

"Sadly no. Oh, the doctors now think she might have caught a summer cold. Ugh, she's always been so dramatic." Lady Beaumont shrugged, more carefree than Susannah had ever seen her. "But I've returned early at the Duke of Huntington's behest. He wrote specifically to ask me to be present this evening. Julia sent a similar letter."

Susannah doubted the duke would have urged Constance to return just to watch him break off with her daughter. Julia might have done such a thing, but not Huntington. That meant...the duke had not understood her. In fact, now that Susannah considered it, he must have misconstrued her words dramatically. Perhaps he'd thought she was *urging* him to become formally engaged to her.

Her mother hugged Susannah and tittered about the supper Julia had planned when it was all done. Oh, it *must* happen tonight, didn't Susannah agree? But why on earth was she so silent?

"I'm a bit overwhelmed, Mamma. Might I go lie down until they return?"

Lady Beaumont allowed it, and Susannah went to her room and lay curled on her side upon the bed. What was she to do now? Could she simply run away to Rafe's, hide above Mayfair in his elegant flat? Should she refuse to come out to meet anyone tonight, claim she had a dreadful illness? Should she fake her own death?

But Susannah wasn't that shy, placating girl anymore. She couldn't be.

All her life, she'd striven to be the perfect daughter, the perfect debutante, the perfect society girl. She had tried her best to want what other people wanted and to ignore her own desires. It had almost led her to catastrophe, and she had to stand firm. She had to face this.

As the sun dipped into twilight, casting shadows upon the canyons of the London streets, a knock came at Susannah's door.

"Miss Fletcher?" a maidservant said. "Beg pardon, miss. Their Graces and the Duke of Huntington have returned. They'd like to see you in the library."

Susannah hadn't even changed for dinner, but she didn't care.

She walked downstairs as if heading to her own execution. Already, tears were swelling her throat shut. Was she about to hurt Julia and alienate her mother forever? Was she about to ruin her life with one brief word? Would she look back upon this moment decades from now and curse her own stupidity?

What if Rafe didn't love her the way she loved him? What if he wouldn't marry her? He still hadn't proposed, even after their passion this afternoon. Why wouldn't he propose? She should have said something. If only Susannah could have secured that proposal, she would walk into this so much stronger.

She opened the door and found the Ashworths, her mother, and Huntington assembled and in high spirits. To her horror, Susannah saw that Julia had ordered a bottle of champagne and a row of glasses to be placed upon a silver tray. She almost turned and fled, but Julia had noticed her. It was too late.

"Darling! Do come in. We missed you at the races today." Susannah's stepsister embraced her and smoothed her hair. "Dear me, you look a bit peaky. Are you well?"

"I..." Susannah wanted to say she was sick, so sick, could they do this another time, whatever this was? But Huntington was with her now, bowing in a gentlemanly fashion over her hand. Susannah could feel the wheels of the evening turning, the momentum too much to stop now. It was rather like Felicity's foot-wheel things. She could not slow down, and soon she'd dash the garish, cherry-blossom vase of her life to the floor and shatter it to pieces.

It was a poor metaphor, but an apt one.

"You haven't even dressed for dinner?" Her mother clucked her tongue, her irritation evident but also subdued. After all, Huntington was present.

"You'll want to change soon, Zan." The corners of Ashworth's gray eyes crinkled in merriment. "Our cook's put together a real feast this evening."

"Oh?" She tried to pretend ignorance. "Why would she do that? Is there an occasion?"

Julia slipped her arm through Gregory's, the pair of them beaming in the face of impending bliss. Lady Beaumont sat upon the sofa, fluttering her fan in breathless anticipation.

"I hope there might be a cause for celebration." Huntington stood before her, a giant of a man, with all the wealth and power that his title and estate entailed.

It would make the people Susannah loved most so very happy if she were to marry him. And once again, Susannah felt herself bending beneath the weight of expectation. What right did she have to refuse something everyone else would kill for? What made her so bloody special?

She wished Rafe were here to stand alongside her, support her, tell them, yes, he was going to make her his wife and there was no bloody force on earth or in heaven that could stop them.

But Rafe wasn't here. Susannah felt sure she'd be sick.

"Perhaps I'd better go and change right now." Susannah began to back away toward the door. "We can discuss things at dinner, perhaps."

"I was hoping for a moment of your time, Miss Fletcher." The duke appeared bemused. "There's a rather important question I want to put to you."

Scream and faint! Tell them you're the Red Duchess!

Spontaneously combust! Do something, anything to get out of this!

"Um. Wh-What is it?" Susannah felt liable to collapse.

The duke noticed, but seemed only more pleased, perhaps because he assumed she was trembling on the precipice of bliss, ready to fall. He led her to a chair and seated her in it... then slowly knelt before her.

A scream tried to escape Susannah's mouth but lodged inside her throat and stuck there. This was going to happen. She couldn't stop it.

"Miss Fletcher. When my father died ten years ago, he made me promise something. He asked me to swear that I would choose only the best possible mistress for Moorcliff Castle, and a true lady for the Huntington bloodline."

"I see," she wheezed. This had all the quality of a nightmare.

"I think I've already told you I'm a selective man. I'll take only the best for myself and, more importantly, for my family. Over these ten years, I've searched for an ideal duchess, a woman possessed of all the qualities needed to both make me happy and to honor my father and family name. I've searched for a woman with youth, beauty, intelligence, kindness, great talent, and exquisite feeling. In addition, I've looked for a true lady, elegant in birth and breeding but, even more so, graceful in her every word and deed. I have also hoped for a woman I could call a friend. No woman of the *ton* I have ever met had every quality I desired in a wife." He paused and smiled. "Until you, that is."

"I..."

Lady Beaumont's cheeks were already wet with joyous tears. Julia relaxed in Gregory's embrace, both blissful as they watched this scene unfold.

"I believe you to be among the finest ladies of my acquaintance. There is no girl I respect more, none I esteem greater, and certainly none who could make me as happy as you. My hope is, with time, you will come to feel for me as I feel for you. I flatter myself that perhaps your feelings are already in accordance with mine. Not merely romantic feelings, but the beliefs in duty and honor and tradition I hold so dear. A mutual desire to see the Huntington line continue in strength. A commitment to Moorcliff Castle and to everything that it represents to English history."

Her mother nodded to every other word, like a music enthusiast at a concert overtaken by sublime playing.

"Your Grace." Susannah wanted to burst into tears because he really was so bloody good and kind. He just wasn't Rafe; it was his only failing. But it was also the only one that mattered.

"Please, just permit me one thing more." The duke drew something from his pocket and held it up for her inspection.

It was a ring that sported a square cut emerald.

The jewel was the size of Susannah's thumbnail, a jungle green with a ripple of cerulean blue through the center. It was a gorgeous piece of jewelry.

"This belonged to my mother, the late duchess. It is one of the most valuable objects I own, both in terms of wealth and sentiment. There is no other woman in the world who should wear it but you. Miss Fletcher, will you grant me the honor of your hand in marriage?"

In the span of a second, Susannah watched her entire life tumble before her eyes, brief as it was. Playing with Julia in Pennington Hall as a child; working hard at her pianoforte as a summer rain pattered upon the roof; meeting Rafe, kissing Rafe, lying with and loving Rafe; fights with her mother; her triumphs as the Red Duchess; and now this.

It was as if every single moment she'd ever lived had been leading to this instant in time. There were two paths laid out before her, one that wound away into brilliance and sunshine, the other twisting deeper into a dark and unknown wood.

If she took the sunlit path, Susannah saw and knew every single bend it would take. She could see the whole rest of her life happen before she'd even lived it.

Down the path into the woods, she had no bloody clue where it would lead. Would it be happiness or ruin? She had no idea. But that not knowing was part of the excitement of it. She'd be leaving everyone behind if she went that way, wouldn't she? Not just her mother, but Julia and Gregory.

Susannah knew her stepsister would love her no matter what, come to accept her no matter what, but the thought of wounding Julia hurt her like nothing else could. And more than that, the terror of the unknown was finally sinking its fangs into her.

What kind of fool turned down a once-in-a-lifetime opportunity to be a duchess? She could regret these next few seconds every day for the rest of her life.

"Susannah?" Lady Beaumont's impatience showed through her pleasant façade. "What do you say to His Grace?"

"I..." But when she felt herself wavering, about to capitulate and say yes, she remembered Rafe.

The words he'd spoken to her today, the passion in his kiss.

He was a man who'd been bruised and beaten by the world but had never allowed himself to become defeated. He'd made a life he wanted by seizing every opportunity that came his way, damned be the consequences. He was the bravest man she'd ever met.

If she wanted to be worthy of a man like that, Susannah needed to be brave, too.

"I can't," she whispered.

The faces of those before her would have been comic if the whole thing hadn't been so wretched.

Huntington looked astonished, Gregory befuddled, Julia's mouth had fallen open, and her mother was gearing up for one of the great screams of history.

"Beg pardon?" Huntington said.

"I'm so sorry, Your Grace. I, I can't do this." Susannah got to her feet and nearly toppled over but managed to keep her balance.

"I don't understand." Huntington lowered the emerald ring, confusion now playing over his features.

"She doesn't feel well, Your Grace. Look at her, the poor thing's almost falling over. She must be feverish. She can't know what she's saying." Lady Beaumont spoke in a honeyed voice but gave Susannah a look that was all poison.

"Darling, what are you saying?" Julia murmured.

"I'm saying I can't marry you, Your Grace. I'm sorry." Susannah began weeping, blubbering, even. "I should have told you sooner."

"Susannah!" Lady Beaumont shrieked. "Go to your room this instant!"

Julia and Gregory were speaking rapidly, and her mother was stomping her feet, and the Duke of Huntington looked as though the devil had stepped up and spit in his porridge. Another of Julia's famous sayings. And suddenly, that was it. With only a few words, it was done. Susannah was free.

And right now, more than anything, she needed to see Rafe.

"Please forgive me. Everyone. Forgive me," she said.

Then, as her mother screeched and Julia called her name, Susannah raced out of the library, down the hall, and shoved out the front door. She didn't take her bonnet, her coat, or her gloves; she merely raced into the street and ran, unheeding the strange and scandalized looks she attracted.

Susannah almost laughed as she realized how wrong she'd been.

The prospect of a life with Rafe hadn't been a stretch of dark, lonely woods. She'd been lost in those woods her whole life.

Now, finally, she was going home.

Chapter Twenty-Two

The club would be opening in half an hour.

Rafe had never felt in such good spirits as he finished tying his cravat and combing his hair. When he looked in the mirror now, he didn't see a malformed gremlin; he saw a man of business, a man with the love of a beautiful woman.

He'd see to it that the club opened smoothly, and then he'd be off. He'd take his carriage and drive over to the Duke of Ashworth's, pay a call upon the family at an unexpected hour. He hadn't asked for Susannah's hand this afternoon, and that had been a mistake. She needed to know Rafe was a man of honor.

Tonight, Rafe left that miserable orphan behind, the urchin lying upon a cold floor in winter. He abandoned the thug who'd broken skulls and bashed kneecaps. He knew he was worthy of something now, because Susannah believed he was.

He was going to make her happy for the rest of her bloody life.

As he tromped down the stairs all the way to the club's first level, Rafe even hummed a tune. He wasn't much of a musical fellow, but he was in such high spirits he couldn't help himself. He didn't recognize the song until he reached the bottom of the stairs and laughed.

It was "Little Mary Beth Lost Her Spoon."

"Shame that poor bastard never got to hear it," he said, and whistled as he headed down the foyer toward the bar.

Rafe halted when he heard a banging on the club's door. He frowned, checked his watch. It was still seventeen minutes to opening.

"Come back in twenty!" Rafe yelled, grumbling to himself as he trudged on. "Bloody drunks."

"Rafe! Let me in!" Susannah's voice was music itself.

Rafe quickly unbolted the door and opened to greet her. The girl practically fell into the front hall, looking a right mess. She was still dressed for the afternoon, without even a bonnet or a pelisse. Her copper curls were flyaway, and her cheeks were flushed from running. She must have bolted through the city streets like some wild thing.

"What the hell?" Rafe said.

"I did it." She gasped and fell against his chest.

Rafe held her, petted her hair, his mind whirling. He couldn't even find the will to close the bloody door; he wanted only to listen to her. "You told them, then? About us?"

"The duke proposed, and I rejected him." She was crying and trembling, but she kissed him. She kissed him over and over, her lips as warm and sweet as ever. "My mother was so angry, I'm sure she'll never see me again. And Julia, oh God, I can't believe I hurt her like that."

"Fuck them. Fuck everyone." He dropped his cane and took her face in his hands. He wiped the tears away with his thumbs, marveled at this living work of art before him. "It's over, then? His Grace is sent packing?"

"I've been such a bloody fool," she cried. "I was so afraid and unsure of what I should do, but now I know. I want you, Rafe. I want to be with you, and no one else. There's nothing more I want in this world, not money, not travel, not anything."

"Susannah," he growled. She was right, her name was like summer air. It was like life and growing green things, and as he pressed his mouth tight to hers, he felt fire coursing through his veins. He held her, savored her taste and feel. He canted his hips against hers, let her feel the hardness she inspired in him. Susannah gasped in sweet shock to feel it.

"I love you," she moaned, tilting her head back, letting Rafe kiss along her neck. "I love you, love you."

"I love you. I adore you. You're mine now." Rafe kissed her so hard it hurt, slid a hand along her body, clasped her round, perfect thigh.

He hitched her leg around his waist, loving the squeal of shock she gave. He wasn't going to be able to last all the way back up those bloody stairs. He needed her now, needed to have her in a private salon, or a fucking closet. Hell, he'd take her here. Let those drunk sods come in to gamble and flirt and see him making love to the most exquisite woman in London.

Their kisses grew hotter, harder, greedier. She clutched his lapels, then moaned in gratitude as Rafe slid the coat off and pressed her so near, let her feel how his heart beat for her. Only for her.

Rafe traced his fingers along the swell of her bosom, dipped them below her neckline, until he could feel the tight, ruched bud of her nipple. "Mine," he whispered.

"Yes, Rafe." She sighed, her eyes fluttering shut. And then...

"*Bastard!*"

Someone stood in the doorway, mere feet from Rafe and Susannah. The Duke of Huntington looked ready to commit murder. The normally genial man wore a look of pure, teeming rage as he beheld Rafe embracing the woman he'd failed to make his intended.

"Your Grace?" Susannah cried out in shock, turning and pressing her back against Rafe. It was as if she were shielding him. "Why have you come?"

"You seducer!" The duke glared at Rafe. "You...you defiler of innocents!"

"Save your breath, Duke." Rafe put himself before Susannah. He had to protect her, not the other way around. "This isn't some melodrama. The girl and I are in love."

It was so bloody pathetic, wasn't it?

Rafe watched the Duke of Huntington lose what he wanted for perhaps the first time in his life. Rafe might have savored his victory, lorded it over the aristocrat, if he didn't feel the smallest bit of pity for Huntington. After all, to lose Susannah Fletcher would be misery itself.

"Your Grace, please," Susannah cried.

"I've come to retrieve you, Miss Fletcher." The duke's voice softened when he spoke to her. "Your stepsister and your mother don't know where you've gone. They're alarmed at the thought some tragedy has befallen you."

"It's not tragedy. As I told you, Your Grace, it's love." Rafe put an arm out when Susannah tried to leave, blocking her exit. No, she would not go with this man. She was staying with him, here in the Wolf's Den where she belonged. So long as Rafe had Susannah, the world could not get at him.

"And you, Miss Fletcher? Do you love this man?"

"I do. Please, Your Grace, I'm so sorry for all that's happened."

"How long has this relationship lasted?" The duke looked so wounded that even Rafe felt sorry for him for an instant. He wasn't shouting at the girl; he seemed frankly heartbroken. Poor sod.

"Not long. But Mr. Winters and I have worked together

since May." Susannah gave a weary sigh. "I am, or I was, the Red Duchess."

The duke stared at Rafe and Susannah in stunned disbelief, then quickly resolved himself. Striding forward, the man pulled out a gray velvet glove and slapped Rafe hard across the face with it. Rafe would give the bloody duke this much: his slapping game was top-notch. That damn well hurt.

"*Your Grace!*" Susannah shrieked.

"You've insulted this young woman and dishonored her." Huntington looked at Rafe with pure, seething scorn. "I can't allow that to go unpunished. Hampstead Heath, tomorrow at dawn."

"There was no insult," Susannah said.

"Miss Fletcher, honor can't allow me to behave any other way." At least the duke spoke kindly to Susannah. Rafe would've killed him otherwise, but it was clear Huntington didn't blame her for this scene unfolding. He held out a hand to the girl. "Please. For your mother's and Julia's sakes, return to Carter House with me now. I wish only to escort you. I make no other claim."

Rafe watched Susannah falter then; he knew she loved her family, knew she'd do anything to keep them from worry and pain. Irritated, Rafe snatched up the glove from the floor.

"I'll meet you on the Heath, your Dukeship." Rafe sneered.

"No. Rafe. Your Grace. This is all a mistake," Susannah cried.

"His Grace is right about one thing. You ought to go home." Rafe looked at the girl, needing to be strong for her right now. "We'll sort the rest out. Your stepsister doesn't deserve to be frightened, does she?"

"No." Susannah watched him with pained eyes. "But…"

"Miss Fletcher. Please join me." The Duke of Huntington held open the front door and gestured for the young lady to go outside. At least he wouldn't force her. Susannah wavered a moment, and Rafe selfishly wanted her to forget her stepsister and family and stay with him. But Susannah wasn't like that. She might've been prepared to head for the Continent alone, but she wasn't going to cause a scene and then disappear. She wouldn't knowingly hurt anyone like that.

She turned and exited the club. Huntington followed, closing the door behind them.

Rafe stood there, his head hung low, his mind spinning.

For five seconds, Rafe had held everything he wanted in his arms.

Now he was going to pay with his life for the privilege of loving her.

Chapter Twenty-Three

For much of the ride back to Carter House, Susannah and Huntington were silent.

She peeked at him from time to time and found him a block of marble, a noble statue with no emotion on his features. Susannah wanted to lower her head and say nothing, rush upstairs to her room and bar the door and let them all yell at her from the hallway while she wept into a pillow.

But that was how little girls handled things. And Susannah was no child, especially not now.

"I'm sorry," she said at last. Susannah cleared her throat. "But you mustn't duel him."

"We don't need to discuss it, Miss Fletcher." Huntington spoke kindly to her, and that infuriated Susannah. She didn't want to be treated with delicacy. She wanted to have a proper conversation.

"Well, I do wish to discuss it."

"Very well." He sighed. "Then please tell me why."

"Why what, Your Grace?"

"Why would you relinquish your virtue to some vile seducer?"

Lord, he talked like a melodrama sometimes.

"Because I love him." It was a simple answer, and a devastating one.

"Yes. So you said." He winced as though she'd landed a blow, and Susannah felt a bit rotten. "But how?"

"What do you mean how? Is it because Rafe is common? A businessman?" She felt indignant on his behalf.

"No. I'm simply trying to work out why or how you would know such a person in the first place! You say you have been the Red Duchess all this time?" The duke continued to watch the London streets pass by through the window, obviously trying to sort this out in his head. "Why would you be? Was it a game?"

"No game. I worked for Rafe because I needed to earn money. He was going to pay me five thousand pounds to perform at his club as the Duchess."

"Why did you need five thousand pounds?" He was amazed. "Didn't you know that I was on the threshold of proposing to you?"

"Yes. I did." Susannah couldn't hold back the tears of fear and rage and misery much longer.

"I thought we understood each other."

"I understood you, Your Grace. But you never understood me." Tears coursed down Susannah's cheeks.

"What on earth do you mean? Miss Fletcher, what have I failed to understand?"

Susannah could not hold the tide of truth back a second longer.

"I don't love you! I can't love you!" She hid her face in her hands and wailed until she was sick with it. "And I'm sorry, because I like you ever so much and you're one of the most decent fellows I know, but I don't want to marry you. I can't."

She wondered how angry he'd be now, or how hurt.

Would he now threaten to expose her to the rest of the

ton, ridicule her? Would Huntington spread ruinous gossip, ensure that every decent door in London was shut to her forever after? It was no more than she'd deserve, but Rafe had done nothing wrong. She needed to defend him. Beg for his pardon. But first, she needed to allow the duke his anger.

"Miss Fletcher. Susannah." Huntington took her hands down with an exceedingly gentle touch. There was no wounded pride or bellowing now. He seemed only sincere. "Explain all this to me from the beginning, if you please."

So she told him.

She told him of the feelings of helplessness and hopelessness she'd struggled against while he courted her. Susannah told him of her secret dreams of the Continent and freedom; she recounted how she'd met Rafe at the Hunter's Ball, of his need to obtain the Corner Castle, of his generous offer.

She regaled the duke with the stories of her fears and triumphs on the stage, of falling in love with Rafe. She did not go into unnecessary detail, but she could tell he understood their passions had been consummated. She was a bad, loose woman, perhaps, but she genuinely loved that man. And Susannah told the duke how she'd gone from wanting freedom and travel to wanting Rafe, wanting him more than she'd ever craved anything in her life.

Then the story was done, and she felt drained of all energy.

She couldn't have imagined how wonderful it would feel to confess all her hidden truths to somebody. Susannah slumped against the cushions in an unladylike manner and waited for Huntington to condemn her.

"Why didn't you simply tell me before?" The duke was not angry; he seemed vaguely horrified. "Miss Fletcher, why did you not tell me my suit was in vain?"

"Because my mother would have killed me, for one," she blurted out. Oh damn. Well, that certainly wasn't a lie. "And Julia and Ashworth were so excited by the idea, and everyone in town seemed so thrilled. And in addition to being a duke, you're also one of the most admirable men I know, and quite attractive, and everything a young woman is supposed to want." The tears fell again, and the duke kindly offered her his handkerchief. "I felt certain I was being selfish and awful."

"Because you could not love me."

"Not in the way you should be loved by your wife. I'm sorry. I'm so, so sorry."

Huntington appraised her from his seat opposite, looking as large and handsome and severe as Jupiter might have if Jupiter were a duke instead of a god.

"You have nothing to apologize for," he said at last.

Susannah blinked and blinked again. Surely she'd only imagined those words; he could not have meant them. "Beg pardon?"

"I took your own feelings for granted. It seemed impossible to me that you would not love me. Indeed, I've been brought up my entire life to imagine any woman would commit murder for a chance to be a duchess. I see now how utterly egotistical such thinking is."

"None of this would have happened if I hadn't been such a coward. If I'd simply told you how I felt."

"In truth, Miss Fletcher, I would have reacted as most in the *ton* likely would. I'd have either thought you touched in the head or playing feminine tricks to push for a quick engagement. But knowing now you risked your reputation nightly merely to earn enough money to purchase your freedom, I see what an arrogant assumption that would be." Huntington bowed his head to her. "Please forgive me for being such a conceited fool."

That was probably the worst part of all this—that Susannah was hurting a decent man. It didn't matter that the duke was, well, a duke, or handsome, or vastly wealthy.

It didn't matter that he was reputed to have been

something of a rake in his time, with a list of brilliant conquests. Underneath it all, he was fundamentally decent. And Susannah hated more than anything to disappoint decent people.

But she couldn't marry him merely to spare him disappointment. That would be a disaster for both of them.

"Only if you'll forgive me for being cowardly, Your Grace. I let all this happen because I was too afraid to say what I felt." Susannah bit her lip, screwing up her courage just a touch more. "Please, don't punish Mr. Winters for my own lack of honor."

"I'm sorry, Miss Fletcher, but I must meet him on the field. He took advantage of your innocence and trust. I can't allow a man like that to go unpunished."

"Don't you understand what I've been telling you? We love each other."

"Has he asked for your hand in marriage? Has he attempted to do the responsible thing?"

"We…we're not engaged yet," she muttered. "But I'm certain we will be, and soon!" But now there was nothing to be said or done; Huntington had made up his mind and would follow his honorable course to its fatal conclusion.

As the carriage stopped before Carter House, Huntington took her hand in his, respectfully.

"I give you my word, no one will ever hear from my lips what you've told me tonight. Not Ashworth, not the duchess, not your mother, not another living soul. Whatever I can do to protect you from scandal, I will."

"Then please don't duel Mr. Winters, Your Grace. Please!"

But the duke shook his head. "It's a question of honor and duty."

"I understand Rafe Winters. I understand him better than I understand myself. I'm telling you that he's a good man. Please," Susannah said as a servant opened the carriage door. "Please don't hurt him."

"Susannah?" Julia stood by the open door, looking more stricken than ever. "Darling, come inside. Thank you for bringing her home, Huntington."

"My pleasure, Your Grace." Huntington bowed to the ladies as Susannah reluctantly stepped out of the carriage.

She felt Julia's arm wind around her shoulders and stifled a sob. Why was everyone being so bloody nice to her? She didn't deserve their kindness. Rafe did, yet they all blamed him for Susannah's misadventures. It wasn't right.

"Please!" Susannah cried, but Huntington closed the carriage door and drove away down the street.

"Come inside, dearest. We need to speak with you," Julia whispered, hurrying Susannah back inside the gates of Carter House.

Susannah hung her head, utterly dejected.

She didn't care if they punished her now, didn't care if they cast her out and never saw or spoke of her again. Susannah deserved isolation and poverty if that's what it all came down to. Just so long as they didn't harm Rafe.

...

Rafe stood in the front hall of the Corner Castle, amid a mess of ladders and planks of wood. The renovations had already begun, sucking away more of his blasted money. Jacks had been right about one thing: this undertaking was going to bleed Rafe of every last penny he'd saved. It was a true gamble, maybe the biggest of his life.

No, that was wrong. Susannah Fletcher had been his biggest gamble. Loving her had led to his redemption, and now it'd be his ruin as well.

He leaned on his cane and held that damned duke's velvet glove in his hand.

So, His Grace the Dunce of Huntington thought Rafe had seduced Susannah, eh? Of course he did. Huntington probably thought Rafe saw Susannah as a sweet misadventure, or maybe a fat load of cash. He didn't know, couldn't know. Rafe saw salvation itself in Susannah's beautiful amber eyes.

But creatures of the underworld like Rafe weren't made for salvation, were they?

Seeing as he was about to die for her, Rafe had to believe Susannah Fletcher was worth risking Hell for. *Ah, fuck*. It was something he already knew to be true.

Rafe startled at the sound of breaking glass. *Shit*.

He strode into the front foyer and found a broken window gaping back at him. Shards of glass littered the floor, illuminated by the London streetlamps, and in the middle of all the carnage lay a stone. Some horrible urchin had decided to break one of his windows? He'd nab the little bastard.

But then Rafe noticed the piece of paper tied around the rock with a bit of string. He undid the note and read:

Hope this cleans up the last of the gambling debts.

Rafe frowned at the note, written in a prissy, loopy, upper-class sort of hand. What kind of urchin wrote in that style?

Rafe's stomach sank as the memory rushed back over him. Those three toffy-nosed prats who'd beat up on Celine and tried to rough up Susannah. Those rich little bastards who'd said Rafe was no gentleman. What did they mean by this, those goons?

Rafe realized he could read this note quite easily, even in the dark. In fact, the world around him was growing brighter with every passing second. Warmer, too. The whole front foyer of the Castle was lit with a rosy, orange glow.

Much like the glow of fire.

No!

Rafe hurried out onto the front steps and saw, to his horror, that the Den was engulfed in flames. Smoke poured out of windows, and fire licked its way up the walls, devouring the curtains and the finery within.

Rafe imagined that from here he could see the fire demolishing everything he'd built over the last five or six years. His priceless paintings, his crystal chandeliers, his satin bedclothes and fine, tailored suits—all gone in a puff of smoke.

But more than that, he thought of Jacks and the people inside that bloody inferno.

With a roar, Rafe hurled himself across the street and toward the fire, even as his blasted knee hurt. Hands grabbed him, men pulled him back, but he cursed them and tried to break free, shoving people off with his cane, threatening them with his fists.

"Rafe!" Jacks shouted.

Oh, thank God. His friend rushed over to him, held him in a tight hug. Though Rafe wasn't one for big displays of emotion, he hugged her back.

"The others?" he croaked.

"Everyone's safe, thank God. The club wasn't too full yet. We managed to get everybody out."

He shut his eyes. That was some relief, at least. But…

"But…" Jacks said, echoing his fearful realization. "The Den's gone. It's gone, Rafe."

She couldn't stop the tears, just wept and wept as he patted her back. Rafe stood amid the growing crowd of onlookers as people called for water, for someone to do something.

As Rafe stood there and watched his world burn down before his very eyes, he realized his fairy tale had well and truly ended.

The Wolf's Den was gone. And so was Susannah Fletcher.

Chapter Twenty-Four

Obviously, Rafe didn't get a moment of sleep the entire night and rode out to the dueling pitch on Hampstead Heath in the same clothes he'd been wearing since yesterday afternoon. As a matter of fact, these were now the only clothes he owned. At least they were fine; he'd have a nice suit to be buried in.

"You've got to call this bloody duel off," Jacks said as she tied up their horses. Rafe saw the duke, his second, and the black-coated figure of a doctor on the other side of the field. The morning mist was already burning away as the sun rose.

"There's no reason to. I've got nothing much to live for now," Rafe said. He cursed as Jacks slugged him in the shoulder.

"Don't be an ass! What am I supposed to do without you, you bastard?" But she was trying not to cry.

"You'll do what needs doing." Rafe sighed. "What I would've done. You'll sell the Corner Castle for the best price you can find and hope it's enough to cover the costs of rebuilding the Den. Everything I own's yours, Jacks, even if that now amounts to a pile of burned bricks and a derelict building. But you'll restore the club, I know you will. You'll do just fine without me."

"You bloody fool."

"That I am."

Rafe and Jacks went to meet Huntington and the other men.

The duke towered above every other man there; bloody sod had to be almost six and a half feet tall. Rafe was one of the tallest men in London, and this duke was the only man who'd ever made him feel small.

That thought made Rafe want to take true aim and fire his pistol through Huntington's rich, titled heart.

"Gentlemen," the doctor said, eyeing Rafe and the duke. "I'd like to offer this opportunity to resolve your differences without violence. Surely there's no need to draw this out to its bitter conclusion."

"I'm afraid there's every need, doc." Rafe never looked away from Huntington as he spoke. "His Grace here's had his pride wounded, and he needs to put me in the ground to make up for it."

"The reason we're here has nothing to do with my pride." Huntington frowned. "It has everything to do with a certain young lady's honor."

"Maybe we could try talking this out?" Jacks whispered to Rafe, but he wouldn't be budged.

It wasn't that he'd lost the Den, or all his treasures; it was that Susannah had apparently allowed Huntington to come here and kill Rafe for the sake of her own honor. She'd abandoned him, and that was the only thing in this world that could make Rafe Winters want to give up.

"You got those pistols, then?" Rafe pointed to the wooden box that Huntington's second held.

Rafe recognized the young man, Percy Randall, from the Wolf's Den. Another of the rich clients who liked a good drink. Mr. Randall glared at Rafe as he opened the wooden case and revealed the two pistols. Rafe went to choose his weapon.

"Wait." Huntington canted his head to the left, appraising Rafe. "I've another proposition for you."

"And that is?" Rafe didn't want to waste time; this was the perfect hour for dying, and he didn't want the light to change too much. He was an artist at heart.

"I will call off our duel," the duke said slowly, "if you will agree never to see the young lady ever again. If you agree to do so, I shall pay you."

"Pay me?" Rafe's lip curled in disgust.

"Pay him how much?" Jacks sounded eager.

"Twice what you offered to pay the girl. Ten thousand pounds. On the condition, of course, that you never see her or speak to her again."

"Rafe." Jacks grabbed his arm. "We need to talk about this."

She had a point. Right now, ten thousand pounds would do so much for him. It'd keep him solvent while he tried to repair the club. Maybe he didn't even need to sell the Corner Castle. If he had that kind of money, Rafe could rebuild his club and maintain the dream he'd cherished for so long. He could be the man of business and the gentleman he'd always wanted to be.

If he agreed to never see Susannah again.

Perhaps she didn't wish to see him? Perhaps…perhaps she'd even asked Huntington to extend this offer to Rafe. Yes. To try to save Rafe's life, in a cowardly and sly way. She wanted him to live, but she wasn't brave enough to live with him.

"Well, Mr. Winters? What do you say?"

"I say you toffs don't have the market cornered on honor, Your Grace. You don't need to pay me to keep away from the girl. I'll do it for free."

"Is that so?" Huntington appeared almost surprised. "Rather a noble statement, Mr. Winters."

"Noble's got nothing to do with it, remember? I'm a cheap seducer, or a vile villain, or whatever the bloody hell you said yesterday. Why not draw your pistol and finish me right here, the way you obviously want?"

"Rafe!" Jacks clenched her fists, clearly imagining she was choking the life out of him. Rafe was open to that way of dying as well. He was flexible. "We need the money. You know how much we need it!"

"Some things aren't for sale." Rafe leaned on his cane, cursing when it sank into the damp grass and almost tossed him off-balance. There was a reason he wasn't much of an outdoorsman.

"I must admit, that's an admirable statement." The duke appeared deep in thought as Percy Randall shut the wooden case with the pistols.

"Can we hold off on the duel, then?" Randall asked the duke.

"Gentlemen, you need to decide quickly. We shouldn't linger once the sun's fully up," the doctor said.

"Let's do it. Come on!" Rafe was impatient for the end now, but Randall stepped away with the case, almost like he was withholding a sweet.

"The young lady told me you were a good man, Mr. Winters. I'm beginning to suspect she may have been right."

"Oh, don't go patronizing her *and* me, you bloody fool." Rafe ignored Jacks's angry shushing. "I did all the things you accused me of. I'm a seducer, a defiler, a villain, and a cad. Go on and shoot me through the heart for her precious honor and your pride. Go on!"

Ah, but Rafe should have known that anything he truly wanted would be denied him. That was how the upper classes always did it; they'd twist you up with their laws and words until you were literally begging for your own death. England was a bloody ridiculous country.

"She asked me to spare your life." The duke nodded grimly. "I believe I shall grant her that request."

"Oh, don't be so damned noble!"

"Come on." Jacks tugged at Rafe's sleeve, trying to drag him after her. "We ought to get out of here. Oi! You want to get snatched for dueling?"

Even though Rafe wanted to scream with frustration, he had to admire this duke a little. He had listened to Susannah, played this game by her rules. He'd be a good custodian for her honor, tarnished though it was. In fact, Rafe couldn't quite believe that the duke would be so forgiving of a fallen woman that he'd still make her his duchess. Right? Or was Huntington so in love with the girl he'd forgive her even this?

"Just do me one favor, Your Grace."

"Name it."

"Take care of the girl for me." A lump swelled in Rafe's throat. He wasn't about to start weeping and wailing. "See to it she's happy."

"You don't need to ask such a thing, Mr. Winters. I consider her safety and well-being a duty."

Right. Shit, Rafe had never seen anything like it before, a duke overlooking a girl's impurities to safeguard her. Then again, Susannah Fletcher was worth any amount of forgiveness. She was too beautiful and good and fine to be real.

Besides, now Rafe was a penniless fool instead of a wealthy businessman. There was nothing he could offer Susannah that would be worthy of her time or love.

"Do me a favor and give her the ten thousand you were going to give to me." Rafe turned from Huntington and the others and walked the long way back to his horse. "She'll put it to good use, I'm sure. And tell her goodbye from me."

Rafe walked away with his life spared in exchange for a broken heart. It wasn't much of a trade.

Chapter Twenty-Five

Susannah sat at the table, staring into a bowl of lukewarm porridge as Julia and her mother continued to speak to her and argue with each other.

After Huntington had returned Susannah last night, she'd had to sit and endure the endless rounds of pecking questions and, on her mother's part, half-formed threats.

Lady Beaumont had told Susannah that she would be sent to a nunnery, cast out into the street, put in prison, and, perhaps the strangest threat of all, returned to a shop somewhere and exchanged for a new and better-behaved daughter.

"Stop talking nonsense!" Julia had cried, her tolerance for Lady Beaumont's peculiar threats never terribly robust. "Zan, darling, we don't want to punish you. All we want is to understand precisely what's happened."

"And if the explanation should not be sufficient, punishment will again be on the table!"

Susannah could not bring herself to answer, no matter how much she wanted to. To answer a little bit would mean having to answer all of it, and while she could imagine telling

Julia the shocking truth, Susannah truly believed her mother would burst into flames, should she know the full extent of Susannah's debauchery.

So after dodging questions and pleading to be allowed to go to bed for a few hours, she'd finally been granted her wish and had lain awake the entire night, weeping and fearful of what the dawn would bring.

Would Rafe be dead? Would the duke? And what would happen to the winner of this hideous duel? If only she could get away and ride out and tell them both to stop this foolishness! Men's greatest problem was that they didn't listen enough to women.

Come the morning, a maid had entered Susannah's chamber and told her the Duchess of Ashworth and Lady Beaumont wished to see her to continue the less-than-cheery interrogation.

With a sigh, Susannah washed and dressed and went down to breakfast, where she found her mother hacking away at a wedge of grapefruit as though it were Napoleon Bonaparte himself.

Meanwhile, Julia stood and embraced Susannah the moment she entered. "Now dearest, please. I know you're tired, but you must explain this to us. I haven't been able to sleep a wink!"

"I shall never sleep again," Lady Beaumont said gravely.

"I've barely been able to sleep for days." Susannah was teary as she sat down before a cup of tea and some toast.

"This is not a competition, Susannah! Which of us has procured the least amount of rest should not be up for debate! After all, as the eldest party here, my lack of sleep trumps all the rest of you!"

Julia did her best to ignore Lady Beaumont. She'd had ample practice throughout her life.

"Please, Susannah, just tell us what happened." Julia

petted her stepsister's cheek. "Why did you reject the duke, darling? And where on earth did you go yesterday?"

"I can't tell you." Susannah hid her face. "I'm too ashamed. And frightened."

"What do you have to be frightened of?" Lady Beaumont demanded, looking like nothing so much as a dragon wielding a grapefruit fork.

"Perhaps you should leave Susannah with me a while, Constance. She might be more forthcoming," Julia said, her patience evaporating.

"If you think I will abandon my daughter in her greatest hour of need, you are quite ridiculous! This has always been your problem, Julia. You've indulged her again and again, filling her head with fancies about her music and her talent and, I don't know, the south of France!"

"The south of France is not a fancy. I assure you, it is a real place," Julia drawled.

"Of course it is, but the way you always made it sound when Susannah was a girl! Hmmph. What kind of decent English girl should ever dream of going someplace hot and surrounding herself with foreigners? Especially *French* ones?"

Susannah didn't want to listen to Julia and her mother go back and forth, tossing arguments at each other like lit satchels of gunpowder, waiting for the moment something would properly explode.

All she could think of was Rafe, particularly as the sun climbed higher in the sky. What if Huntington was already dead? Or Rafe? Who would call upon Susannah to let her know he had survived? Or even worse, what if no one called ever again?

What if one man died and the other fled the country for the rest of his life?

Oh, this was all her fault. Why had she done this? The

wail of misery and the fury and the shame built and built inside her until she felt she might burst.

Then, finally, she did.

"I don't love the duke!" Susannah cried. Both the other women fell silent and stared at her. Susannah rushed on. "I didn't want to marry, especially not him. Not because he isn't a wonderful man, but because I'm not in love with him. I've tried and tried, but I couldn't make myself fall in love."

Why not? She couldn't live with the lies any longer. "And there's something else you should know. *I* am the Red Duchess, or at least I was. That's why I've been so tired and spending so many nights with Lady Henry Douglass this Season. The owner of the Wolf's Den said he'd pay me five thousand pounds to perform as the Duchess nightly to help him close a business deal. I did it because I wanted enough money to leave England and go traveling, the way I've always yearned to. But something else happened. The owner of the Wolf's Den, Mr. Rafe Winters, and I have fallen in love."

Susannah almost broke down in tears at the words, but she struggled on. "I love him more than anything in the world, and I could never marry the duke when I felt that way for another man. When I rejected the duke's proposal yesterday, I ran to the Den to see Rafe. The duke followed me, and he challenged Rafe to a duel, and I imagine that's what's happening right this second." Tears spilled down her cheeks, but Susannah felt so bloody relieved at being able, at last, to speak the truth. "The Duke of Huntington and Rafe are fighting a duel, and I only pray to God neither of them dies."

Susannah bowed her head in shame, unable to see the kind of horror and shock Julia and her mother were feeling. They must feel so betrayed, so hurt.

Susannah screamed when her mother slapped her hard across the face.

"You spoiled little wretch!" Lady Beaumont barked, the very picture of righteous indignation as she pushed her chair back and went to smack Susannah's cheek once more.

But Julia rose and blocked her mother from Susannah. While Susannah wept in shock, her hand pressed to her stinging cheek, she heard Julia ordering Lady Beaumont out of the room and out of Carter House.

Servants came in, and the two women continued snarling at each other until Lady Beaumont had been removed from the premises. Then it was only Julia and Susannah alone together, with a cooling pot of tea and a half-eaten wedge of grapefruit as company.

"I'm sorry." Susannah couldn't look at her stepsister. "You can throw me out, too, if you wish. I deserve it."

But Julia knelt beside Susannah's seat and gathered her into her arms.

"Oh, my poor baby." Julia hushed Susannah's crying and kissed the top of her head. "I'm so sorry, dearest. Why didn't you ever tell me any of this?"

Julia's petting and her kindness only made Susannah cry harder. Julia helped her stand and took her through to the morning room, where they sat side by side upon the sofa. Susannah rested her cheek on Julia's shoulder and cried and cried.

It was as much of a release as it was crying from sadness. Susannah hadn't realized how much that secret had been draining the life from her all these long months.

"Now, now. It's all right."

"It's not all right." Susannah sniffed and then wept harder while Julia rubbed her back. "I'm the reason they're both going to be killed!"

"I know Huntington well." Julia hugged Susannah tighter. "He's an honorable man, and he's wise. I don't think this will go as badly as you fear it will."

She was right, Huntington *was* a good and wise man, and that made Susannah feel infinitely worse.

"You must think me such a fool to have rejected his proposal."

"No! Dearest, I don't think that at all." Julia lifted Susannah's face and wiped her cheeks. "In truth, I'm the fool here, not you. I had no idea you didn't want to marry the duke!"

"And if you'd known?"

"I'd have supported any decision you made. Perhaps I wouldn't have understood it—to be fair, I still don't entirely understand." She kissed Susannah's forehead. "But we're two very different people, and I love you as you are. There's nothing you could ever do that would change that."

Susannah hugged Julia tightly, and Julia petted her hair and hushed her for a few minutes more. How could Susannah have been so foolish? Of course Julia would never turn her back on her own stepsister. Then again, Susannah hadn't believed Julia would abandon her; Susannah just hadn't wanted to disappoint her.

The doors opened, and Felicity skated inside. Quite literally.

"Felicity! How many times must we tell you, not in the house?" Julia sounded weary rather than angry.

"I've added brakes, Your Grace! I couldn't wait to try them on." The girl held out her arms and waved them this way and that to keep her balance. When she started rolling too quickly toward the opposite wall, Felicity tilted her heels back.

Susannah saw the adjustment that had been made; the girl had screwed a kind of padded cushion to the heel, which stopped her when it made contact with the floor. Quite ingenious. The only problem was that the sudden stop sent Felicity tumbling backward and rolling across the carpet.

"Well. I suppose I'm grateful she's broken no vases." Julia sighed. "Today."

"It's scarce past breakfast. There's still time," Miss Winslow said, breathlessly rushing into the room with a worn rather than frightened air. She began pulling the wheeled shoes from Felicity's feet. As the child argued about her need to experiment, the governess noted Susannah in tears and frowned. "Miss Fletcher, are you well?"

"I'm afraid dear Susannah has rejected the duke's offer of marriage," Julia said quietly.

"Oh?" Miss Winslow's face went from pale to flushed to pale again in the space of a few seconds. She appeared to wrestle with herself to keep from smiling, or perhaps weeping. The woman's obvious relief gave Susannah a bit of joy. Even if everything else was gone to pot, someone had been made happy by all these events.

But then again, Miss Winslow would hardly be happy if the duke died. Susannah's thoughts flew back to Rafe on the dueling pitch, and the worry and the fear returned with furious vengeance.

"I have to know what's become of Mr. Winters," she said to Julia.

"Perhaps Ashworth can find out." Julia rubbed her shoulders. "He's an old hand with dueling. He'll manage to keep a cool head about all this, I'm certain."

The doors boomed open again, and the Duke of Ashworth appeared before them all in a state of pronounced fury.

"*What's this I hear about that woman striking Susannah?*"

"Gregory, I have dealt with that! We need you to look in on Huntington and see what's occurred," Julia said.

But Susannah knew Ashworth had never liked her mother, and this allowed him all sorts of indulgence for that dislike.

Indeed, her dear brother-in-law had never seemed so delighted to be so angry. He strode across the chamber, headed for the breakfast room door. Susannah hadn't a clue where he thought he was going.

"She will leave my house at once!" he snapped.

"I've already ordered her out." Julia sounded cross now. "Will you stop pacing about like a bloody peacock and listen to me?"

"I'm sorry, my love, but I can't allow such audacious behavior to go unpunished."

"You are not about to challenge Constance to a duel."

"Are women allowed to duel, then?" Felicity asked Miss Winslow as the governess hurried them both from the room. "Because that's splendid! I must practice my form."

Susannah didn't know what Ashworth paid Miss Winslow, but she suspected the woman deserved a rise.

"Don't be absurd," the duke said to his wife. "Of course we shan't duel. But the time has come to retrieve my stick."

Julia rolled her eyes in exasperation. "Not this mother-in-law stick business again," she muttered.

"I don't intend to strike her, but she deserves a good poke." Gregory was all bristling rancor as he charged into the breakfast room. "I shall poke and poke at her until she is gone from my house!"

"I told you I've already sent her away! Aren't you listening?" Julia chased after her husband, slammed the door shut behind them, and Susannah listened to their muffled and increasingly ridiculous argument.

Susannah was left quite alone and allowed her thoughts to spin. She bit her lip and clasped her hands beneath her chin, praying to whoever would listen to please keep both Rafe and the duke safe. She couldn't bear anyone's blood on her hands, especially not theirs.

"Miss Fletcher?" Miss Winslow had stepped back into

the room and approached Susannah almost shyly.

"Yes? Is anything wrong?" Susannah wiped her cheeks.

"I...I suppose I wanted to say I'm sorry for whatever trouble you've found. I hope that it will all be resolved quickly."

The governess was such a self-contained person, but Susannah could feel how much she wanted to reach out. Perhaps she wanted more information on what had become of Huntington.

Susannah took Miss Winslow's hand and sat her down on the sofa.

"The trouble's all my own making. But thank you." She squeezed the woman's fingers. Then she added, "The duke's a good man. It wasn't his fault I couldn't return his affections."

"No, of course not." Miss Winslow drooped a little.

"But I don't think men often know what's best for them. Perhaps in time he'll see what's right before his eyes."

The governess turned bright red and cast her eyes to the floor. Susannah had never in her life seen someone so shy. "Oh. I don't know what you mean, miss."

"All I mean is he'd be a tremendously lucky man." Susannah winked, and Miss Winslow smiled a little.

"Some things just can't be, though."

"I don't believe that," Susannah said. Again, she thought of Rafe and the man she'd originally thought he was. The man she knew him now to be was the opposite of that snarling, greedy creature. If someone like Rafe could come from the mess his life had been and transform himself, surely anyone could. "I think much of life is whatever we make of it. At least, it's what I choose to think."

The governess nodded.

"Perhaps you're right, miss." Miss Winslow was a bit startled when Susannah wrapped her in an impulsive hug, but soon reciprocated. "Thank you," she whispered.

"Now then. What on earth has happened to Julia and Ashworth?"

Indeed, the duke and duchess had become miraculously silent.

"Ah. Perhaps we might vacate the room." Miss Winslow stood. "The duke's valet says that when an argument between them falls silent, it usually means they've, well, begun to make up with each other. "

Susannah had a good idea what "making up" looked like between the Ashworths. Hopefully none of the maids would go through to clear the breakfast dishes for a while. Giggling, Susannah hurried away with her arm through the governess's.

They were on their way to the schoolroom, where Miss Winslow had sat Felicity down and instructed her to begin copying some French vocabulary, when Peele appeared.

"Excuse me, Miss Fletcher. The Duke of Huntington has called to see you. I've put him in the western salon."

Susannah's heartbeat tripled. If the duke was here, alive and well, what did that mean for Rafe?

Chapter Twenty-Six

Huntington was pacing before a window when Susannah entered. He faced her and bowed immediately.

"What happened, Your Grace?" Her voice was weak with fear.

"The duel did not take place. Mr. Winters and I discussed the matter, and I believe you were right about him. He is a better man than I imagined."

Susannah could have collapsed to the rug and screamed in elation, but all she could muster was a weak "Oh thank God" before sitting down. Huntington sat beside her, his gloves in his hand. He regarded Susannah with silent concern.

"What did he say, exactly?" She could scarcely find her voice.

"I decided to see how mercenary he was and offered him money. Ten thousand pounds, in fact. Twice the sum he offered you to act as the Red Duchess. The only condition would be that he never see or speak to you again."

It was like being lanced in the heart. Susannah whimpered, afraid of what she'd hear next. "I see. Did…did he take it?"

Huntington shook his head. "He did not."

She couldn't stop trembling with the relief. Rafe had turned down a small bloody fortune. He must have done it for her, yes? Mustn't he?

"Did Mr. Winters say anything about me?"

The duke cleared his throat. "He asked me to give the ten thousand to you instead, as he felt you'd make good use of the money."

Susannah frowned. Well, that wasn't the most romantic thing. "Anything else?"

Huntington sighed. "He asked me to say goodbye to you on his behalf."

"Goodbye? But I don't understand. He turned down the money, didn't he? That means he wanted to see me again. Yes?"

Goodbye? Rafe had said goodbye to her through somebody else? But why? He had his club, his Castle, and he would have had her. The duel had been called off, he'd refused Huntington's money on principle, but he still turned away from Susannah?

"Frankly, I'm as stunned by the fellow's behavior as you, Miss Fletcher. He wasn't what I'd expected in the slightest." The duke seemed confused. "One moment he spoke as a criminal of the lowest sort, the next as a man of honor. I don't understand him at all."

Most members of the *ton* would never understand Rafe.

Huntington was a decent gentleman, but he still couldn't comprehend that virtually all the "differences" between him and the owner of the Wolf's Den came down to the circumstances of their birth.

"Was he angry with me?" she whispered.

"No. He seemed more resigned than anything." The duke sighed and studied his gloves. "He'd a request. He asked me to look after you and ensure your happiness. I promised him

I would do so."

"Thank you." She wanted to scream. All these "noble" men passing her around as if she were a sack of flour or something drove her to distraction.

"I know you don't love me." He wasn't self-pitying, merely honest. "But if you wished to be protected from all possibility of scandal, I would still marry you."

"Even knowing I couldn't feel what you wanted me to feel?" She was amazed. "Even knowing that I'm, well, damaged goods now?"

"As I told Winters, I'll do whatever is necessary to safeguard you. And rest assured, even if you don't marry me, I'll see to it no harm comes to you."

"You're a wonderful man, Your Grace. Truly. I'm sorry that I couldn't give you what you wanted."

Huntington bade her think nothing of it.

Susannah saw what perhaps attracted Miss Winslow to this duke, something beyond the obvious like handsomeness and wealth. He was, in many ways, the epitome of honor. Though he was a bit too staid and tradition-minded for Susannah, she got the feeling he'd make a splendid husband for the right woman. Again, she hoped the bloody fool looked up one day and noticed who was standing right before his eyes.

"I also intend to gift you the ten thousand that would have been Mr. Winters's. That, at least, I hope you'll accept from me."

"Goodness!" To say this morning had been overwhelming would be a gross understatement. "I can't ask that of you."

"It would be my pleasure. I'm proud to have discovered the Red Duchess, after all." He laughed. "I must say, I'm now also proud of my initial suspicion you might be the Duchess."

"You were very observant, Your Grace. Thank you for everything. Truly."

Huntington kissed her hand and took his leave.

Susannah sat in the window for a long while afterward and stared out onto the rose garden. She had everything she'd wanted at the start of this endeavor.

She had the money she'd sought, freedom from the duke's proposal, with Julia and Gregory firmly on her side. Perhaps her mother would never see or speak to Susannah again, but she could hope that, with time, she'd come to understand.

Tell her goodbye for me. She could hear the way Rafe might speak those words before turning his back on the duke and walking away.

Had he been bitterly disappointed with her? Perhaps he never wanted to see her again after Susannah had left with the duke yesterday evening. Suppose Rafe thought her a coward now? Perhaps he believed her unworthy of his love.

A tear dropped from Susannah's cheek and onto her hand. She wiped it away, irritated with herself for all this crying.

She had the freedom she'd craved, and now she didn't want it.

Susannah fought with herself the rest of the day, wondering if she ought to go down to the Wolf's Den and see Rafe. Perhaps it had been a misunderstanding. Perhaps Huntington had misunderstood Rafe's message to her.

Or perhaps Susannah had never fully understood Rafe. Perhaps he'd seen this as a test on her part, and she'd failed it. Or maybe he believed having been challenged to a duel, Susannah was more trouble than she was worth.

Or perhaps he simply wasn't the marrying kind.

Susannah couldn't very well force him to marry her, though good society would disagree with her on that point. She hated the idea of forcing anyone to do anything against their will, particularly something as important as marriage.

If Rafe didn't want to be with her for the rest of his life, he certainly wouldn't make her happy if they *were* wed.

By the mid-afternoon, Susannah was too tired to hold her head up a second longer. She'd gotten no sleep the night before, and the gray cloud of misery that hung overhead drained her of the last little bits of energy. She could have slept for days, if not weeks.

Julia had food sent to her room, and later that night came and sat beside Susannah on the bed. Susannah cried, and let her stepsister pet her hair and shush her until, mercifully, she fell into a dreamless sleep.

...

The next morning looked a bit brighter, though Susannah still felt as if her head were filled with rocks. She stumbled down to breakfast, yawning her way through tea and some coddled eggs. Julia usually breakfasted in her room, so it was only Ashworth for company.

"Morning, Zan. Are you feeling better?" he asked, looking concerned as she nearly drooped into her plate of eggs.

"Mmm. I'm still a bit tired is all. No post has come for me, has it?" She clutched her spoon, hoping against hope, but Ashworth shook his head.

"Perhaps I ought to call on Winters," he muttered.

"I think I should like for everything to revert to normal as quickly as possible," she said.

Ashworth made a sympathetic sound and passed Susannah a section of the newspaper. She stifled a grin; Gregory saw nothing remarkable about a woman reading the news. As he'd told Julia, he liked a girl who was well-informed. She'd told him it was one of his more charming traits.

"At any rate, he's got even bigger problems than me to

worry about." Ashworth sipped his coffee. "What with that bloody fire."

Susannah dropped the article she'd been reading. Tea began to soak into the paper, but she didn't care a jot.

"What did you say?" Her heart was a mallet against her ribcage now. What had happened to Rafe?

"The Wolf's Den burned down. Some fire the night before last. No one knows how it started." Gregory glanced at her in curiosity. "It was in yesterday's paper."

"But…" Susannah's head felt both heavy and light. "Why on earth would he turn down the ten thousand pounds, then?"

"Zan, what the bloody hell are you on about?"

She quickly told him of her meeting with Huntington, and how Rafe had turned down ten thousand pounds in exchange for never seeing Susannah again. And if Gregory had the timing correct, the duke would have made his offer *after* the Wolf's Den had burned down. To save his fortunes, all Rafe needed to do was promise to stay away from Susannah forever.

It had been a promise he refused to make. And now, if his club was gone, and with all the money he'd spent on renovations for the Corner Castle, why, he wouldn't have a penny to his name when this had finished. Perhaps he wouldn't want to tie her down to a struggling man…

Susannah pushed back her chair and rushed for the door. She stopped, returned, and took the soggy papers out of her tea. She gave an apologetic curtsy to Ashworth, blew him a kiss, and then raced off again.

"Where are you going?" he shouted.

"To the Wolf's Den! Or what's left of it."

"Well, let me finish my coffee and I'll have my carriage take us there! Don't be in a rush. The place will still be burned down when we arrive."

Chapter Twenty-Seven

Rafe stood across the street from the wreckage of the Wolf's Den, and he thought of Susannah.

Even if he never saw her again, it gave him some pleasure to imagine her living the life she'd always wanted. Perhaps she'd go as far as Russia, or even on into China. She'd have a life of adventure, so many stories of other cultures and countries. Perhaps other lovers, by the time she was finished. Perhaps she'd find a man who was as good as she deserved, who'd spoil her with everything Rafe could no longer provide.

Imagining that bit gave him no pleasure at all.

The former club was now a pile of rubble and burned brick and ash. Rafe did notice that part of the front doorway was still standing. Most of the sign had been knocked away, but a few words of it remained on the tarnished plaque.

FANTASIES MADE FLESH

But it was as he'd told Susannah, wasn't it? You couldn't live on fantasies. Sooner or later, you had to return to reality.

He used his walking stick to shove a few bits of burned debris out of the way and discovered a smoked and cracked crystal pendant from one of the chandeliers. The Rose

Room was gone now, as was the pianoforte at which the Red Duchess had played.

The Bow Street Runners were looking for the arsonist, but Rafe knew the true bastards would never be brought to justice. He imagined Wembley and the other sods had hired some low-life scum to smash his window with a brick and set fire to his establishment. They'd have paid the dregs of the streets, the kind of men with unmemorable faces and names. Even if, by some miracle, the criminals were found, Rafe knew those who'd hired them would face no penalty. It was the way of this sodding, bloody world.

I should have listened to her, he thought. *Susannah had those bastards in their place when I just had to come out and bash them with my cane. If I hadn't done that, none of this would've happened.*

Then again, it had been satisfying to strike a blow against the pricks who'd hurt Celine and attacked Susannah. Perhaps that moment of satisfaction had been worth all of this. Perhaps Rafe wasn't the great, canny businessman he'd always thought himself. He'd let feelings get in the way of his plans.

But Susannah had taught him to feel, and feel fully. Much as he wanted to regret that, he knew he never would.

Again, he pictured Susannah wandering the canals of Venice, laughing gaily with ribbons in her vibrant hair, and he felt a touch better. At least she was free.

"You look a sight." Jacks shuffled over to him, her hands in the pockets of her coat. She nudged a pile of ash aside with her boot and drew nearer to him. "No sleep again, I take it?"

"You've got real powers of observation, Jacks." Rafe enjoyed teasing her a bit; it took some of the edge off. "You might become a Bow Street Runner yourself, you keep it up."

"I doubt it. That lot would resent the fact I look so much better in uniform than they do." She chuckled and slung an arm around his shoulders. Rafe wasn't much for being touched, but he made an exception for those he really loved. Jacks was one of them. So was Susannah.

But Susannah was gone.

"Do you want the bad news first?" Jacks asked him. "Or would you rather hear the bad news?"

"Hmm. Long as I've got a choice, let's start with the bad news," Rafe said.

"Very well. I've spoken to Corkus and his blokes. They don't see you rebuilding the Wolf's Den in its entirety for less than twenty thousand pounds. Maybe even thirty."

And Rafe had already put every spare penny he had into buying and restoring the Corner Castle. *Brilliant.* "That's quite bad. I need a change of pace; what's the *other* bad news?"

"Ah, well, for some variety, I've discussed the sale of the Corner Castle with some of the agents, and they think the market looks quite bad. Doesn't help that the building opposite the place just burned down like a candlewick. At the most, we'd get three thousand pounds for it right now. Probably less. That's if we get any offers at all, which is unlikely. And seeing as we no longer have the Den, we can't cover the rest of the costs of the Castle's renovations."

"I see." Rafe pondered a moment. "I think you're hinting that we may be a tad fucked."

"We're more than a tad fucked. We're fucked all the way to the hilt."

Something about Jacks's cheery way of cursing made Rafe laugh despite all the hell around him. Jacks laughed because of his laughter, and they leaned against each other. It was good, he realized, to have at least one decent friend on his side.

"Looks like we're starting from nothing again, Jacks." Rafe shook his head. "Don't suppose you'd appreciate me telling you I was damned wrong about everything?"

"This is a moment I've awaited for years," she drawled. "If we had any champagne left, I'd open a bottle."

"You won't be touching a drop for a while. Neither of us will. Starting today, we sit down and strategize the best path forward. We'll have it all again, Jacks. Never you worry."

She slung an arm around his neck and hugged him. "I never worry about you, Rafe. Might want to kill you sometimes, but I never worry."

He growled and shoved her off, letting Jacks return to her business with the moneymen inside the Corner Castle.

He went back to standing at the ash heap that used to be his sanctuary. A few months before, losing his home and his club would've been the greatest tragedy that could befall Rafe Winters, but now he could scarce feel the pain of it. Things could be replaced, after all. Buildings fell down and got rebuilt.

But love was different. Once a heart broke, you couldn't trade it in for another. And his was busted and would be for a long time to come.

Rafe.

He could still hear Susannah's musical voice calling his name. He could've listened to his name on her lips the rest of his bloody life. He closed his eyes and, even now, swore he could hear her calling him over and over. Rafe, Rafe...

"Rafe Winters! Will you turn around please?"

That was no memory. Susannah was snapping at him from a mere few feet away. She climbed down from the Duke of Ashworth's carriage and hurried to meet him. Somehow, her beauty had tripled since last they'd met, possibly because he'd been damned sure he'd never see her again.

But here she was, dressed in a snow-white gown and a bonnet trimmed with cherry blossoms. She was the picture of sweetness and innocence, the epitome of maidenly virtue.

"You must be the deafest man in London!" she cried.

She also had a sharp tongue on her sometimes, which only increased Rafe's attraction.

"What the bloody hell are you doing here?" he asked.

"That's not the warmest opening you could have chosen!"

The Duke of Ashworth was watching them from the confines of his carriage, allowing space but still chaperoning. He managed to glare menacingly and read his paper at the same time, a rare gift.

"Susannah, why are you here?" he asked again. Susannah didn't answer right away, as she'd been stunned by the utter destruction of the Wolf's Den.

"Oh, Rafe. I'm so sorry," she whispered. Tears glinted at the corners of her eyes. "How did this happen?"

"Some bastards wanted to run me out of business. I'm not exactly famous for making friends," he muttered. He wasn't going to tell her about Wembley and his wretched friends, not just now. Rafe wanted to nurse what remained of his pride.

"I hope they catch the fiends!" Her cheeks reddened with fury. A beautiful sight. Even in the midst of all this sorrow, she made him want to smile.

"Never mind that. What are you doing here?" He could feel his heartbeat in his fingertips.

Had she come to fling herself into his arms? Beg his forgiveness for running off with the duke that night? Kiss him to distraction, until he was so delirious with desire that he shoved Ashworth out of his own carriage so Rafe could have all of Susannah in private?

"I've...I've come about a business proposition," she said.

"Excuse me?"

"I learned about what happened with the Wolf's Den, and I had an idea to help you rebuild."

"I don't need your help," he said shortly, which probably wasn't bloody true, but he didn't care. The last thing Rafe wanted was a contractual partnership with Susannah; why didn't she put her arms around his neck and kiss him? He could try making the first move, but the sting of her possible rejection would undoubtedly finish him off.

"Just listen to me, will you?" she cried. "I have the money that you need to rebuild your club and keep the dream of your hotel alive."

"No, you don't. It's why you were working for me in the first place. Don't you remember?"

Perhaps she meant the ten thousand Rafe had asked Huntington to give her. Fuck, that's what this probably was. She intended to assuage her guilt about abandoning him by handing over His Grace's gracious check? Rafe would rather die. Fuming, he walked away from her, his cane tapping on the paving stones.

"Aren't you going to listen to what I have to say?" she asked, chasing after him.

"I don't want your ten thousand. Take it and see the world with it."

"This isn't about that money! I'm talking about my dowry."

That froze Rafe, made his stomach cramp.

Right, she'd mentioned that before, hadn't she? Her father had set up a dowry that, when she married, would become available to her.

"Look, I know you said you'd a great deal of cash." He faced Susannah, attempting to spare her feelings. "But you don't know the kind of money I've got to spend before I'm even ready to begin again. The club's gonna cost upward of thirty thousand pounds, and as for the restoration—"

"My dowry is ninety-two thousand pounds," Susannah said with great primness and elegance.

Rafe blinked at her, and then blinked at her again. He tried to speak a few times, but the lines of thought kept getting all crossed together.

"That'll buy you a fair few pianofortes," was what he finally said. Rafe had never heard of a dowry that huge before.

"Yes. More than that, it can restore your fortunes. Can't it?" She worried her lip and looked up at him with a pleading, winsome expression.

Such sweetness. Such care in that face of hers. And she wanted to help him? Give him the money he'd need? Hell, Susannah could write off all his costs with that money and still have plenty left over for a wealthy, comfortable life.

Except there was only one catch, wasn't there? It was as she'd told him back in May, when she agreed to perform at his club.

She needed the job because she couldn't get access to the money unless she got married or turned thirty-five. And as she had more than a few years to go before achieving that birthday, there was only one way she'd found to get her hands on the money.

"You say the dowry would be your money," Rafe muttered. "But that's not quite true, is it? Wouldn't it be your husband's money?"

Susannah scoffed. "Well, I suppose in the legal sense, yes. But why would that matter?"

He hadn't thought Susannah could be this daft. "It matters because your husband likely wouldn't want you spending half your bloody fortune on my club!"

"Whatever are you talking about?" She seemed bewildered. "Why wouldn't he?"

Rafe could just picture it, His Grace the Duke of Huntington marrying this girl and allowing her to use half her dowry for a little pet project.

After all, Huntington himself was vastly wealthy; what'd it matter to him if his little wife carved off forty to fifty thousand pounds for her own personal use?

Worst of all, perhaps the duke had encouraged Susannah to make this offer to Rafe. A chance for His Grace to rub salt in Rafe's wound one final time, to show Rafe that the duke would always be on top. That he, Rafe, could only live according to the whims of some rich tosser and his beautiful young bride.

The thought that Huntington would *let* Susannah do anything felt like a knife directly under Rafe's ribs. He shook his head and turned his back on Susannah again, trying to get away.

"Look, tell the duke I don't need anyone's help in my affairs," Rafe said. "Tell him I've already got a buyer for the Corner Castle lined up, and it's gonna pay more than I need to restore the Den."

"Are you out of your mind?" Susannah sounded like the embodiment of indignation. "Come back here! Rafe!"

He didn't know where the hell he was going, as he had no club to retreat inside anymore. He should probably make for the Castle.

A depressing meeting with Jacks and the financial blokes would be a parade compared to getting his heart stomped on all over again.

"Look, go back to your duke and have a nice life!" Rafe said.

Susannah gripped his sleeve and tugged on him to turn around, nearly sending Rafe to the street. Damn this girl, she was impossible!

"I'm not marrying the Duke of Huntington." Susannah shook her head. "How in the world did you get that idea into your skull?"

Rafe had no good answer for that. Instead of sounding like a prat, he chose to say nothing and glower at the girl. Glowering usually got him out of a bad situation.

"Then how are you getting your hands on the dowry?"

Rafe asked.

"Oh, you bloody fool. By marrying *you*!"

Time seemed to freeze; the streets of London seemed to hold their collective breath, the birds to fall silent, and the Duke of Ashworth to stop turning the page of his paper in mid motion.

"Well. That would..." Rafe still couldn't speak properly. "What did you say?"

"Men," Susannah whispered to herself in irritation. Then, "I'm proposing marriage to you. Isn't it obvious?"

Chapter Twenty-Eight

When Susannah had glimpsed Rafe standing against the ash heaps that used to be his club, she'd been filled with such a rush of love and longing that she could scarcely control herself.

She'd run to him, shouting his name, only for Rafe to not hear her and then turn hostile before stomping away from her. Susannah had known the worst sort of fear then; that Rafe truly didn't want to marry her, or that he didn't want to see her again at all. That when Huntington had relayed Rafe's goodbye, it had not been for the sake of his pride or her security, but out of a genuine desire to break ties with her.

So when she realized Rafe had somehow got it into his head that she was now engaged to Huntington, Susannah could have wept with relief. But first, she needed to get it through this brilliant man's dense skull that they were getting married.

"I'm proposing to you. Isn't it obvious?" Susannah cried.

"In general, it's supposed to go the other way around, isn't it? The man usually proposes to the girl."

"Would you have gotten to where you are today by

playing by everyone else's rules?" Susannah couldn't resist teasing him a little.

"You mean with a burned down club and a giant bloody house that won't fetch a good price on the market? Maybe. Who knows?"

"Oh?" Susannah folded her arms in triumph. "I thought you said you'd found an excellent buyer for the Corner Castle."

Rafe shook his head and cursed under his breath. "I hate when women listen to the things you say."

"Then why not allow me to speak now?" she said. "I want you to marry me so that I can give you what you need to restore your fortunes."

That seemed to make him only more sullen. What *didn't* create excessive sullenness in this man?

"I'm not going to do that, Susannah. I won't have you sacrifice your life and your dreams for my sake!"

"That's not what this is." How frustrating could one man be? His stubbornness was one of the things Susannah most admired about him, but every now and then she wished she could shake some sense into him. "I love you, you great fool!" Susannah's breath caught when she noticed Rafe did not respond right away. "Oh God. You still love me, don't you?" she whispered.

"You need to ask a question like that?" That wintry gaze of his softened ever so slightly. "You know I do. You know how much, too, I hope."

A knot of tension in her chest finally loosened. So long as that were true, she could manage anything.

"If you love me, and if I love you, what could be more reasonable than to get married?"

"It's not the being married. It's the reason for it! You said it yourself; it wasn't just about love. You want to help me restore the Wolf's Den and the Castle, get everything all set up for myself. But what about what *you* wanted? Those dreams of Venice in the spring and Rome in the autumn, what about those?"

Susannah couldn't stop smiling. "You remembered?"

"Of course I did. I listen to everything you say," he grumbled. Rafe caught her face in his large, warm hand. "I hang on every word you speak, damn it."

She giggled. When Susannah leaned up to kiss him, though, Rafe pulled away.

"You were supposed to see the world and lead a life of adventure," he said. "I want you to have what you want."

"Why can't I travel *and* help restore your dream? Why does it have to be one or the other?"

"Because a man like me will tie you down in the end. My life's here, in London, with Jacks and the rest. This is where I made my fortune, and where I'll make it again. I can't go abroad and travel the Continent with you, not while the place is being rebuilt and probably not for years to come. I can't ask you to sacrifice yourself for me like that. I took enough from you as it is."

Susannah gently skated the tips of her fingers along his jaw, reveling in the coarseness of his stubble. Rafe's eyes shut, and he gripped her gently by the wrist. He didn't remove her hand, but he wouldn't let her continue to touch him.

"I'm still rather young," she said. "I imagine there will be years yet for seeing the world. I know one thing, though. I could never be happy without you, Rafe. You are what matters to me more than anything now."

"Don't say things you don't mean," he whispered. But he turned his face to kiss her palm, his eyes closed as if in prayer. "Susannah."

Again, her name on his lips sounded decadent. Like summer air. Like freedom.

"Rafe. If you don't want to marry me, I'll understand.

But please don't go around telling me my own mind and heart. I've had them far longer than you have."

"I've your heart, then?"

"Stop asking useless questions. You know you do."

He let go of her and tapped his cane upon the sidewalk again and again, a habit whenever he was deep in thought. Rafe narrowed his eyes, scanning the stones in the street as if they'd offer up some secret information to him.

When his mind was leaping about, he always looked down. Right now, he seemed to be calculating something tremendous.

"We've got a problem," he said. Susannah sighed; that was no great shock.

"What is it?"

"You're not going to give me anything."

"Rafe, be serious. I want you to have your club again."

"Let me finish, you chit." But the way he said it was sweetness itself; he might as well have called her his gracious darling. Susannah's face warmed as he took her hand and kissed it, kissed the backs of her fingers one by one, speaking in between kisses. "That money's not going to be yours, and it sure as hell won't be mine. It's the both of ours, and I'm bringing you on as a partner, along with Jacks. You'd better get used to work, my girl, because I don't intend for you to sit idle in our marriage."

"I should think not." Susannah could have reeled from the sheer happiness. Rafe slid an arm around her waist and drew her nearer to him.

"The Wolf's Den will be our club, as the Corner Castle will be our hotel."

"Yes. Your dream is my dream now."

"As yours is mine." Rafe gazed deep into her eyes. She'd always thought of that pale blue color as winter, but now it seemed the fair shade of a morning in spring. The time of year when life returned, and warmth as well. "And I tell you this: after we've rebuilt and made ourselves richer than the king, you'll see Venice in summer and Rome in the autumn and Vienna and Russia and everywhere else you've ever wanted to go. I never thought of myself as a traveling man before, but I'd be damn pleased to take in the world with you at my side."

"Why Mr. Winters. Was that a proposal of marriage?" She giggled, so happy that she could scarce stand still. Lifting onto her toes, she wrapped her arms about his neck. This must make quite a shocking sight to the Mayfair streets, but Susannah had finished with *ton* propriety. The rest of her life would be lived for herself, and her family...and Rafe. Rafe most of all.

"I suppose it was. You want me to get on one knee? I bet those fancy dukes get on one knee when they propose."

"Seeing as we're in the street and you've only one good knee, I don't think that would be a fantastic idea." She brushed her nose against his just the once, and noticed how that simple, affectionate gesture seemed to rouse something primal in him. Susannah loved that she could bring out the beast in this man. "But already, that was the most romantic and poetic proposal of marriage I've ever received."

"So I outdid the duke, then?" He grinned, wolfish in his greedy joy. "I'm not ashamed to say that makes me proud."

"Well. Pride's a sin, I suppose. But it's one we can work on. Together."

Susannah held her breath as Rafe kissed her lips.

Once again she fell into his embrace, tumbled into it with joyous abandon, but it wasn't just about fire now. His touch filled her with light as well as with heat.

Even as Susannah already yearned in every bone of her body to lie under him again, to feel the sweet fullness of him inside her, she also merely loved touching this man and kissing him. Speaking with him. Looking into his eyes.

"Just so we're clear on the matter," he growled, "Miss Susannah Fletcher, will you do me the honor of becoming my wife?"

"Yes, Mr. Winters. Nothing would give me greater pleasure." She pressed her forehead to his, luxuriating in the strength of his arms around her and the feeling of utter safety he inspired.

Susannah didn't remember what he said to her, or what she replied. She only knew she was happy, deliriously so, and felt she would remain so for a long, long time. Probably the rest of her life.

"Hallo," the Duke of Ashworth said, standing directly beside the embracing pair with a smile on his face and a folded newspaper in his hand. "I'm assuming a satisfactory agreement has been reached?"

"I've asked Mr. Winters to marry me, and he's accepted." Susannah grinned, knowing Rafe loved it when she was cheeky.

"You little minx. I was the one who proposed to you." He kissed her neck in satisfaction, a quick kiss that left her shaking to her foundation.

"I think this calls for champagne, then. Also, we might want to get off the street. I'm a liberal-minded man, but I'd rather give these London nitwits as little to talk about as possible."

"I shan't argue with that," Susannah said.

"Well, Your Grace." Rafe stiffened a bit when Ashworth was around. "Hope you're not too disappointed, having a man like me in the family."

Yes, especially as Ashworth's best friend had been rejected in all this. Susannah did feel so very sorry for Huntington; his wounds had been totally undeserved. She hoped he would find happiness, and soon.

"Are you good at billiards?" Ashworth asked.

"I'm better at cards."

"Oh, we shall do very well together, then! Now if you don't mind, I'll see my sister-in-law home. Why don't you come for dinner tonight to Carter House? I know my wife will be delighted."

Susannah put a hand to her mouth. Ashworth was being more than decent about the whole thing.

"You don't have to embarrass yourself, Your Grace. I know how those *ton* bastards love a gossip, and I know this'll set enough tongues wagging already."

"First, you ought to know that, as a former rake who's been shot at by all the best people in town, I don't care a jot for gossip. And second, as my future brother-in-law, I insist you address me more informally. From now on, please refer to me as Bertie."

Rafe frowned. "That's not your name, though."

"No, it's not, but I always rather liked the sound of it. I'm hoping to persuade Julia to adopt it."

"If she were here now, Julia might tell you to stop talking nonsense." Susannah laughed.

"Ah, it's as if my dear wife were speaking through you. It brings a tear to my eye. Well, Winters?" Ashworth extended his hand. "See you at eight?"

Rafe stared at the hand as though it were a snake that might bite him. Susannah knew he was accustomed to not trusting the aristocracy, but hoped that, with time, the Ashworths and their odd, modern sensibilities would make him feel welcome. She had no doubt that's precisely what would happen.

"All right, Bertie. See you then." Rafe shook.

"Julia won't like this Bertie business," Susannah told Ashworth as he helped her back into the carriage.

"My dear, you're only just newly engaged. When you're

as happily married as I, you'll discover a willingness to put up with your husband's eccentricities."

Susannah smiled as she leaned back and watched the streets of Mayfair roll past her window. In the distance, she saw Rafe standing before the ruins of his club, but there was no grimness in him now.

For someone who'd lost everything, Rafe Winters was smiling as if he had gained the whole world.

Chapter Twenty-Nine

The wedding was quite small, and Lady Beaumont did not attend.

All of Susannah's letters to her mother had been returned unopened to Carter House. That was the only point of melancholy in Susannah's life these days.

'I don't suppose she'll ever forgive me,' she'd said to Julia only yesterday, during the last fitting for her wedding dress.

"There's nothing to forgive. You're the one who should forgive *her*, my love. Remember that." Julia had gazed upon Susannah in Mrs. Maxwell's shop and smiled wistfully. "And she will miss what an extraordinary bride you make."

Julia and Ashworth, Lord and Lady Weatherford, Miss Winslow, Jacks, and Lord and Lady Henry Douglass were the only attendees. The Duke of Huntington, naturally, did not attend.

The last Susannah had heard, the duke had returned to Northumberland the day after learning of her official engagement to Rafe. Before he left, she'd made certain to send over a letter that was both formal and tender, thanking him for his goodness in all this and apologizing profusely for his disappointment.

The duke had responded with a kind and proper note that promised her a wedding present. Before Ashworth had walked her up the aisle this morning, he'd told her that Huntington had elected to pay for all the rest of the Corner Castle's renovations. Susannah had been gobsmacked.

"We can't possibly accept!" she'd said.

"I'm afraid it's already arranged. He's rather a slippery creature, Huntington."

"Rafe will be horrified."

"In all truth, horrifying Winters might have been part of the duke's aim." Ashworth had grinned at her as their procession up the aisle began. "My only request is to be in the room when you tell him."

Now, at their wedding breakfast in Carter House, Susannah had the distinct pleasure of revealing all this to her new husband while her brother-in-law sipped champagne and recklessly eavesdropped.

"He can't bloody do that!" Rafe looked as horrified as she'd imagined he would. He hadn't looked so offended even when Huntington had challenged him to a duel. "I can't allow that."

"I'm afraid you must, my love. This is the kindness we need to do him after the debacle of last month." She stroked his cheek and loved how he softened at her touch.

"Well. He'll have to accept a percentage of the profits," Rafe grumbled. "I'll make him rich, the bastard. That will teach him a lesson."

"Yes. He'll be quite disciplined." Susannah kissed him, feeling again that fine, buzzing sensation in her veins, as though she were filled with champagne. Every time her new husband touched her, it was like a celebration. Rafe kissed her cheek and whispered in her ear.

"How long until I can get these bloody clothes off you?"

"All good things to those who wait." She kissed the tip of his nose.

The rest of the reception passed quickly, seeing as how there were so few guests. Annabelle had happy tears in her eyes as she embraced Susannah before departing.

"And to think you owe it all to my dreadful sense of direction!"

"Yes." Susannah giggled. "If you hadn't taken the wrong path in the Wolf's Den that night, I wouldn't have met Rafe. Thank you, Annie. I'm only sorry that my last carefree Season as an unmarried girl wasn't more fun for you."

"Nonsense. We're both happily married now. Married women get into *so* much more mischief." She practically licked her lips at the thought. "Besides which, you're going to co-own the Wolf's Den. Next Season, we'll scandalize everyone in town."

Susannah found she couldn't wait for that.

When the party ended, Rafe called for his carriage.

The newlyweds were taking a small house near the club and the Castle while the renovations were finished. Susannah's honeymoon would be spent surrounded by carpenters as she discussed drapery and ornament with interior designers. It certainly wasn't Venice, but she found herself blissfully excited at the prospect, because it was her own life. Her own business.

Her own husband.

"Well, Mrs. Winters?" Rafe said when they were settled side by side and driving through the London streets. "Was our union everything you'd hoped for?"

"I can't recall a more perfect day." She kissed him.

"Good. Then I'm hoping this'll solidify that feeling." Rafe slid a long, black velvet box from out of his pocket and presented it to her. "I'd already commissioned this before the club burned down. It was only just completed, or I'd have given it to you sooner. But then again, it seems like a good wedding present."

"What is it?" Susannah opened the case and gasped. It was a bracelet strung with rubies, every one of the stones as large as a fingernail and cut to glisten like the sun. She lifted the bracelet and held it to the light, watching the vibrant dazzle of the gems' surfaces. Small diamonds encircled the rubies, glittering like ice amid the fire. "Oh, Rafe. It's sensational."

"I think the design's quite good. But I'm proudest of the engraving."

Puzzled, she flipped the bracelet, expecting to see their initials or something. Instead, he'd had musical notes engraved in the gold. Susannah's heart almost stopped when she realized that he'd selected one of the sweetest moments in the piece she'd written down for him—her piece, the one she'd played during their first rehearsal.

Her music was immortalized in gold and jewels. She bit her lip as she felt the tears threaten to overwhelm her.

"So that's why you wanted a copy of my work," she whispered.

"I wanted to give you something that's as unique and gorgeous as you are." Rafe spoke low and gently, kissing the top of her head as she studied the jewelry. "Of course, if we hadn't married, I likely would've had to sell it to help rebuild the Den."

Susannah giggled as she clasped the bracelet around her wrist. She wiped one tear away before it fell.

"I'm awfully glad you didn't have to sell it."

"As am I."

Susannah took his large, rough hand and squeezed it.

"You asked me if our union was everything I'd hoped."

"Well. Isn't it?"

"Almost."

He frowned. "Almost isn't good enough. What do you

need?"

She kissed him on the mouth. "You."

Rafe didn't stand on ceremony, but quickly rolled the shutters down, enclosing them in the dark, safe cocoon of the carriage.

Susannah allowed him to pull her over to him, to straddle him on the carriage bench. They kissed deeply as he reached down and fumbled at his trousers while she pulled up her skirts, and in a second she felt the burgeoning tip of his excitement at her entrance.

"This is heavenly," she whispered, sinking around her husband inch by exquisite inch. He kissed her neck, and she adored that he was still rough and unshaved.

Rafe kneaded her breast, slipping it free from the constraints of her gown and laving her nipple with the tip of his tongue. As he continued to tease and torment her in the most sensational manner, Susannah moved her hips up and down and rode him.

Their lovemaking combined with the rhythmic jolting of the carriage created a glorious friction that soon had Susannah panting and moaning, climbing the heights to her ecstasy.

"This is good," he hissed as he thrust as deep into her as he could. "Susannah, you're a miracle."

She kissed the line of his jaw as she picked up the pace, relishing the way he groaned as they made love.

"Do something for me," she gasped, the pleasure almost blinding her.

"Anything."

"Say my name again."

"Susannah."

"No, the other one."

Rafe grunted in understanding, clutching at her hips as he helped her move faster along his length.

"Mrs. Winters," he whispered. Those words sent the most delightful shudder through her whole body.

"Yes, Rafe. Yes, my darling."

He kept saying her name over and over until they climaxed in the same instant. Susannah pressed her cheek against his, her fingers caught in his hair as she spent herself of every last drop of pleasure.

When they'd both finished, they held each other a moment and tried to get their breath back. She smiled to feel him still so hard inside her.

"Thank you," she said.

"No, thank you. That was fantastic." He seemed boneless with pleasure.

"I meant thank you for my name." She kissed his lips. "You said once that you were sorry to be depriving me of a title, but you've given me the most perfect title I could possess." She looked into his eyes. "Mrs. Winters. It suits me well."

He ghosted the back of his knuckles along her cheek and kissed her with the most exquisite tenderness.

"Then I ought to thank you, too. You gave me the greatest treasure I could ever possess." He kissed her lips once, then twice. "Yourself."

Susannah wrapped her arms around his neck, happy to at last be setting off on a grand adventure.

One Year Later

Rafe could not have pictured a more perfect opening night.

As he stood at the top of the grand staircase and surveyed the posh crowds that filled his lobby, he knew he'd finally arrived. He snagged a glass of champagne from a passing waiter's tray and toasted to the whole lot of them.

The Mayfair Castle, as his hotel was now called, had been restored to a glory even its former masters could never have imagined. Every surface was gleaming marble or polished brass, every bit of texture was silk and velvet and satin.

They served the most delectable dishes and the finest wines, and guests were free to walk from one pleasure palace to the other across the street. The Wolf's Den had reopened, to even greater success than before. Its salons were never empty, its gambling tables never vacant.

Much of that had been Susannah's doing.

The woman was diabolically clever, really. She'd suggested they use the scandal she had created in rejecting the duke and marrying Rafe to their advantage.

Any other woman would have hidden her face from good society forever more, resigned to being an outcast, but she'd known how to handle everything.

In order to help raise funds for the Den's restoration, she'd had Rafe advertise a select series of Red Duchess concerts that sold out at once. It was also advertised that at the final concert the Red Duchess's identity would finally be revealed.

With Julia's and Gregory's knowledge and approval, Susannah unmasked herself before a breathless crowd of London's finest and wealthiest people.

She'd also encouraged Rafe to have the press there to record every detail, and to interview Mr. and Mrs. Winters on their strange and beautiful courtship.

The Duke and Duchess of Ashworth loudly proclaimed their approval, as did others like the Henry Douglasses and the Weatherfords. The combination of bombast and tacit approval from the right sort of people launched Rafe and Susannah from pariahs into the upper stratosphere of society. Perhaps they would never be nobility, but they were respectable. At long last, Rafe had the strangest sort of respectability conferred upon him.

And with respectability came money.

When the Mayfair Castle had neared completion, so many people wanted to stay for its opening weekend that they needed a lottery system.

The press recorded every move the Winterses made with ecstasy, loving the romance of the whole affair. With Rafe's taste, Jacks's bookkeeping, and Susannah's ideas, the whole of London soon fit nicely into the palm of their collective hand.

The Wolf's Den and Mayfair Castle were packed and would remain so every night. Rafe and Susannah had also ventured further into real estate, now owning rows of those tasteful townhouses and flats in select, genteel corners of the city.

Already, they were letting rooms to the second sons of

earls and gentlemen of independent means. But more than that, Rafe had been able to fulfill his promise to open housing for working mothers and women from hardscrabble pasts.

The flats were clean, healthy, and would not cost the ladies a penny. All his dreams had come to fruition in a matter of months.

And he owed it all to his wife. Rafe scanned the room, hungry for a glimpse of Susannah. She'd gone to meet with Julia and Ashworth, and he'd decided to hang about on the landing and watch his triumph from the perfect angle.

"Suppose congratulations are in order?" Jacks asked, leaning upon the marble balustrade as she peered into the wealthy masses below. She'd dressed especially fine for the evening, in a waistcoat of midnight blue satin and a fitted jacket to match. Rafe stood beside her.

"Congratulations to us both, you mean."

"To all three of us. I must hand it to you, Rafe. That Red Duchess was the find of the century."

In every possible way. Every day with Susannah was delirious fun, and every night a sensual delight.

In fact, he'd ordered the most luxurious suite to be prepared for himself and his wife this evening.

Normally they'd go home to Grosvenor Square, only a block or so down from Carter House. They'd return to a townhouse furnished with a pianoforte and filled with paintings by the great masters, with crystal goblets and silk tapestries, a house stuffed with all the treasures Rafe could ever have wanted.

But as he'd told her before, nothing he owned was as much a treasure as Susannah herself.

And there she was, hurrying up the steps to meet him. She looked gorgeous in a gown of red satin, a ruby pendant glistening upon her neck. He'd given that to her yesterday, a gift for their anniversary. Then she'd worn it and nothing else as they made love. He wouldn't mind a repeat performance.

"Isn't it wonderful?" His wife happily slid into his embrace. "By the time we're finished, the crowned heads of Europe will be staying here."

We. Rafe loved to hear that word on her lips. We, meaning they, meaning Rafe and Susannah. And Jacks, of course, but mostly Rafe and Susannah. He kissed his wife discreetly as Jacks blustered about needing to find champagne and looking at the time and so on. She hurried off as Mr. and Mrs. Winters surveyed their new fantasy kingdom.

A true fantasy made flesh, Rafe thought as he gazed at his delectable wife.

"Oi. Got a surprise for you." He kissed her again.

"Mmm, I wonder. Is it perhaps upstairs? In the Emperor Suite?" She nibbled at his chin. "Waiting to be unwrapped?"

"Oh, it is," he growled. "But I've another surprise."

"What is it?"

"Now that the businesses are both running strong, Jacks can more than manage them on her own for a spell. I was thinking of taking you on that proper honeymoon at last." He kissed her cheek and whispered the locations in her ear. "Italy, and Greece, and even on into Turkey if you'd like. I've always wanted to see the warmest climes in Europe and Asia."

After all, people wore fewer clothes in hot weather, and he liked seeing as much of his wife's figure as he could.

"Oh, Rafe. That sounds like heaven." Her eyes were soft with joy as she kissed him. "But…"

"But?" He frowned.

"But I'm afraid we have to postpone that trip for a while."

Well, if she wasn't the most baffling creature alive.

"I thought this was what you wanted more than anything."

"It is. But I'm afraid I can't travel while I'm in such a delicate condition." She grinned mischievously.

"What? What do you mean by delicate?"

And then the realization struck him, full force. He held her in his arms.

"You're not...?" He swallowed. "Are you?"

"Expecting? Yes." She kissed him, unashamed of her affection in front of all society. "I thought we could do with another project."

"Oh, you thought right." He kissed her again and again, the world around him bright and cheerful, friendly and kind in a way it never had been before her.

"Happy anniversary, Mr. Winters."

"Happy anniversary, my love." He kissed her greedily. "And many more to come."

Acknowledgments

Massive thanks to my editor, Jen Bouvier, who helped me so much in bringing this book to life. Thanks also to Rebecca Friedman, agent extraordinaire. Thank you to Lydia Sharp and Liz Pelletier for invaluable insights. Thank you to the Entangled team, including Bree Archer, Jessica Turner, Curtis Svehlak, Elizabeth Stokes, Heather Riccio, Riki Cleveland, and Nola Carmouche. Thank you to my family and friends for putting up with my erratic writerly habits and for providing me with coffee and tea on demand. You make it all worthwhile!

About the Author

Lydia Drake is a reader of all things romance and a drinker of all things tea. A New Jersey resident, her favorite activities include taking the train to New York City, scouring used bookstores, spending time with her family, and wrangling her hyperactive cockapoo puppy.

Also by Lydia Drake...

CINDERELLA AND THE DUKE

Discover more romance from Entangled...

THE BEAST AND THE BOOKSELLER
a Once Upon a Wallflower novel by Eva Devon

All of London gossips about the Duke of Montrose. But he's also the most important patron of the centuries-old book shop that belongs to Miss Elizabeth Sharpe's family. Now she's been charged with delivering books to the Gargoyle of London herself. Garrett Maximilian doesn't give a tinker's damn what society says about him. But nothing makes him feel more alive than Miss Elizabeth tartly criticizing his books. The duke's glower fascinates Elizabeth. Worse, he looks at her with a dark hunger that makes her shake with desire. But Elizabeth's father has sinister plans in store for his daughter...and this beastly duke might be her only salvation.

Four Weddings and a Duke
a novel by Michelle McLean

As the middle sister in a bevy of swans, Lavinia Wynnburn is quite content being the odd duck out. Until the Duke of Beaubrooke turns up the morning after a ball, asking for her hand in marriage. Alexander Reddington doesn't particularly care for social niceties, nor is he particularly good at them. But when he stumbles into the same corner as a socially awkward wallflower, he knows he's found the perfect wife. Only, Alexander's shy new wife is finding her new position surprisingly exciting and keeps accepting every invitation that flutters past their door. And worse luck, he might even be falling for her. Now he must hide the truth about why he really proposed… before his unexpectedly happy marriage is dashed to pieces.

EARLS RUSH IN
a novel by Jennifer Haymore

The beloved "sunshine" of the ton, Miss Charlotte Chapman, is trapped in a carriage with the best friend of her deceased brother. The reclusive Earl of Trevelyan has a reputation for being something of a beast in society's circles, but nothing—nothing—will stop him from rescuing Charlotte from her disastrous engagement. He promised his best friend that she and her sister would be looked after. Protecting her from himself is quite another matter... Now, thanks to their upended carriage, they're stranded at a country inn—which has only one room left.

One Night with an Earl
a Daring Ladies novel by Tina Gabrielle

Determined to lose her virginity before she turns thirty, Ana visits London's most exclusive brothel under the veil of anonymity. Her night with the Earl of Drake was unforgettable and he wants more. But when she discovers his family is responsible for her father's death and subsequent family ruin, Oliver must persuade her to trust him now, and forever.

Printed in the USA
CPSIA information can be obtained
at www.ICGtesting.com
LVHW091709280824
789533LV00005B/28